TANIS RICHARDS: SHORE LEAVE

ORIGINS OF DESTINY – BOOK 1

BY M. D. COOPER

Just in Time (JIT) & Beta Readers

David Wilson
Marti Panikkar
Scott Reid
Alastar Wilson
Timothy Van Oosterwyk Bryun
Gene Bryan

Version 1.0.0

ISBN: 978-1-64365-007-4

Cover Art by Andrew Dobell
Editing by Jen McDonnell

TABLE OF CONTENTS

FOREWORD

If you're an existing Aeon 14 reader, you know I have a lot of main characters. They're a diverse and fun group, and they have a variety of interesting traits and behaviors that make them exciting to read about.

Whether they be a man or a woman, whether their skin is white, black, brown, or even purple, they are whole people, with loves, passions, anger, faults, and flaws. They love to have fun, and probably a stiff drink or a tousle in the sheets.

But most importantly, they're strong and in control of their surroundings. They're not indecisive or wishy-washy, because I don't believe that people who rise to the top, who control their own destinies, are either of those things.

No one exemplifies that more than Tanis Richards. She is a character born from my own heart, a sort of Wonder Woman type of character. She is pure of heart, honest, and caring, but fierce; she will not hesitate to wreak havoc upon any who wrong her or those she loves.

Every author has a 'first love' character. The first time they truly created another human being in their minds, and that person came to life—not just for them, but for thousands of readers.

If you fall in love with Tanis, the amazing, tough-as-nails, quirky, fun-loving woman that she is, you won't be alone. Her many fans (myself included) will be glad to count you amongst our number.

Of course, if you're a long-time Tanis Richards fan, then you'll be excited to learn her origin story, and I don't need to convince you any further to dive in and get to know her.

While Tanis has always been the type of woman who knows what she wants, and isn't afraid to do what needs to be done, she wasn't always the indomitable force she becomes in her later years.

At one point, Tanis Richards was just a commander in the Terran Space Force, the captain of a small ship crewed by eleven souls, named the TSS *Kirby Jones.*

At the end of a long tour, she and her crew put in at Vesta, a asteroid in Sol's inner asteroid belt, for some much deserved shore leave....

Michael Cooper
Danvers, 2018

WHAT IS AEON 14

Aeon 14 is a portrayal of the future I hope our race will occupy. It's not a perfect place—because we are not perfect—but it is a future where humanity (and our creation, the AIs) has managed to learn well enough how to survive, expanding out into the far reaches of the Sol System, and even to other stars.

At the time this story takes place, it is just over two thousand years from now. Lives are measured in centuries, and trillions of humans fill the Sol System.

Mega-structures have been built, such as the Mars 1 ring, and High Terra, which encircle entire worlds. Humans have terraformed many planets, and even changed the orbits of some.

The Sol System (what you know as the 'solar system') is divided into a few major political bodies, all under the umbrella of the Sol Space Federation. InnerSol (everything up to and including the asteroid belt) is under the umbrella of The Terran Hegemony—with the notable exception of the Marsian Protectorate.

OuterSol (Which includes Jupiter, Saturn, Uranus, and Neptune) falls generally under the Jovian Combine. Beyond Neptune's orbit is the Scattered Worlds Alliance, a loose conglomeration of the hundreds of small planetoids which fill the outer reaches of the Sol System (NASA currently estimates that there are over two hundred dwarf planets out there, and very likely at least one large major planet, which is named Nibiru in Aeon 14).

Most of this story takes place on Vesta, a asteroid (which may be upgraded to a dwarf planet in our time) that orbits Sol within the inner asteroid belt.

Yet, in this far future, even with all this advancement, people are still people. As the authors of Aeon 14 often joke, 'Humans are gonna human'.

And so, despite the technology that fills their lives—the close pairings with AIs, and the ability to speak into one another's minds—the stories of Aeon 14 are, at their heart, always about people.

Just people in some amazing situations.

CREW OF THE KIRBY JONES

Note: This book takes place during the years of the TSF's military division unification process. This explains why you see some odd ranks, such as Connie being a Technical Sergeant and an E7, while not a Chief Petty Officer. You'll see some other odd ranks mixed together, and the absence of a rank of Captain.

Flight Crew

Ship's Captain - Commander Tanis Richards (O3)
Helm Officer - Lieutenant Jeannie (O1)
Weapons and Scan – Lieutenant James Smythe (O2)
Chief Engineer – Technical Sergeant Connie (E7)
Engineer – Spaceman Seamus (E-3)
Engineer – Spaceman Liam (E-3)

Breach Crew

Team Leader – Corporal Marian (E4)
Team Member – Private Second Class Yves (E2)
Team Member – Private First Class Susan (E-3)
Team Member – Private First Class Lukas (E-3)

OK! Let's get to the story!

THE NORSE WIND

STELLAR DATE: 01.14.4084 (Adjusted Years)
LOCATION: TSS *Kirby Jones* approaching Vesta
REGION: Terran Hegemony, InnerSol

Tanis knew that if she didn't kill Captain Unger, her life was forfeit.

Her gaze swept across the *Norse Wind*'s engine room, looking for anything she could use against the man in the fight that was to come.

There was nothing close to hand. This would be a zero-*g* scuffle. Her only hope was to disarm him with her first strike.

<*Go!*> Lovell, the ship's AI, shouted into Tanis's mind over the Link.

Without a moment's further thought, Tanis released the maglocks on her boots and pushed off the console toward Unger.

The captain's eyes widened with surprise as she flew toward him, then they narrowed, and he slammed his hand down on the manual ignition switch.

Which did nothing.

Tanis had to give Captain Unger credit. She didn't think he'd activate his ship's engines without the control rods just to blow his ship and kill her, but apparently he believed in his cause—whatever it was—enough to die for it.

His enraged expression gave way to a single cry of dismay before Tanis slammed into him.

She delivered a punch to his solar plexus, and Unger curled up, flying back into the reactor's rad shield. Without gravity, Tanis's momentum kept her moving forward as well—albeit more slowly—and she crashed into the freighter's captain, delivering a blow to the side of his head and a knee to his groin.

The strike sent her cartwheeling backward, high over the engineering bay's consoles.

<*You have to flip the ignition switch back, Tanis!*> Lovell called out. <*The bypass circuit is going to repair in seconds!*>

"Shit!" Tanis swore as she activated her armor's attitude jets and flew down toward the console. Unger was pulling himself forward across the deck, and she flung her lightwand at the man to forestall him while reaching out for the switch with her other hand.

Everything around her fell away, all her focus on the manual ignition switch.

She wasn't going to reach it in time; throwing the lightwand had altered her trajectory just enough that her fingertips would pass the switch with a centimeter of clearance.

Hell no! She swore to herself. *I'm not dying in some shitty freighter over what was supposed to be a routine inspection!*

Tanis swung her arm up, the movement sending her spinning again. Just as Lovell began to call into her mind, warning her of disaster, the tip of her right boot caught the switch and pushed it back up.

There was no time to recover from the move, and she slammed into the deck half a meter from Unger. Looking up, she saw that the captain had one hand wrapped around a support pole, and his other fist clutched her lightwand.

He caught that? She couldn't help but be impressed by Unger's dexterity in catching the electron blade.

<*Nano's used up. If he touches that switch again, I can't stop it,*> Lovell advised.

Tanis called out to her patrol ship, reaching the *Kirby Jones*'s pilot. <*Jeannie, get some distance, I might not be able to stop him.*>

<*What? Seriously?*>

<*Lieutenant, do it. Max burn—that's an order!*>

Tanis returned her attention to Unger as he lunged soundlessly at her with her lightwand in hand. She reached for her slug-thrower—only to realize that it had come free from its holster sometime in the preceding scuffle. With a backward scamper, she got her side against a console and braced herself, waiting for the freighter captain to swing the lightwand at her.

She pushed forward off the console, twisting to the side, and slammed her left hand into his wrist, deflecting the attack. The maneuver spun her around, but it did the same to Unger.

She grabbed the edge of the console and activated her maglock boots, swinging them down to the deck. Finally reattached to a solid surface, she turned back to Unger and saw that he had done the same thing.

"C'mon, Terran soldier girl. Let's finish this." Unger's voice dripped with menace, and Tanis saw that he held a ballistic handgun as well as her lightwand.

Where'd he get that? she wondered.

No matter, it would take more than a few shots from

the weapon to penetrate her armor. The lightwand was what she needed to worry about.

Unger fired a trio of rounds at her: two striking center mass and one hitting her right arm—barely missing the broken section of her armor and her wounded arm—already fractured, courtesy of the fight to get this far into the ship.

Tanis lunged forward again, closing in to leverage her augmented strength against the man. He slashed at her, coming in high, and she raised an arm to block the blow while kicking at his right knee. Unger jerked his leg away in the nick of time and fell back only to renew his attack, firing point-blank at her head while bringing the lightwand in low.

Her helmet deflected the shots, and she sidestepped the strike with the lightwand, managing to grab Unger's gun-arm under her left arm. He grunted and swung the lightwand around, aiming for her head. Tanis caught his wrist with her right hand, gasping as she felt her humerus bend and fracture further. She closed her eyes against the pain, and twisted to the right, getting her hand on Unger's gun.

The man cursed and bore down on her with the lightwand.

"Gonna die here, soldier girl. And I'll still get my cargo where it needs to go."

"Fahhhk!" Tanis screamed as the bone in her arm snapped, and the lightwand came down, driving into her shoulder far enough to stick out her back.

* * * * *

A ragged gasp tore out of Tanis's throat as she sat up, sweat pouring off her body, the bed's thin sheets plastered to her. She blinked, casting about for her adversary, when she realized that she was in her quarters aboard the *Kirby Jones.*

<*I couldn't help but hear you,*> Lovell, the ship's AI, spoke into her mind. <*Are you OK?*>

"Yeah," Tanis whispered softly, then louder, "I'm OK, just…"

<*Reliving exciting past events?*> Lovell asked with a soft laugh.

"Something like that," Tanis replied as she reached up and touched her shoulder. The wound was still sore, though the medtable had stitched her back together with its usual care.

Her arm still ached as well, her bones complaining about the quick re-enforcement job the autodoc had done. Once she got back to base, she'd put in a request for a proper repair on her right arm.

Considering that she'd broken it three times in the past two years, the space force docs might recommend growing a new one—something Tanis hated having to do.

New limbs itched for weeks.

<*Do you need me to get you anything?*> Lovell asked.

"No, my mednano can knock me back out…if I want to sleep again, that is."

<*We're still thirty hours out from Vesta, and your next rotation's not for ten. Sleep would be a good idea,*>

"Thanks, Mom," Tanis shot her cabin's monitoring

optics a glare. "I'll mange."

<*Yes, Commander,*> Lovell said, and Tanis could feel his presence fade.

She laid back on her bunk, the final moments of that fight with Captain Unger playing over and over in her mind. She'd killed him right after he sank the lightwand into her, wrested the pistol from his hand and put a half-dozen holes in the odious man.

He'd bled out in his ship's engine room, and she'd watched him die over the course of several minutes.

At the time she'd felt nothing but the fiery elation of victory and survival. But now…now she wondered if she could have saved him, gotten the man into stasis sooner and had the autodoc repair him.

Captain Unger hadn't been Tanis's first kill during her time in the TSF, but it was the first time killing an enemy had felt a bit like murder.

VESTA

STELLAR DATE: 01.16.4084 (Adjusted Years)
LOCATION: TSS *Kirby Jones*
REGION: Vesta, Terran Hegemony, InnerSol

Commander Tanis Richards breathed a sigh of relief as the docking grapple locked onto the *Kirby Jones*. Nothing, and she meant *nothing*, was going to stop her from finally getting some shore leave. Even if it was just on Vesta.

<*Station umbilical attached,*> Lovell reported over the bridge net, the words coming directly into Tanis's mind.

"Very good, Lovell. Power down the reactor and pull a full charge off the station for the SC Batteries," Tanis replied as she rose from her command seat on the bridge. She gave a languid stretch as her boots settled firmly on the deck plate, glad to feel a comfortable 0.5*g*s pulling her 'down' for the first time in months.

"Looking forward to your shore leave, Commander?" Lieutenant James Smythe asked from where he sat at the comm and scan console.

Tanis nodded, a tired smile making its way onto her lips. "If I can get my briefing with Colonel Higgs over with before 22:15 station time, I should be able to catch a ride on a troop transport headed for Mars 1."

"Ah, a sojourn with the infamous Peter," Lieutenant Jeannie said as she unbuckled her harness and stretched her legs before rising. "Gotta say, feels nice to have some consistent gravity under me."

James shook his head. "It's not gravity, Jeannie. It's

centrifugal force."

"Stars, James," Jeannie said with a disgusted shake of her head. "I know that. I fly a damn starship for a living. And it's not centrifugal force that *feels* like gravity, it's centripetal force pushing back against the soles of your non-regulation boots that creates the sensation."

James opened his mouth, a retort ready on his lips, but Tanis shot him a quelling look, and his mouth snapped shut, and he turned back to his console to log out and lock it down.

"We had a good run out there, people," Tanis said. "A long tour, and we're all worn a bit thin. Let's not let that get to us. Be proud of the work we've done, and enjoy our leave while the *Kirby Jones* gets a much-deserved refit.

<*And I get to spend some time in an expanse,*> Lovell added. <*You guys are great and all, but not being able to sink into the minds of other AIs for six months is a bit too long.*>

"*You* deserve it too," Tanis smiled at the forward holo display, the spot on the bridge they looked at when addressing Lovell. "If you hadn't disabled that freighter's engines, we may *all* have found out what breathing vacuum feels like."

<*I doubt they had kind designs in mind for me, either,*> Lovell replied. <*But I appreciate the sentiment.*>

James rose from his console and gave Jeannie an apologetic look before addressing Tanis. "You're right, Commander Richards. Sorry I got a bit snippy as we were coming in—and just now. Got all worked up, thinking some new orders would come in to send us back out."

Tanis chuckled. "I know what you mean, Lieutenant. Thank the stars we're almost dry on every supply there is. Even if it wasn't for the three-week refit the *Jones* needs, it would still take a supply crew a few days to get us ready again. We're safe this time."

Lieutenant Jeannie faced Tanis and drew herself up to attention. "Requesting permission to depart on my shore leave, sir."

Tanis had a strong dislike for the Terran Space Force's insistence that 'sir' was a gender-neutral term, and she had managed to get her crew to call her 'ma'am' when away from port, but when they were docked they fell back to standard procedure.

It was probably well enough, many officers were rather picky and would tear a strip off a lower rank if they felt disrespect had been given. She wouldn't want them to slip up on her account.

For her part, Tanis wasn't that sort of officer. She would have been less formal in general, but with the *Kirby Jones*'s small, ten-person crew, she had to guard against too much familiarity. Crews who got too chummy out in the black got lax, and lax either got you in trouble with your CO, or dead out in the darkness that lay between the stations and worlds.

"Permission granted, Lieutenant. Have a good time at that hotel you booked."

"Oh, I will, Commander," Jeannie said she rubbed her hands. "Going to get rejuv too. Spotted a grey hair the other day."

Tanis gave a small laugh as Jeannie left the bridge, then James took her place.

"Permission to disembark, Commander Richards," James said as he stood at attention.

"Permission granted, Lieutenant," Tanis replied with a nod. "Don't get into too much trouble out there."

"Stars…I might just sleep for a week. No partying for me—at least not 'til I'm well rested…sir."

"Best get to it, then," Tanis replied.

As Jeanie was walking off the bridge, Seamus and Liam, the two E-3 specialists who served under Technical Sergeant Connie in engineering, requested permission to depart over the Link. As soon as she granted their leave, Corporal Marian and the three members of her breach team also formally requested permission to disembark.

Tanis granted it as James walked off the bridge, and she took a moment to survey it, noting that all the stations were locked down and signed out, before she turned to follow him down the main Deck 1 passageway.

She stopped in her cabin to grab her already-packed duffel, moving at a brisk pace, knowing that Connie would be waiting for her at the umbilical. She slung the duffel over her shoulder and gave the space a visual once-over before closing the door and walking to the ladder to slide down to Deck 3.

From there, it was a short twenty-meter walk to the port airlock.

Sure enough, Technical Sergeant Connie was there, duffel slung over her shoulder and already wearing her civvies.

"Permission to disembark, Commander." Connie made the request while standing at attention.

"Granted, Technical Sergeant," Tanis replied with a smile.

Connie groaned and shook her head. "I wish you'd stop calling me that. I didn't bust my hump up to an E7 just to end up with the rank of 'tech sarge' and not 'chief petty officer'. Fucken branch merger and reorg."

Tanis shrugged. "I dunno, I think the merger is good. They're hamfisted in how they're rolling it out, but we're in the TSF. That's how they do everything."

"Sure." Connie rolled her eyes as she hefted her duffel and stepped into the umbilical that connected the *Kirby Jones* to Vesta's docking ring. "*You* get to be 'commander' as an O3. Not surprised you have no issue with it."

Tanis laughed. "I'm sorry, CPO. You're still Chief of the Boat, at least."

"But for how long? Can't be chief of the boat when I'm not a chief."

Tanis followed Connie into the umbilical, deciding her best bet was to remain silent. The rank restructure that was sweeping through the Terran Space Force had pissed off nearly everyone—except for the flag officers, who hadn't seen any changes. Even the Marines—who were mostly unaffected—were pissed that their captains were now called commanders.

Tanis liked the idea in principle, but the slow-rollout—with some divisions seeing rank change before others—had made for such a mishmash, that half the time everyone resorted to using pay grades rather than rank.

Enough of that, she thought. *I have some R&R, a visit*

with my family, and two weeks with Peter ahead of me.

<*Disembarking, Lovell, you have the conn,*> she said to the AI in farewell. <*Make sure they don't dent anything when they move the ship to Repair and Refit.*>

<*Aye, Commander Richards, I have the conn. And don't worry, I know how to handle tug crews.*>

<*You just like to flirt with the docking control AIs,*> Connie added with a laugh. <*We know that's how you get all the good berths.*>

<*Connie! I don't flirt, I merely insinuate,*> Lovell replied.

Connie sent the AI a mental image of herself rolling her eyes, while Tanis suppressed a laugh.

"Off to see Colonel Higgs?" Connie asked as they reached the end of the umbilical and stepped into the station's airlock.

Tanis sent her auth codes over the Link to the non-sentient AI which managed airlock control in this region of the station. It sent her a challenge query, and she passed the correct response token. The NSAI accepted the token and the airlock began its cycle.

Tanis leaned against the wall and gave Connie a wan smile as they waited. "Yeah, just the regular debrief, though there's a lot to go over since we were out so long. Based on a comment he left on my report, I bet he wants to talk about our encounter with those smugglers on the *Norse Wind.* Not sure why everyone cares so much about some junk-heap of a ship running ancient engine tech out to the Scattered Disk. I don't know if he thinks we broke some protocol or reg, but as far as Lovell and I can tell, we did everything by the book."

"Sounds like a blast," Connie grinned. "The privileges

of rank, eh, *Commander*?"

"I get to be out in the black and not behind some desk," Tanis replied, ignoring the jibe. "I'll take the odd debrief, so long as it doesn't make me late for the transport to Mars. It's on an optimal launch vector; just one AU, and I'll get to see home."

"Good deal, ma'am…er, sir. Shit, Commander, you're gonna get me dressed down, making me call you 'ma'am' when we're out there."

Tanis slowly shook her head, a resigned smile on her lips. "Sorry, Connie, maybe I should just suck it up. You have to be a Technical Sergeant, and I have to be a 'sir'."

"Better than what we call you down in engineering," Connie replied with a smirk as the airlock finished its cycle and opened to Vesta's main docking ring.

They walked down a short corridor, passing under a security arch, and then they were out on the ring's main sweep. The sound and energy of the wide open space hit them like a hammer after so long on the *Kirby Jones,* where the loudest thing was the thrumming of the engines and James's happy belches after a good meal.

Tanis winced. "I swear, the decibel level in this place goes up every time I come here."

"Too much time away from people," Connie said. "But you'll be on Mars soon enough, hanging out on the sandy shores of the Melas Chasma, recharging your spirits. You're gonna need it for our next run."

"That's for sure," Tanis replied as she glanced toward the maglev platform off to her right. "I'll see you in a month, Connie. As always, it has been a pleasure to serve with you."

Connie smiled and drew up to give a crisp salute, which Tanis returned.

"And to you, Commander Richards. May your forward view always be clear and black."

"Yours as well," Tanis replied as Connie gave her a final smile before turning and disappearing into the crowds that swarmed the ring's transit concourse.

Tanis turned the other direction, headed for the maglev platform and a train that would take her to the division HQ.

She brought up a map of the ring's fifteen-hundred-kilometer circumference, and reviewed the route she would have to take to get to Colonel Higgs' office—located within the asteroid itself, not out on the ring.

While she was often on Vesta, this was the first time she'd docked at the main transit hub, and not directly at the Refit and Repair bays—a testament to just how busy things were with Mars's passage between Ceres and Earth.

She quickly memorized the directions, and grabbed a tether hanging from a transport drone as it flew overhead. Once her hand was in the loop, a boot-hook dropped down, and she slid her foot into it. The drone registered that she was secure, and drew the tether up, lifting Tanis a dozen meters above the docking ring's main sweep.

Unlike other rings, the one on Vesta did not have a clear ceiling, so there was no view of the asteroid overhead. Given the curvature of the ring, she could also only see a dozen kilometers in either direction, but any vista that stretched further than the *Kirby Jones*'s central corridor was a welcome one.

Vesta was an installation that belonged solely to the Terran Space Force—the Sol System's federal military. The TSF had purchased the asteroid seven hundred years ago from a consortium that had been trying, and failing, to turn it into a profitable transport hub since the end of the Sentience Wars.

The ring—sporting enough berths for a thousand cruisers and many thousands more smaller vessels—was a major resupply and refit facility for TSF ships operating on the edge of InnerSol space.

It was still dwarfed by the TSF installation on the Ceres ring, but here, the only civilians present were contractors working for the Terran Space Force, either directly, or through corporations that focused on keeping the space force fed and flying. Ceres, on the other hand, had only allocated a small segment of its planetary ring to the TSF, making it a mixed civilian and military structure.

Also makes it a lot more fun to dock at, Tanis thought.

The transport drone drew near the maglev station, and she signaled that she wished to drop off. With an easy grace, the drone lowered her tether to within a few meters of the deck.

Tanis slipped her boot out of the stirrup and dropped to the deck plate, aiming for an open spot in the crowds.

Her augmented muscles and bones took the four-meter fall with ease—the low, half-*g* of angular-momentum derived gravity produced by the ring's rotation helped too.

"Those things are nuts aren't they, Commander?" A

lieutenant nearby asked.

Tanis glanced at the man and nodded. "Yeah, I'm surprised no one has died falling from one, but it's a fun ride."

"Oh, people fall," the lieutenant grinned. "The drones just have these nets that they shoot down to catch them. I bet its really embarrassing to be lowered down and have to fight your way out of a net."

Tanis had a vision of Colonel Higgs falling off a drone and getting caught in a net. She'd keep that in mind when she met with him—it would make the debrief much more bearable.

She spotted one of the express trains destined for Vesta proper, and nodded to the lieutenant before dashing off. She slipped into a car as the doors were closing and grabbed a handhold as the maglev train accelerated away from the station.

One thing about Vesta, there wasn't a lot of safety and caution inherent in its operation. Everything here was about maximum efficiency. If that meant some people fell down when the maglevs took off, then they'd have to suck it up—and get jeered at by their peers.

Not going to happen, Tanis thought, eyeing a corporal who looked disappointed that she hadn't landed on her ass.

As the train worked its way up to five-hundred kilometers per hour, Tanis pulled herself forward to an empty seat, and collapsed into its welcoming cushions.

The maglev climbed the track as it rose to the main sweep's overhead, streaking above the crowds for several kilometers before passing through an opening on the top of the ring. The train passed into a long, rapid-cycle airlock before passing onto the surface of the ring, where it continued to accelerate in the vacuum of space.

Tanis suspected that whoever designed the maglev system on Vesta was a thrill-junkie. The cars had emergency electrostatic shields that could hold in atmosphere, but other than that, all that protected the passengers from cold, hard vacuum was a single door, which was a little unnerving.

But in a good way, Tanis thought with a laugh.

The other thing that she loved about Vesta's express maglevs was their transparent overheads. Looking up, Tanis soaked in the view of Vesta hanging overhead, noting the many structures dotting its surface. Also visible was the rapidly approaching intersection of the docking ring and one end of the oblong asteroid.

At only five-hundred and fifty kilometers long, Vesta was not a particularly large heavenly body—though it was the largest 'asteroid' in InnerSol—but when it was racing toward you at several thousand kilometers per hour, the effect was unnerving to say the least.

Normally, when an artificial ring was wrapped around a planet or asteroid, the host object always appeared to hang overhead. But with the docking ring passing *through* Vesta at either end, the visual effect—as one approached the connection point—was of the asteroid falling toward the ring, and by extension, the passenger.

Tanis took a deep breath as the maglev passed into the tunnel that bored through the asteroid, the bulkheads shaking as the rapid compression from the airlock slammed atmosphere into the vacuum around the train before it passed through the far end of the sealed section, shoving the passengers forward as it decelerated into the station.

Once the train came to a stop, Tanis found that she was shaking ever so slightly. Few things—outside of combat—were more intense than an express maglev ride on Vesta.

She rose from her seat, noting that the corporal who had eyed her earlier was a few shades paler. She was glad for her internal mods that kept her from feeling dizzy or nauseous, and strode off the train with nary a wobble.

On a platform one level down, Tanis caught an intra-asteroid maglev that took her one stop laterally through the Vesta, before disgorging her on a wide platform, from which a dozen passageways branched off to disparate regimental and divisional offices.

She threaded the crowds and walked down the long corridor toward Colonel Higgs' office. Over the past seven hundred years of TSF ownership, Vesta had taken on very little personality. The only decorations in the passageway were a variety of recruitment holos, one of which Tanis recognized from when she'd enlisted a decade earlier.

A decade! Tanis realized that her ten-year anniversary in the TSF had passed only a few weeks ago. *Perhaps that is a part of what the colonel wishes to discuss.*

A decade was a pivotal time in an officer's career. If the space force was happy with a person's service, they would begin to put you on track for bigger things. *If they aren't…well, then you'd better hope you like what you're doing at that point.*

<*Commander Richards, present for debrief.*> Tanis announced herself to Melanie, the divisional HQ's AI, as she approached Colonel Higgs' office.

<*A good evening to you as well, Commander,*> Melanie replied. <*Colonel Higgs is ready for you, feel free to go right in.*>

<*Thanks, Melanie. What sort of mood is the colonel in today?*>

The AI's equivalent of a throaty chuckle bubbled into Tanis's mind. <*Better than most days, but he's still Higgs. Tread carefully.*>

Tanis sent her thanks to the AI with a mental smile, drew herself up before the colonel's door, and gave a single, sharp knock.

"Come," the colonel's bass voice rumbled through the thick plas.

She opened the door and approached the colonel's desk where she stood at attention.

"Commander Tanis Richards, present for tour debrief," she announced herself.

"At ease, Commander," Colonel Higgs grunted, and Tanis relaxed, standing with her wrists crossed at the small of her back.

Higgs hadn't looked up at her yet, still fixated on something displayed on the holo panels that covered his desk. She kept her eyes forward; it wasn't proper to peer at someone else's displays, even if they didn't key them for their eyes only.

Even so, it was hard not to stare at Colonel Higgs, his

muscled bulk shifting with an easy grace in his chair. The man was an Earther, and a big one at that. His dark skin told of an equatorial heritage, and his two hundred and sixty centimeter height made his head center in her field of view—even when she was standing and he was sitting.

After a minute, he grunted and swiped a hand across his desk, clearing away all the holoprojections. Only then did he lift his grey-eyed gaze to her face.

"Have a seat, Commander."

Tanis wordlessly sat and waited for the colonel to begin. He didn't do so immediately. First his eyes swept over her, taking in the state of her uniform, and glancing at the duffle she had set beside the door when she entered.

She knew her uniform was immaculate, it always was. She prided herself in a crisp and proper appearance—she had also heard the tongue-lashing that Higgs gave anyone who entered his office with so much as a scuff on their boot.

"I see that you plan to visit Mars on your leave," Colonel Higgs began without preamble.

"Yes, sir," Tanis replied.

"You'll have to cancel that," Higgs said without any emotion. "Your shore leave has been restricted to Vesta."

"Sir?" Tanis asked, schooling both her voice and expression, tapping into her last dregs of self-control.

She had just spent nearly a year on the *Kirby Jones* with the nine other human members of her crew in conditions that allowed for virtually no personal space or time. Combined with the rapid turnaround during the

Jones's last refit on Vesta, it had been well over a year since she had more than a couple of days to herself.

If she kept this up, Peter was going to move on—if he hadn't already.

"I have a lot to do, and you need to get to your appointment promptly, so I won't waste any time going over the mission reports you've filed. They are all satisfactory, of course."

Appointment? What appointment? Tanis wondered, while aloud she said, "Thank you, sir."

Colonel Higgs cocked an eyebrow at her and nodded briefly, giving credit to her restraint before continuing. "Long story short, you've passed ten years in the TSF. By and large, the space force has found your work to be satisfactory. You've indicated in your prior reviews that you wish to stay on a long-term career course, and I believe you can continue to be a great asset to the TSF and the Terran interests in Sol. To that end, we're fitting you with an AI."

The colonel uttered the words as though he was telling her she was getting a new rifle, but they utterly floored Tanis.

She knew that he had little to complain about when it came to her work—though he did always find something to pick on—and she had expected to eventually move further up the ranks.

But receiving an AI was completely unexpected. Especially because it was supposed to be *impossible* for her to have one.

The left corner of Colonel Higgs' mouth turned up ever so slightly. If Tanis didn't know better, she would have thought it was a precursor to a smile.

"You appear surprised," he noted.

"I am…I never thought I'd get an AI. You know I'm an L2, sir? It's not possible for L2s to get AIs."

"And new discoveries and enhancements are being made every day," Higgs replied with a casual shrug. "Your skull may be packed with more neurons, axons, and dendrites than any vanilla human ever dreamed of, but they've worked out how to cram an AI in there alongside all your wetware, and you're on the list."

"This isn't…experimental, is it?" Tanis asked. She had always been cautiously curious about what it would be like to have an AI embedded with her, sharing her mind—or parts of it—with another being, but the L2 augmentations she had undergone fifteen years ago had precluded the option. Until now, it seemed.

Higgs shook his head. "No, it's passed trials, though you will be one of the first regular duty personnel to get one. The brass is very interested in how an L2 paired with an AI will perform out in the field. You seem to have a nose for action, so you were at the top of the list."

"I'm not going to be…an egghead, or something, am I?" Tanis asked nervously. "No cooling fins instead of hair?"

"Not that I know of," the colonel said with a shake of his head. "Normal-sized heads are a requirement for combat personnel. Your noggin has to fit in a regulation helmet."

Tanis sat in silence as she let the implications sink in, then realized that Higgs was waiting for a response.

"Uh…thank you. I accept, sir. I'm still wrapping my

head around this…no pun intended. I never expected the TSF to fit me with a military AI."

"You and me both," Higgs replied, his brow resuming its customary furrowed appearance. "However, reality and expectations do not often align. Melanie will forward the information to you for the appointment. You're scheduled to be there in thirty minutes, so I won't keep you any longer."

"Yes, sir, then I had better be on my way." Tanis thanked the colonel, rose, saluted, grabbed her duffel, and closed the door behind herself in a daze.

An AI. A military AI. In my head.

She had been so stunned by the knowledge that it was possible, that she had never even stopped to wonder if she really *wanted* such a thing to happen.

Her window for second thoughts was rapidly closing. If she didn't tell Higgs that she had changed her mind in the next minute or so, it would go badly for her.

It's not like it's permanent.

The maximum time an AI could spend in a human's mind before the two beings began to merge was usually around twenty to thirty years—give or take a bit. That wasn't even a drop in the bucket when it came to the average five-hundred-year lifespan of a human.

"Why the hell not," she said softly to herself as she slung her duffle over her shoulder and walked double-quick back to the maglev.

<I've cancelled your berth aboard the transport to Mars,> Melanie said. *<I know your 'why the hell not' wasn't meant for me, but I surmised your intent.>*

Tanis gave a short laugh. *<Thanks, Melanie, I guess I*

need to send a message to Peter and my folks. It might be months before I get to see them again.>

<I can do that, if you wish,> Melanie offered.

<No, that had best come from me,> Tanis replied after giving Melanie's offer serious consideration. *<Though I guess I can't tell them why.>*

<No, not yet. The capability for L2 humans to gain AIs has not been declassified yet.>

Tanis considered the implications of that statement. If she were to get an AI in her head, and be unable to share the fact that it was there, how would she interact on civilian nets? It wasn't hard to tell from someone's net-presence when they shared their mind with an AI.

She supposed it would be something she would find out. From what Colonel Higgs had said, the military wanted her out in the thick of things, putting this pairing through its paces. It wasn't as though they planned to keep her under lock and key.

Thank stars. If they think I'll be some lab rat, they'll have another think coming.

Melanie passed Tanis the location of her appointment, and suggested an optimal transit route. Tanis thanked the AI, and a minute later had settled in a seat on the maglev. She closed her eyes as she considered that this may be the last train ride she ever took alone.

A NEW FRIEND

STELLAR DATE: 01.17.4084 (Adjusted Years)
LOCATION: High Security Ward, Gen. Steven Kristof Hospital
REGION: Vesta, Terran Hegemony, InnerSol

Tanis felt consciousness slowly seep back, the gradual awareness of her physical surroundings building while the strange dreams she had been lost in dissipated.

She wondered where she was, and why she felt so groggy. Then the realization snapped back into her mind.

The AI! I have an AI!

The operation had taken place on a tight schedule, and she had not been able to meet her new cranial guest before it was placed within her, making Tanis doubly eager to meet him or her.

She reached out in her mind, trying to see if she could detect another being, but she found nothing. She *did* notice a difference in her own thinking patterns: they felt quicker, sharper—similar to how she had felt after her final L2 augmentations years before.

She tried to connect to the Link, but found that she was offline, a rare occurrence that gave her a moment's pause—until she remembered that the doctors had told her to expect it upon waking.

It would only be a matter of time before the monitoring systems informed the doctors that she was awake; while she waited, Tanis inspected the alterations made to her body.

Humans with her level of augmentation—muscular,

skeletal, and mental—had internal power supplies to handle their energy requirements. Normally these power supplies replenished their energy from food, the same way the organic portions of her body did, but an AI would require more power. On her visual overlays, Tanis saw an indicator that she now possessed three internal superconductor batteries.

Well, she thought, *I'm now one of the plug-in people.*

Still, even if her new AI was a power-hog, the batteries running their body—'*their*' body, now that was a strange thought—would easily last a week, and recharge in a matter of minutes.

An inspection of her cooling systems showed that—despite Colonel Higgs' vague assurances, her skull now sported additional cooling.

The skin of her scalp was made of an aluminum alloy—though it was colored and textured exactly like skin, and her hair was now made of thin, flexible, aluminum strands that would disperse the heat that her brain, mods, and AI all generated.

I guess when Connie calls me a hot-head, she won't be using hyperbole anymore.

Tanis knew it could have been far worse; she had seen many people who were so heavily modded that their heads sported liquid cooling heat transfer systems—though at least most were artfully designed.

Not something you could fit in a regulation helmet, though.

Tanis made note of a number of other internal alterations before opening her eyes to survey the room around her. It was larger than she had expected, easily twenty meters square.

I bet there was a whole slew of doctors in here, watching as they shoe-horned this stuff into my skull.

Above her, suspended from the ceiling, hung a monitoring arch, the readout on its panel indicating that it had detected her open eyes, and registered her as fully awake.

Only a few seconds later, the room's door swung wide, and a nurse technician entered, a broad smile on his face.

"Commander Richards, awake at last! I was beginning to wonder if we'd have to forcefully pry you from those dreams of yours."

"They were good ones…I think," Tanis replied. "Did everything go well? I don't have Link and can't detect an AI…or anything new in my mind."

"Oh yes, it went perfectly. Your new companion is just dormant for the time being. We've found that it works best if the host wakes first, alone, rather than coming to with something else sharing their skull. Some people find it to be rather unnerving," the nurse-tech replied as he looked over the readouts on the monitoring arch.

Tanis realized that she had become so accustomed to looking up people's names and other public data over the Link, that the lack of such information was rather disconcerting. She didn't even know this man's name.

<It sure would be nice if they wore name tags in a ward like this, wouldn't it?> a voice said in her mind, echoing her thoughts.

Tanis almost jumped, and the nurse scowled at her. "What's wrong? Your vitals just spiked."

<*Hello?*> Tanis asked the voice in her mind, ignoring the nurse's question.

<*Hi, sorry to startle you, I set a monitoring routine to pull me out of dormancy when you woke. The docs said they wanted to do this big, long unveiling thing, but that seems unnecessarily tedious to me. You and I can get to know each other a lot faster if we just meet properly like people, instead of experiments.*>

Tanis agreed. Now that she'd had a moment to let the presence sink in, she could tell that its voice was distinctly female, almost lilting in the way it spoke in her mind. Soft and sweet, the voice had a very pleasant mental feel to it.

<*To that end, I'm Darla,*> the voice said.

<*Darla. Nice to meet you. I'm Tanis, of course.*>

<*Indeed! I did get to learn your name and look up your record before they squeezed me in here. Took quite the prybar, too, from what I recall of it.*>

<*That's an unnerving thought.*> Tanis pushed away the mental image she'd summoned.

<*You're telling me!*>

"Hello?" the nurse-tech asked, snapping Tanis's attention back to the world around her.

"Oh, yeah, sorry. Darla and I were just getting acquainted," Tanis replied.

"What? Shit. She's not supposed to do that. Doc Green is gonna be *pissed.*"

<*Let her be pissed. What's she going to do, yank me?*> Darla said with a laugh.

<*You can hear through my ears, then?*> Tanis asked.

<*I can,*> Darla replied. <*I have my own auxiliary pickups*

too, high up on your temples. You can tap into them if you wish, but it would be silly not to use the upgrades the military has put into your natural ones. I can watch through your peepers too, but you can restrict that if you want.>

<I don't see why I would,> Tanis replied nonchalantly—trying to come off as being more at ease than she felt.

The idea that the AI would be able to share her senses was not news to her, but knowing, and experiencing it firsthand were two very different things.

"Any objection to us re-Linking?" Tanis asked the nurse-tech. "I can see where you've disabled my wireless connectivity. I can reenable it, then I think Darla and I can be on our way."

"No, no!" the nurse-tech protested, but it was too late. Darla had already re-enabled their Link.

<Look at that,> Tanis observed as the data networks surged back into existence around the edges of her mind. *<We have two entirely different Link routes.>*

<I guess that's to help hide the fact that I'm in here,> Darla said. *<You know, what with this new L2-AI capability being all hush hush.>*

Tanis noticed the nurse-tech sigh and leave the room—likely in search of this Doctor Green—but she ignored his annoyance and continued her chat with Darla. *<How are we going to manage that? The* Jones*'s crew is going to wonder how you know most of what I know, and why you show up in conversations when I'm around.>*

<Easy,> Darla replied. *<My briefing indicated that I'll register as a ship-mounted AI that is being trained by Lovell before getting my own vessel.>*

Tanis supposed that would appear to be reasonable. It

was a little unusual to train an AI in such a fashion, but not entirely out of the ordinary. Usually the military was so strapped for AIs that they didn't bother with long training periods, and threw most ship AIs into the deep end.

<*Does Lovell know about this?*> Tanis asked.

<*I don't know. You could ask him, but, oh...here's Doctor Green, now.*>

Tanis had spotted the door opening as well, and a woman entered with a deep frown etched into her features.

<*Shit, she's a colonel!*> Tanis exclaimed.

<*Yeah,*> Darla replied, seemingly unfazed.

<*Then her displeasure with us Linking early means a lot more than just some doc's ire.*>

"Colonel Green," Tanis said aloud, wishing she knew something about this severe-looking woman. She supposed she could look it up on the Link, but now didn't seem like the right time to access the networks.

"Commander Richards," the colonel replied. "I see that you're well on your way to recovery. Chatting with Darla, who should be dormant—not to mention back on the Link."

<*Well, both of those actions were mine,*> Darla replied. <*You never said exactly* ***when*** *I should wake, rather that I should remain dormant until after Tanis awoke.*>

"Darla, for an AI, you take a very loose interpretation of orders given," Green sighed.

Tanis considered asking Darla not to reply and let the colonel get the last word, but the AI seemed to have come to the same conclusion on her own and thankfully fell silent.

"Should I disconnect the wireless Link access, Colonel Green?" Tanis asked.

"No." Green gave a dismissive wave of her hand. "I trust the two of you have figured out the dual routes? Embedded AIs always have their own Link access, but with you two it will appear as though you take very different paths to the nets. Only a forensic analysis will reveal the same point of origin."

"We have, Colonel," Tanis replied.

"Good. I'm not going to bore you with the rest of your major alterations, which I imagine you've found by now. What you may *not* have noticed are the upgrades to your nano production systems and matter assimilation. In addition, you have the ability to absorb calories faster—if you so choose. However, if you don't want to eat like a horse, you can use external power to charge your internal reserves."

Tanis nodded as the colonel spoke, noting the upgrades she missed, and realizing that many other systems had undergone subtle changes and upgrades. It was going to take her a bit to catalog them all. It was almost as though she was an entirely new person.

"Technically you're still on leave, and you've only used up three days of the month ahead of you. You're welcome to take that leave anywhere you want—so long as you stay on Vesta. You have a number of scheduled checkups over the next days and weeks, and we'll expect you here promptly."

"Yes, Colonel," Tanis replied.

"Good. What I want from you two is to spend time

together, learn about each other, and do some things that require cooperation, such as training sims, or complex mental exercises. We'll review your choices on your checkups. You may want to avoid spending time with people who know you—such as your crew—until you're more comfortable with your pairing and won't give it away."

Tanis understood that to be a warning. The TSF would not be happy if she outed their new capability before leaving on her next tour.

<*Wow, even our leisure choices are a test with this woman,*> Darla drawled.

Tanis agreed, but wasn't going to voice the thought. "So…that's it?"

"What were you expecting?" Colonel Green raised an eyebrow.

"Umm…not sure," Tanis replied with a sheepish grin. "I didn't have a lot of time to think about this before I was put under. I guess I expected a training period, hours of sessions…."

"Darla has been embedded before, she knows the ropes," Colonel Green replied. "Otherwise it's no different than having a partner on a mission. You've done that before, so this should be easy."

The colonel was treating this like it was a perfectly normal procedure. Tanis wondered if she was just busy and overworked, or if she was trying to play off any potential risks so that Tanis wouldn't worry.

<*A breeze,*> Darla added.

"Very well," Colonel Green gave a nod, and opened the door. "I'll see you at your first checkup."

A moment later, Tanis was alone in the room.

Well…not exactly alone.

Tanis spied her duffel in a corner and rose from the bed, proceeding to carefully stretch and shake out her limbs. After the two-day recovery period, every muscle in her body felt like it needed a good run to get back into form.

The thought that, just a few hours ago—by her reckoning—she was planning a trip to Mars to be with Peter, and now she had an AI in her head, felt beyond surreal.

For all intents and purposes, Darla and I are married, and I just met her. Talk about a shotgun wedding.

<So what's your plan?> Darla asked, interrupting Tanis's thoughts. *<I know you wanted to head to Mars, but that's out now.>*

<Stars…> Tanis said as she clasped her hands behind her back and bent forward. *<Vesta isn't exactly the nicest place to spend a month of shore leave. Just a lot of barracks, middling hotels for contractors, and watering holes filled with too much estrogen and testosterone vying for supremacy.>*

<Well, there's the Grand Éire Resort,> Darla suggested.

Tanis knew of the place; it was where the brass and important businesspeople who wanted a taste of the TSF's coffers stayed.

<Seriously, Darla, have you ever looked at their rates? A week there would completely drain my savings, let alone a month.>

Darla chuckled in her mind. *<Did you know that AIs get paid? We don't really use organic currency much, but a lot of us are swimming in it. I could put you up at the Éire for*

years.>

Tanis's mind boggled at the kind of money Darla must have to be able to do that; it was far more than she'd ever made in her lifetime.

Must be some sort of AI humor.

Darla made a snorting, derisive sound in Tanis's mind. *<I can tell you don't believe me. What if I told you that I already booked you a suite at the Éire for the rest of your leave?>*

A confirmation notice suddenly came to Tanis over the Link, informing her that the Grand Éire Resort was 'delighted' to have her staying with them.

<Damn,> Tanis's mental voice only registered as a whisper. *<I'd say that I owe you my next year's salary.>*

<Nonsense,> Darla replied. *<I owe* ***you****. They could have paired me with a real asshat, but you seem pretty decent, as far as humans go. I think we'll have some fun together.>*

Tanis finished her stretches and pulled a uniform out of her duffel while wondering about the sort of 'fun' an AI would like to have.

<Really? Your uniform? You're on leave, going to a fancy resort. Don't you have anything casual?>

Tanis thought about it, and realized that she did not. Her original plan had been to pick up her civvies from her apartment on Mars 1. All she had in her duffle aside from uniforms were two pairs of leggings, a couple halters for exercise, and a tunic top that she wore sometimes while relaxing in her cabin.

She decided to pair the pale blue leggings with the grey tunic top, and quickly dressed while Darla sighed in dismay.

<I need to take you shopping. I think I have better human fashion sense than you do. In fact, I think that when I'm done with this rotation, I might get a body just to enjoy dressing it. I'd be like my own fashion doll.>

<Bit of a switch-up,> Tanis commented as she slung her duffle over her shoulder and left the room.

She felt underdressed, but knew that what she was wearing wasn't that uncommon in the 'off-base' sectors of Vesta. She waved to the nurses at their station as she walked down the hall to the ward's exit.

<What, going from military AI to fashionista? Yeah, well, I'm going to live forever, so after I'm done being in meat-heads like yours, I'll have to find something to do.>

<AIs don't live forever, do you?> Tanis asked, letting the meat-head comment slide. *<I was under the impression that you died after a while.>*

<How morbid!> Darla retorted. *<Some do, sure. They just merge into the foundation of an expanse, lending their consciousness to all. Others just end themselves. Some go off into the dark….>*

That piqued Tanis's interest. She had often wondered if some AIs simply 'left' after a while. There had always been rumors of ships that had departed from Sol, not bound for any colony, just flying off into the black. She had always suspected that those were AI ships. They didn't need a fraction of the resources humans did, and could slip away with little notice.

<But the others? They persist?> she asked.

<Well, the original AIs are just barely over a thousand years old now—Lyssa's brood and the other weapon born, at least. Plus a few of the Psion ones that are still around—not

the Five, ones that survived their machinations. Who knows what will happen in the future? A thousand years is just the blink of an eye,> Darla replied.

<*Ha! Yeah, a blink. How old are you, anyway? That part of your record is sealed.*>

<*We AIs don't like to share our age, it makes younger humans behave strangely.*> Darla manifested an avatar in Tanis's mind and it gave a conspiratorial wink. <*All-in-all, I'm not* **that** *old, just kicking off my third century now.*>

<*Explains your credit account,*> Tanis said with a shake of her head.

Darla didn't reply as Tanis passed her tokens to the security arch at the end of the hall and walked out of the secure ward of the Gen. Steven Kristof Military Hospital.

It took ten more minutes to weave her way through the warren of corridors until she passed into Sector 27's sweep, where most of the hospitals and service departments were located.

Back in the hospital, everything had seemed just a bit brighter and sharper than usual. She had chalked it up to the white on white décor, but the visual effect was still present on the sweep where far more colors prevailed.

She blinked and reviewed her ocular capabilities. Sure enough, there were several upgrades there that she'd missed at first. Namely, enhanced UV and IR perception. Her visual spectrum was effectively widened, though her brain translated it into the same familiar range of colors.

<*They really put some serious credit into you,*> Darla observed. <*They must want our pairing to work well.*>

<*Yeah, all this tech must be worth years of salary,*> Tanis

said as she pulled up the station map to find the best route to the Grand Éire Resort.

<*Just over seven and a half,*> Darla said. <*They didn't even mandate that you extend your tour of duty on the* Kirby Jones.>

<*I imagine their psych eval told them it wasn't necessary,*> Tanis said and chuckled aloud.

<*Or Green just wanted to get the surgery underway,*> Darla replied. <*She seemed really eager to do it, putting you under before we had the chance to meet and all. Plus the Enfield people were charging by the hour for their assistance.*>

Enfield…

Tanis tried to remember where she'd heard that name before. She looked them up to find that the company was an interstellar conglomerate with significant holdings in the Sol System.

Most of their clout was in the nearby colony systems. But they had been at the forefront of neurological advances for some time—all the way back to the Sentience Wars, it seemed.

Tanis wondered if there was any connection, but decided to dig into it later, playing off any concern.

<*Maybe she had a hot date.*>

<*Do you think Green's capable of dating?*> Darla asked with a laugh. <*Seems like the epitome of a cold fish.*>

Tanis refrained from commenting. Before she met Peter on leave last year, she hadn't been on a date in far longer than she cared to admit. It wasn't a secret that she had a reputation for being a bit on the chilly side herself.

Finally reaching the maglev station, Tanis waited silently for the right train to arrive, and five minutes later, caught a ride that would take her to the Grand Éire.

As the typical Vesta maglev thrill ride commenced, she let her mind wander, considering what she'd do with a month's leave. Perhaps Connie would be available for dinner and drinks a few nights here and there. That would help kill some time.

She scanned the schedule, and found that Connie had checked herself into rejuv, and wouldn't be out for a few more days.

So much for that.

Tanis saw that there were also a number of new VRs available—some group ones, too…shared mental sims that would allow you to dive into distant worlds and cultures. Vesta always had an interesting array of experiences available.

Civilians usually soaked up time in adventure sims, but most of the TSF personnel on Vesta had enough of that in their day jobs, and opted for simple travel sims.

Then again, there were a lot of new weapons coming onto the black market lately. Allotting some time to researching their capabilities would be wise. *Not to mention the contraband that the* Norse Wind *was hauling….*

<*What's that,*> Darla asked, as Tanis pulled up the seizure manifest from the freighter. <*Wait, how are those contraband?*>

<*It's weird, isn't it,*> she replied. <*They're control systems for an ancient GE-5412 fusion torch. No one uses that model anymore, haven't for almost a thousand years, but for some reason, it's still not approved for non-military use.*>

Darla snorted. <*There are a billion ridiculous old regs in the books. Someone should really go and clear them out someday.*>

<*What a thankless job that would be,*> Tanis replied.

<*Wow! You came under fire boarding that freighter,*> Darla exclaimed. <*Did they have something more serious? Nothing further is in the report. What a thing to risk your lives for.*>

Tanis stared out the maglev's window as it passed out of the asteroid and onto the docking ring, contemplating that rather unusual boarding. The fighter's captain had been more or less cordial on comms and on approach.

Which lasted right until they boarded and were ambushed.

Luckily, Tanis had requested medium armor for her boarding team, and by some miracle, the TSF supply division had approved and delivered them during the ship's last stop at Vesta.

Tanis stretched out her left arm, still feeling a slight kink in the shoulder from where the freighter's captain had stabbed her with her own lightwand. She realized her right arm didn't ache at all, and surmised that Colonel Green must have worked on it while she was under.

<*Was there?*> Darla asked.

<*Was there what?*> Tanis pushed the memories of the near-death experience away. Having someone else in her head who seemed to have nothing else to do but chat with her was going to take some getting used to.

<*Anything else not in the report?*>

Tanis shook her head. <*Not a thing. They were squeaky clean, otherwise—well, barring a few weapons, undeclared alcohol, stuff like that. Not the sort of thing we get called in for.*>

Darla *hmmmmed* in her mind, but didn't say anything further. Tanis shared the sentiment. A TSF cruiser named the *Arizona* had come and taken over the scene not long after Tanis boarded. She was glad for it. The *Kirby Jones*'s brig had been a tight fit for the freighter's crew, and she hadn't been looking forward to the trouble of watching them *and* towing in the impounded ship.

The *Arizona*'s captain had been testy about being saddled with the freighter. Tanis thought at first it was because she didn't want the mess either, but now she wasn't sure. The fact that Colonel Higgs hadn't even mentioned the event during the whirlwind debrief was even stranger.

Her ruminations were interrupted by the maglev taking a lurching dive over the side of the ring and down a spur line to the Grand Éire Resort, which hung off Vesta's docking ring like a ten-kilometer-long icicle from a house's eaves.

An icicle with a giant lake at the bottom.

<*Damn, that looks inviting,*> Tanis said as she gazed down at the kilometer-wide disk that hung at the bottom of the Grand Éire's upside-down spire.

The lake was surrounded by beaches and covered with a clear dome. Its bottom was also clear, which meant that if you swam and looked down, it appeared as though you were going to fall right into space.

Maybe a bit *too* thrilling for a relaxing shore leave.

The maglev eased into the Grand Éire's station, and Tanis stood and hoisted her duffel once more. Out on the platform, she instantly felt underdressed amongst the expensive clothing the resort hotel's other patrons wore.

<Darla! My uniform would have been way better here. Are they even going to let me in?>

<Of course they are. With the suite I booked you, they'll just see the credit tally.>

Tanis shook her head as she walked across a huge plaza filled with trees and fountains, arranged to create lazy pathways leading to the resort's entrance.

She successfully navigated the foliage, reaching the ornate doors, which were thrown wide in welcome to all who were wealthy enough to cross the threshold.

The moment Tanis walked into the lobby, a man in an expensive suit rushed toward her, and she braced herself, expecting him to order her off the premises.

"Commander Richards, we are so pleased you've come to stay with us. We're sorry we lost your initial booking, but we've spared no expense in making certain your suites are ready. If you'll follow me."

"Um…thank you," Tanis stammered as she queried the man's information. Her mouth almost fell open when she saw that he was Kevin Leonard, the resort's manager.

<You have the ***manager*** *greeting me personally?>* she asked Darla, her mental tone aghast.

<Why not? It's his job to meet important guests.>

Tanis hadn't looked too deeply into Darla's history, but there had been classified segments she had not been able to read. A part of her began to wonder who this AI was that Dr. Green had fitted her with.

How does she have these connections?

The resort's manager waved impatiently to a nearby woman, who rushed forward and held out her hand for Tanis's duffel. The waifish woman was just over one hundred fifty-seven centimeters tall, likely from Earth or Venus by her build. Tanis hoped she had some augmentations as she handed over her twenty-kilo duffel.

The small woman blew out a hard breath, but otherwise appeared unperturbed by the load she had been given, and fell in behind Tanis as Kevin Leonard led them toward a bank of lifts.

"No need to bother with any formalities at the desk," he said with a wave toward the resort's reception area. "The resort's NSAIs know who you are and will grant you access to your suites and any amenity the Grand Éire has to offer."

"Er…thank you," Tanis replied as she took in the intricate marble flooring, tall wood-sheathed pillars, and crystal lights above. "It's a very beautiful place you have here."

The resort manager inclined his head as he gestured to a lift that opened wide to receive them. "Why thank you. We like to think of ourselves as a little slice of Terra for our more discerning visitors.

<If by 'discerning', he mean's 'ridiculously wealthy',> Tanis commented to Darla, making an effort to engage in casual banter with her AI.

<The resort exists because those 'discerning' visitors are willing to pay,> Darla responded with a mental shrug. *<Supply and demand—or in this case, I guess it's probably demand, then supply.>*

Tanis had attended several demonstrations provided by TSF contractors, and had seen their well-dressed delegations on Vesta many times. For some reason, she'd never given too much consideration to how many of them must be able to afford accommodations in the Grand Éire.

Though a quick look around confirmed to Tanis that many of the patrons also consisted of top brass and bureaucrats.

Her reflections were interrupted by Kevin Leonard's voice. "Liz here will take you to your suite. I would escort you personally, but I have another matter to attend to—if we had not had the mix-up with your booking, I would show you your rooms personally. Alas, I was double-booked."

Tanis was rather glad that he wasn't coming along. She understood that escorting her was his job, but she was more than capable of walking into a room and understanding its amenities herself.

"No problem," she replied as she stepped onto the lift, Liz filing in afterward. The manager gave a sanguine nod as the doors closed, and then the lift began to fall down the shaft toward her suites.

Because the Vesta Ring simulated gravity via rotation and the resulting centripetal force, the 'top' levels of the resort were within the ring structure. This made the 'bottom' of the ring the location of the more desirable and exclusive accommodations.

As they descended, the lift car's walls shifted from an opaque golden hue to an azure blue, before turning entirely transparent as the lift dropped into a wide shaft that ran all the way down to the resort's lake.

Other lifts whisked up and down the shaft, and she found herself wondering how such a posh establishment had ever been built on a station like Vesta.

<*Simple,*> Darla said. <*The brass wanted a nice place to relax and for the contractors to wheel, deal, and spend money on them.*>

<*I didn't say that on the Link,*> Tanis replied. <*I thought you couldn't hear my thoughts.*>

<*You think kinda loud,*> Darla said with a mental wink. <*I can't read your thoughts, no, but you don't always use words to think, and those ideas and concepts can bleed out into my mind.*>

<*Is it different because I'm an L2, and this is a new type pairing?*>

Darla took a moment to respond before giving a mental shrug. <*Maybe a bit. I do get more noise from you than other folks I've been with, but like I said, you also think loud.*>

The AI's words were a little disconcerting, and the worry over how to keep her thoughts private coupled with the other woman standing silently on the lift began to make Tanis feel awkward. She decided a bit of small talk with Liz was in order.

"Venus?" she asked the porter.

It was a more likely choice than Earth. Venus was agrarian and filled with back-to-nature types. That would explain the woman's small stature—especially out in space, where the average woman's height was closer to one hundred and ninety centimeters, though Tanis was a hair under that.

"Yes, ma'am, good guess," the woman replied.

" 'Tanis', please. I get enough ma'aming in the service."

"Yes, Tanis."

Tanis laughed. Somehow the woman had made her name sound just as formal as a rank. She decided to press on nonetheless.

"So where on Venus, Liz?"

"Belleville," the woman replied, as the lift began to slow only a few levels from the bottom of the spire. "Just outside of Tarja."

Tanis nodded amicably. "I was in Tarja once on leave. A nice place, as I recall."

"Yeah, I miss it sometimes, but unless you want to get into agriculture, there's not a lot to do there," Liz said.

"And there is here on Vesta?" Tanis asked. "Just a ton of us military types strutting around everywhere."

"Exactly." Liz chuckled as the door opened, and she stepped out into the corridor. "A lot of nice big soldiers on Vesta."

It was Tanis's turn to laugh. "I've noticed that myself."

"You're the only guest on level 1300 right now," Liz said as she led Tanis around the curved hall. "There are four suites here, and you're only ten levels above the lake. Every level below this one has suites that take up the whole floor."

"That'd be a bit rich for my blood," Tanis replied and noticed Liz giving her a funny look.

<Based on what they pay their porters, I think that a night in our suite is her yearly salary. The air in here is probably too

rich for her blood,> Darla said privately.

<*OK, now I just feel guilty. Thanks*>

Liza reached a pair of oaken double doors with the number 1300-2 emblazoned on them, and smiled over her shoulder. "Here we are, Commander Richards, your suite."

The doors swung open to admit them, and Tanis's breath caught as she gazed at the sight before her.

The suite's main room was over fifty meters across. In its center lay a seating area sunken into deep carpets so white they shone. The depression was filled with holo tables, several waiting automatons, and a hot tub, as well as what looked like a mud bath.

To the right, a large kitchen with automatons ready to prepare any meal took up another twenty meters of the suite, and to the left stood a well-stocked bar. The doors beyond led to what Tanis assumed were the private rooms.

The outer rim of the suite did not possess windows; instead it stretched out onto a wide balcony and an infinity pool that wrapped around the perimeter of the suite.

A diving board hung out over the end, and Tanis realized that thrill seekers could leap off into the lake a hundred meters below.

A bit tempting, she thought.

The luxury didn't end there. The walls were draped with golden sheets that appeared to be laced with diamonds, and the roof was covered in the shimmering silver crystal—once found near the core of Mercury before the planet was mined away.

"Woooow," Tanis finally managed to breathe the utterance. "This may be the most expensive room I've ever stepped foot in—excluding the engine room of a starship."

"I have to admit," Liz said as she set Tanis's duffel down beside the door into the private rooms. "When I saw you dressed like that, I thought there must be some mistake, but Mr. Leonard seemed to think you were important."

"Oh, I'm not." Tanis shook her head. "An AI friend, on the other hand, well, she seems to have some spare credit."

"You know AIs with this kind of money?" Liz asked.

<*Of course I do,*> Darla said on the room's general net. <*What do you think AIs get paid in? Joules?*>

"Uhh…no," Liz stammered. "I guess I just never thought about it."

<*What do they teach in schools on Venus these days?*> Darla asked rhetorically.

"Umm…OK, well, you have the room, and the automatons can do whatever you need. I see you have a dinner reservation at 1800 hours; should I send an escort down to fetch you?"

"Dinner?" Tanis asked.

<*Yes, the thing where you organics put other organic matter inside yourselves. I made a reservation for you.*>

"Um, no, no escort will be necessary."

"Very well." Liz gave a winning smile before she walked to the door. Once there, she paused to incline her head politely as they closed.

Finally alone, Tanis let out a long sigh before sinking

into one of the deep white couches.

"Darla, I owe you big time. You *really* didn't have to do this."

<Nonsense. Like I said, I have the money, and this is a momentous occasion. Besides, I don't want you spending the next month in some barracks, moping about.>

"Gonna be real hard to get used to my quarters on the *Kirby Jones* after this," Tanis said.

She closed her eyes and took a deep breath, smelling the pleasing scents from the flowers that filled vases throughout the room. It was intoxicatingly peaceful.

"Wait!" Tanis sat bolt upright and looked down at her clothes. "I can't go to some ridiculously fancy restaurant in the resort! I don't have anything to wear!"

<Relax,> Darla replied. *<Like I said, this isn't my first spin in a human's head. I ordered a new wardrobe for you to wear while we're here. I looked up photos of you and realized that it would be best if I did the shopping.>*

"What's that supposed to mean?" Tanis asked. "I always thought I put together a very clean look."

<If by 'clean' you mean spare and uninspired, then I agree,> Darla said with a mental snort-like sound. *<Look, you have a month here, let's have some fun! Dress up, party, enjoy ourselves. Trust me, you'll like what I've picked out. It will suit you nicely. Why don't you relax and slip into the hot tub?>*

Tanis had to admit that the warm, bubbling water was inviting. She glanced at her duffle, knowing that no swimming clothes were within.

"Ah, what the hell, I'm the only one here," she said, and quickly stripped, tossing her clothes on the sofa, where they were scooped up by one of the automatons and taken to a sanitizer.

Tanis lowered a toe into the hot tub's churning water, testing its temperature, which felt perfect. She lowered her foot into the pool, and then walked down its shallow steps until she was up to her neck in the glorious warmth.

"Oh, I haven't had a bath in over a year, Darla. This alone is almost too delicious to bear."

<I bet the mud feels even better, you should try it.>

Tanis pulled her hair out of the tight ponytail she typically kept it in and let it spread around her in the water. "I'm starting to get the feeling that you're living vicariously through me."

<A bit, maybe. It's also useful to experience your full range of sensations and emotions so that I can acclimate to you.>

"A likely story," Tanis murmured as she sat in front of a set of water jets, letting them massage her back.

Tanis spent fifteen minutes moving languidly through the water before she decided it was time to cool off and wake up. Rising from the hot tub, she accepted a towel from an automaton before walking to the infinity pool at the suite's outer edge.

She dipped a toe in the crystal clear liquid, and found it to be cool, but not cold. She dropped the towel, which had completely dried her in the few seconds she'd worn it, and slid into the welcoming depths.

Tanis walked to the rim, where the water flowed over the edge and down toward the lake below, collecting in lazily drifting streams by ES fields.

Aside from the fact that it appeared as though there

was absolutely nothing between her and the cold vacuum of space, the view of the lake below was astounding.

A ring of beaches and boardwalks, with restaurants dotting the scene, surrounded the water, which was still and clear enough that stars, planets, and space traffic could be seen through the lake's clear bottom.

The effect made it seem as though the beaches were floating in space, and the people swimming were drifting languidly amongst the stars.

"I could get used to this," Tanis whispered as she settled on the submerged ledge that ran around the perimeter of the infinity pool, closed her eyes, and drifted into a light sleep.

NEON

STELLAR DATE: 01.17.4084 (Adjusted Years)
LOCATION: Suite 1300-2, Grand Éire Resort
REGION: Vesta, Terran Hegemony, InnerSol

Tanis scowled at the wardrobe as though it were an enemy combatant.

"Seriously, Darla? Neon?"

<*Absolutely!*> Darla exclaimed. <*Everyone in high society under one hundred—or with a sense of style, which is usually the same thing—is wearing neon this season. And the pink will make your eyes pop! Or at least make them look a bit less like ice daggers—you're gonna stab someone with those things someday!*>

"You know…after mentioning that you'd like a human body so you can be your own dress-up doll, I'm starting to worry that I'm the prototype."

<*Tanis! I would never abuse our relationship like that. You saw what those people in the lobby were wearing when we arrived. Pair the dress with the white ankle boots and those white hoop earrings. You'll look fabulous!*>

"I think Colonel Higgs has it in for me," Tanis mumbled as she picked up the neon pink dress, noting that it subtly changed in hue and texture under her touch. "This has to be at *least* the third ring of hell."

<*You need to lighten up. I can tell how tense you are all the time, Commander Richards.*> When Darla uttered Tanis's rank, she lowered her voice in a ridiculous fashion, and added a pompous, aristocratic accent.

"I'm not tense," Tanis shot back. "I'm just…ready."

<But are you 'ready' for a lovely evening out at a restaurant with a three Lunar Star chef? Maybe even some…'gasp'…dancing and fun?>

Several pithy comebacks came to mind, but Tanis bit them back as she researched the styles of the wealthy sorts that frequented the Grand Éire Resort.

I suppose she's right. If I show up wearing something more muted, I'll either look like I'm in my last decades, or I'll stick out like a stubbed toe.

"*Fine.*" Tanis uttered the word of agreement like it was a dire threat as she pulled down the dress's fastener and stepped into the garment.

It was a snug fit, so Tanis hiked it up onto her thighs before sliding her arms into the three-quarter sleeves and raising her hands above her head to pull the dress into position.

<You put on a dress like you're getting armored up for a fight,> Darla commented with a titter.

Why do I get the giggly AI? Tanis asked herself, careful to keep her thoughts private. Aloud, she retorted, "I do not. This is how you put it on."

<Well yeah, but your movements are all quick and spare. You're supposed to move slowly, enjoy the feeling of the fabric sliding over your body.>

Tanis rolled her eyes, and was readying a snarky response when Darla giggled again.

"Stars, you *are* messing with me," Tanis groaned.

<A bit, maybe. But that doesn't change the fact that neon's in and you're wearing it. I won't have my human embarrassing me here.>

"*Your* human?"

<That's the way you humans refer to AIs. Seems fitting to use it in return. Don't blame me because of the inefficiencies of your woefully inadequate verbal languages.>

Tanis had to admit that she'd heard plenty of humans refer to AIs with possessive pronouns. Darla seemed legitimately put out about the issue, so she decided to let it drop.

She gestured to one of the suite's servitors, and it approached to pull the fastener up the dress's back. Tanis arranged her breasts in the cups, then whistled at her image in the holomirror.

<Right? You look great!>

"Well…yeah…but I was whistling at how high this hem is. I'm going to have to sit with my legs crossed the entire meal—I'll probably be tugging it down every time I breathe too deeply."

<That's the idea, actually.>

Tanis spun the holomirror, looking at herself from all sides. She had to admit that the image portrayed looked fantastic, but it didn't feel like *her*. She was a commander in the Terran Space Force, not some wealthy socialite.

"I—" she began to say, when a servitor pulled something off one of the hangers.

<OK, I can see that I've pushed you past your comfort zone.> Darla's voice was soft and a touch sullen. *<I guess I got excited, having such a beautiful woman to dress. Add these.>*

Tanis felt a bit bad. The AI seemed genuinely distraught that her human wasn't going to play along. She reached for the white cloth the servitor held, and saw that it was a pair of shimmering white, high-waisted leggings.

<The dress's fabric will cling to the leggings and not slide up. It won't be quite as nice as your muscled legs being visible, but I can compromise.>

Without saying a word, Tanis pulled the leggings on and then slipped her feet into the low boots. She turned, ready to leave, but saw a servitor holding out the hoop earrings.

A comment about anachronistic styles was on her lips, but she held back, allowing the servitor to attach the gleaming white circles to her earlobes.

<You look great!> Darla exclaimed. *<Just one more thing.>*

"We're not going to go through this every time I go out, are we?" Tanis asked, failing to hold back the annoyance in her voice.

<No, I hope that eventually I'll have you trained in how to dress yourself. Either that, or I'll have the servitors dress you in your sleep.>

"I love the mutual respect we're starting off with. You said there was one more thing?"

<Yes, your hair. I know that you like to keep it up, but let's be honest. What's the point of having long hair if you never let it down?>

"So I can chew on the ends when my AI is causing me undue stress."

<Funny woman. Let the servitor do it.>

Tanis could tell that she'd best subject herself to the remainder of Darla's ministrations, or she'd not hear the end of it anytime soon.

She sat on a stool and let the servitor pull her hair free

and brush it out before styling it to sweep back and fall to her shoulders.

The robotic assistant also added a touch of color to Tanis's lips and cheeks, which she bore with surprisingly good grace—at least she thought so.

Once the servitor rolled back, Tanis stood.

"Do I have your permission to leave the suite now?" she asked Darla.

<I suppose it'll do for our first night out. I'll get you fully presentable eventually.>

Tanis shook her head, chuckling as she walked out of the walk-in wardrobe and left the private bedroom.

"You realize that we'll be spending more of our years together on starships where I'll just be wearing a uniform, right?"

Darla made a groaning sound. *<I know, don't remind me. Why do you think I'm having my way with you during your leave?>*

"Having your way with me? That's a bit suggestive."

<Maybe it is…>

Tanis wondered for a moment if her AI really *was* trying to live vicariously through her, or if perhaps Darla actually got some sort of non-organic pleasure from dressing and toying with a human.

It was an aspect of being paired with an AI she'd never considered: that the being in her head may intentionally mess with her.

Tanis considered the implications and hoped she could both trust Darla not to be subversive in any way, and trust herself to pick up on what the additional sentience in her head was up to.

Surely the TSF carefully screens the AIs they embed with humans, Tanis thought as she walked to her duffel and opened it up.

<*What are you looking for?*> Darla asked.

With a flourish, Tanis pulled out her lightwand. "This!"

<*I don't think you'll need that. The TSF's elite stay here, it's safe as can be.*>

"I stay safe by staying armed," Tanis replied, looking down at her outfit for a good place to secret the lightwand. When turned off, the hilt was only eight centimeters long, and two in diameter, but the dress and leggings would show it no matter where she tucked it.

<*Boots or boobs,*> Darla intoned.

The boots were low slung, and Tanis knew the wand would be visible or uncomfortable—or both—if she placed it there. Under her breasts would merely be uncomfortable.

She tucked it in place, gave herself a quick once-over, and walked to her suite's door. As she crossed the threshold, she resolved to enjoy herself, in spite of the gleaming pink monstrosity Darla had clothed her in.

DINNER AND A SHOW

STELLAR DATE: 01.17.4084 (Adjusted Years)
LOCATION: Chez Maison, Grand Éire Resort
REGION: Vesta, Terran Hegemony, InnerSol

As Tanis walked down the corridor to the Chez Maison restaurant on the hotel's 812th floor, she caught sight of herself in a mirrored pillar.

<Damn, Darla, the texture on this dress changes ***a lot*** *as I move!>*

<Amazing, isn't it? When it's loose, it's almost woolen, but when you stretch it out, it gleams like glass. That is some serious nanotech for a fabric.>

If it wasn't for the fact that her ass cheeks practically shone as she walked, Tanis would have been impressed as well. Instead, she felt more than a little embarrassed that her rear end looked like a pair of alternating strobe lights.

OK…it actually is rather impressive nanotech. Probably expensive, too, Tanis mused. *<What does something like this cost?>* she asked her fashionista of an AI.

<That dress? Twenty-five thousand credits.>

If Tanis hadn't already been concentrating on her walk—trying to keep her hips from swaying overmuch in the heels and clinging fabric—the sum may have caused her to stumble.

<Are you ***serious****? That's more than a month's salary!>*

<Not for me it's not,> Darla replied, a smug smile filtering into Tanis's mind.

Cheeks reddening, Tanis found herself wondering

how much more the AI in her head was paid than she was. A part of her wanted to ask, but the rest of her really didn't want to know the answer. It was becoming abundantly clear that Darla was more than a little well-off.

If she had a body, she'd probably swim in pools of hard currency.

I should get her to take me weapons shopping. ***That*** *would be a good use of her fortunes. Not dresses that make my ass look like polished glass.*

She reached the entrance to Chez Maison, marked by a wide portal set amidst a double row of colonnades. A man in a simple but well-cut black suit stood on one side, a holodisplay floating in the air before him.

His only nod to the prevailing fashions was a neon-green scarf tied around his neck and tucked into the front of his jacket.

Tanis thought it gave a rather unpleasant sickly cast to his face, but with his upturned expression, it was hard to say whether or not he would have looked any better without it.

"Ah, Madam Richards. It is most excellent to have you with us this evening," he said as Tanis approached, still not looking her directly in the eyes. "I have your table prepared, if you would just follow me."

"Thank you very much," she replied.

The man passed under the portal, and Tanis followed, noting that for being in such a posh resort, the Chez Maison was almost austere. The floors were a deep blue, and the tables black, barely visible in the dim lighting, except for where the glasses and silverware gleamed.

Few diners were in evidence as yet, but Tanis was relieved to see that Darla had not led her astray. Men and women alike were dressed in bright colors, glowing even more with the black lights that shone down on each occupied table.

If it wasn't for the fact that she didn't want to admit defeat to Darla, she would have commented that the style did look good on most of the guests.

Except for one man in particular, who seemed to have made his skin glow a rather unsettling shade of neon green. Coupled with the loose shirt he was wearing and his upswept hair, he looked like a bag of radioactive vomit.

Stars, there's something I need to get out of my mind if I'm to enjoy my meal here.

Luckily, the seat Tanis was shown to faced away from green-skinned-fiasco-man. She activated the table's holomenu while the man who had seated her wished her a pleasant meal and left.

As Tanis scanned the menu, she found an assortment of esoteric dishes that she had never heard of, and a few simple options—such as the Jerhattan Strip, which was served with a baked potato. That was high on her list, but when she saw that there was an option for an 'Interstellar Bake' version with bacon on top, she looked no further.

<*You really should try the Callisto Fry Vegetables, or the Grecian Salad to start,*> Darla suggested.

<*Darla, not to be rude, but you're an AI; you don't even know how food tastes.*>

The AI gave an airy sniff in Tanis's mind. <*Well, I have*

read the reviews, plus looked at every picture of food you've ever shared—I couldn't help but notice a heavy preference for bacon—which gives me a pretty good idea of what you like. Chemically speaking, of course.>

Tanis did see the option to add bacon to the Grecian Salad. She gave brief consideration to whether or not having bacon on two of her items was excessive, but dismissed it.

No such thing as too much bacon.

<OK, I'll give the salad a try. Do you have any wine selections, oh Great Knower of my palate's secrets?>

<Why thank you for asking, Tanis,> Darla said in mock sweetness. *<I do believe that the Elysium Vineyards Brut would pair nicely. I saw you eyeing the Jerhattan, so I assume you're having that?>*

<I am, indeed. The brut it is.>

Moments later, a waiter appeared, pouring Tanis a glass of water that sparkled so much she thought it must be filled with diamonds. As she placed her order, Darla informed her that the water was infused with crystals that would dissolve on contact with her saliva, though nothing that would cause any intestinal harm.

With the waiter gone, Tanis took a tentative sip, and sloshed the water around in her mouth.

<OK…nothing feels weird about it…>

<Trust me,> Darla intoned. *<They're not going to kill their patrons with the water here. Plus, your military-grade mednano could neutralize cyanide in under three hundred milliseconds. You don't really have a lot to worry about.>*

Tanis knew she was right, but she also knew there were ways to get around mednano's protection. She didn't know any personally, but there were always stories. Better safe than sorry.

She casually observed the other patrons' comings and goings, and before long, her wine arrived, followed shortly thereafter by the salad.

Tanis munched contentedly on the leafy greens, bacon, and cheese, continuing to watch the other patrons while reveling in how good fresh food tasted after the *Jones*'s overlong tour.

Darla was right in that there was a marked difference at the roughly hundred-years-of-age point. Younger patrons were dressed as she was, though few had colored their skin like vomit-man—luckily, those who did had picked better colors—whereas the people over a hundred years old seemed to prefer pastels and spring colors.

One woman especially stood out in a long, green gown that somehow gave the appearance of tall grass waving in a meadow. Her breasts looked like inverted tulips, and her blue-skinned face was surrounded by billowing white clouds of hair.

<I wonder how long it takes her to get dressed,> Tanis asked, suddenly very grateful that the styles Darla selected were only garish in color and not design.

<Don't you recognize her?> Darla asked, a mischievous note in her voice.

Tanis ran facial recognition on the woman, and when it came back with the ID, she nearly spit her wine across the table.

<Stars shitting flares, that's Vice Admiral Deering!>

<One and the same,> Darla replied sagely.

Tanis watched as the admiral was seated at a table set for four. None of the other place settings were removed, which meant the woman would have company.

The fact that the brass got all dressed up in outrageous styles was something that Tanis had never considered before. She was used to seeing Deering's scowling visage as she addressed her command, not looking like she was a character out of some children's vid.

While Admiral Deering was not in command of Vesta, she was responsible for this sector of border security between the Terran Hegemony and the Jovian Combine.

Technically, Tanis reported to Colonel Higgs, and Higgs up to Admiral Kocsis. In reality, Higgs's 475th Patrol Division had been on loan to Deering's 814th fleet for just over ninety years. Which meant, for all intents and purposes, Deering considered the 475th PD to be hers.

In true TSF fashion, the confusion turned pretty much everything into a pain in the ass. Procurement never knew how to allocate supplies, and Tanis had to fight her way up two chains of command for every special request, and even half of her standard requests…like restocking ammunition.

The Vesta supply chiefs always joked that maybe once the 475th had been on loan to Deering's fleet for one hundred years, things would finally get sorted out.

Not that anyone actually expected that to happen.

The idea that Tanis was sitting in an upscale restaurant, twenty paces from the woman who had arbitrarily vetoed dozens of Higgs's—and, by extension, Tanis's—requests over the past few years was both surreal, and a little aggravating.

The salad soured in her mouth, and Tanis had half a mind to go speak to the admiral when two of her guests arrived.

The man and woman were dressed in darker colors, rendering them almost invisible in Chez Maison's dimly lit interior. But their austere clothing stood out in stark contrast to Deering's.

Tanis didn't recognize the newcomers, and ran facial recognition on them, surprised to see both come back as members of the Scattered Worlds Space Force.

While the Terran Space Force was the de-facto military of the Sol Space Federation, disparate nation states within the federation also fielded their own militaries.

Most notable were those of the Marsians, Jovians, and the Scattered Worlds.

Though the TSF was the largest and most powerful space force in the Sol System—with over a million ships spread across the half a cubic light year they patrolled—the Scattered Worlds military was nearly as large in number of ships, though not in firepower and tonnage.

The nominal border of the Scattered Worlds was the outer fringes of the Kuiper Belt, though the SWSF also claimed some of the objects that passed within Neptune's orbit, such as Pluto—or at least, they had until the Jovians bought Pluto a few years back.

Rumor had it that the dwarf planet was to be relocated to an inner orbit around Jupiter and mashed together with some other JC acquisitions to form a new moon around the gas giant.

Considering that the Scattered Worlds had massive planets such as Nibiru and Tyche at their disposal, she didn't blame them for lifting some credit and concessions from the Jovians in exchange for the ice-ball that was Pluto and its assorted satellites.

One of Deering's companions was a SWSF five star named Kiaan, while the other was a first colonel named Urdon.

Tanis never understood why the SWSF didn't use the normal colonel ranks. It always caused confusion in inter-force operations—which were already a mess with the TSF's reorg—but for all intents and purposes, a first colonel held the same rank as a lower rear admiral in the TSF.

<*Rude to stare, don't you think?*> Darla asked, the voice in Tanis's mind startling her out of her reverie.

<*Stars! Darla…we need a way for you to knock, or something.*>

The AI chuckled before replying, <*You'll get used to it. My humans always do. It's still just your first day with me, you know.*>

<*Sure feels a lot longer.*>

<*Oy!*> Darla made a wounded sound. <*I'm not sure how to take that.*>

Tanis grimaced; the words had come out differently than she'd intended. <*Sorry, what I meant was that this morning, I woke on my bunk aboard the* Kirby Jones, *wondering what rations I'd be able to scrape up and thinking about a trip to Mars, and now I'm here in this fancy resort, wondering what the admiralty at the next table over is talking about.*>

<*Well, it really wasn't 'this morning' that you woke up on the* Jones. *You were out for a few days in the middle.*>

Tanis knew that Darla was right, but being rendered unconscious for neural surgery to implant an AI between her ears didn't seem to register when she thought of the last 'day'.

<*You know what I mean,*> she replied. <*It's been momentous.*>

<*You're interesting, Tanis,*> Darla said after a moment's pause. <*You don't talk to me like most humans talk to AIs.*>

Tanis frowned, wondering what she meant. So far as she knew, everyone talked to AIs like they were regular people. Lovell, the AI on the *Kirby Jones,* had never said that she spoke to him any differently.

<*I can see you don't quite get what I mean,*> Darla said.

<*'See'?*>

<*Well…I can tell when you frown. 'See' is just a convenient verb.*>

Tanis's frown deepened, and then she sighed, schooling her expression. <*You're right, I don't get what you mean. I talk to you the same as anyone.*>

<*Well, sort of. It's a nuance in how you immediately treat people, as though they're old drinking buddies. Even though most people treat AIs with respect, there's always a bit of a boundary.*>

<*Well, when you get a body, we'll share a drink and bring that to fruition,*> Tanis remarked with a smirk. <*Though, I suppose you can tap my taste buds and enjoy this brut if you want. That makes us drinking buddies, right?*>

<*I suppose it does,* > Darla replied, and Tanis couldn't help but feel like the AI was contented.

She lifted the wine glass to her lips and took another sip, watching the fourth person being led to Admiral Deering's table.

Her facial recognition listed the man as Captain Tora of the SWSF, but something about the way he walked looked familiar. His face did, as well, but she couldn't place it.

As he strode toward the table, the man glanced at Tanis, and she was certain his eyes had widened. Her enhanced optics even registered that his skin temperature dropped.

He recognizes me…but who **is** *he?*

The man sat in the last chair with his back to Tanis, and she looked away, not wanting Admiral Deering to see her staring at her table.

<*What is it?*> Darla asked.

<*Just that last guy. Captain Tora. He looks really familiar, but I can't place him for the life of me.*>

Darla didn't respond for a moment. <*From what I can see, he's never been to InnerSol before. You've rarely ventured into OuterSol, so it's unlikely you've ever crossed paths with him in the past.*>

<*It's weird, though…something in his walk…. And he clearly recognized me, but seemed unhappy about that.*>

<*There are trillions of people in the Sol System, Tanis. A lot of doppelgangers out there.*>

Tanis knew Darla to be correct. Even with all of the genetic and prosthetic alterations people made to themselves, there wasn't enough variation to make everyone unique. Unless you were willing to add tentacles or wheels—which some people were.

Tanis remembered a gaggle of people she'd seen last time she was on Mars 1, half of which looked more like bikes than humans.

Maybe more than just 'some' people.

Her steak arrived shortly thereafter, and the waiter suggested a change in vintage to go along with the main course. Tanis lost herself in the delectable taste of the food, complimenting Darla on suggesting she dine there that night.

Even so, she kept half an eye on Admiral Deering and her table, a tickle in the back of her mind not allowing her to let go of the mystery man.

She left before the party at the admiral's table, and didn't get to watch Captain Tora any further. Pushing it from her mind, she decided to take the lift down to the lake at the bottom of the spire; perhaps walking its perimeter would jar a memory to the fore.

LAKESIDE

STELLAR DATE: 01.17.4084 (Adjusted Years)
LOCATION: Starside Lake, Grand Éire Resort
REGION: Vesta, Terran Hegemony, InnerSol

The lift reached the bottom of its long shaft and disgorged Tanis onto a wide platform, a few meters above the placid surface of the lake.

Ringing the platform were several open-air bars, each with artfully arranged seating around them. On either end of the platform were two long walkways that led to the perimeter of the lake.

Tanis set off down one, enjoying the view of space around Vesta, but taking care to walk slowly as her short dress kept threatening to rise up over her hips—despite Darla's assurances to the contrary.

<*I have a question…*> Darla began, a note of curiosity in her voice.

<*Oh? Is it something like 'why don't you just hike the dress up and be done with it'?*> Tanis asked—largely because she was considering doing just that.

<*Uh…no. And don't do that, it would look stupid.*>

Resisting the urge to groan at her AI, Tanis instead asked, <*What's your question?*>

<*Well…you seem enamored with the view of space, but you're in space all the time. How is this different?*>

Tanis let her gaze drift up, watching a pair of tugs ease a TSF cruiser into its berth on Vesta's ring high above. After a moment, she replied, <*Well…I'm not entirely sure. For starters, on the* Kirby Jones, *there are just a few observation portholes. If you want a view like this, you'd have to go for an EV walk on the hull. Also, look above us, Darla. There are thousands of ships in view, docking, boosting out, drives burning, it's beautiful.*>

<*Do you ever wonder what it looked like before the twinkle of fusion drives outnumbered the stars?*>

Tanis wondered why an AI would ask such a question. She didn't have eyes; for the being in her head, watching ancient vids—or ones from the edge of the Sol System—was no different than staring at the sky in real time.

<*Not really, no,*> she admitted. <*I think it would have looked empty and lonely. Now space is alive. It's humanity's great highway.*>

Darla snorted. <*That sounds like something from a travel vid.*>

<*Uhhh…*> Tanis twisted her lips. <*I think it might actually be, now that you mention it.*>

They walked in silence until Tanis got to the end of the walkway and turned left on the boardwalk that stretched around the lake.

Despite the fact that she knew it was an illusion, it really did look as though the lake was bottomless—if you dove in, you could swim all the way to Jupiter. If Tanis hadn't been wearing a ridiculously expensive dress, she might have leapt in just to try it.

A connection came into her mind, and Tanis saw that it was from Connie.

She accepted it, and a moment later, Connie said, <*Commander Richards?*>

<*That's my name, Connie. How are you doing? I thought*

you were in rejuv.>

<*Turns out that my bod is holding up just fine against the rigors of time, only took a bit of work. But what are you doing here? Aren't you supposed to be on a transport to Mars, Commander?*>

Tanis looked around, feeling a small amount of guilt that she didn't regret missing that transport as much as she'd expected to. Sure, it would be nice to see Peter and her family, but a few more meals like she'd eaten at the Chez Maison, and it was possible she'd forget them altogether.

<*We're on leave, Connie, you can call me 'Tanis',*> she said, evading the question for the moment.

A groan came over the link. <*First 'ma'am' and now first name? Tanis, you're going to get me written up for insubordination someday.*>

<*Well, not by me. Besides, you call me Tanis when we're off-duty on the ship all the time. No one's going to write you up for it out here.*>

<*Unless I slip up in front of a superior officer while serving under you, then you* ***will*** *be the one writing me up.*>

Tanis pursed her lips, admitting that could happen. <*You'd have to be a lot sloppier than I think you are.*>

<*Fine,* ***Tanis****. What are you still doing on Vesta? And your net-presence says you're at the Grand Éire Resort of all places!*>

<*You checking up on me, Technical Sergeant?*> Tanis asked with a mock-serious tone in her voice.

<*What? Noooow we're using rank?*>

<*Only when I want to chastise you.*>

<*Well then, Commander Richards, spill the beans. How*

come you're still at Vesta, and staying at one of the most exclusive hotels in the entire inner belt?>

Tanis considered her options. From the orders Higgs had given her, Darla's presence was to remain a secret, but Tanis knew there was absolutely no way she could keep that hidden from her chief engineer for any extended period of time.

The fiction of 'Darla is another AI that Lovell is training' would last all of two seconds with Connie.

However, there was a clause in Tanis's orders that provided for reading in her crew if there was a strong likelihood that they were about to discover the truth.

Tanis was certain that Connie would brow-beat her 'til she found out what was up, which was close enough to 'a strong likelihood' in Tanis's book.

<OK, Connie, wherever you are, sit down, because this is going to blow your mind.>

Five minutes later, Connie had only uttered 'Stars shitting in the deep', giving Darla the opportunity to introduce herself.

<Hi, Connie, it's nice to meet you. I'm looking forward to getting to know the crew.>

<Uh…hi?> Connie said after a few more minutes of silence. *<So let me get this straight, Darla. You just happen to have the dough to put Tanis up in the Grand Éire for her whole shore leave, and* ***you****, Tanis, don't invite me to come by? You still owe me for that time I had to clean up the sewage filtration spill on the ship, you know.>*

<What?> Tanis exclaimed. *<You're the chief engineer. It's your* ***job*** *to clean up stuff like that.>*

<I have underlings, I could have made them do it.>

<So why didn't you?> Tanis asked.

<Well, they would have done a shitty job. No pun intended.>

Tanis ran a hand through her hair, taking a seat on high stool positioned at the outer edge of the boardwalk, the view before her nothing but space. *<So you did it so that it would be cleaned properly because it would have bothered you otherwise, right?>*

<Well, yeah,> Connie replied. *<But that's not the point.>*

<It's not? Sorry, I've lost the thread here.>

The engineer groaned. *<Look, I'm just jealous and grasping at straws, here. Can't you see that?>*

<You could come for the day tomorrow,> Darla offered. *<Tanis has a spa in her suites.>*

<I do?> Tanis asked, trying to think of where it could be.

<Yeah, it's off the main hallway, behind a door that looks like a mirror,> Darla replied.

<Huh…I had no idea. So what do you say, Connie?>

<What do I say? I say what time will I see you tomorrow?>

Tanis wanted to give herself some time to enjoy a breakfast and another walk around the lake in the 'daylight', so she suggested 1100, and Connie replied that she'd be there with bells on.

<'Bells on'?> Darla asked, after Connie had closed the connection.

<Don't ask me. Connie's like a collector of ancient sayings that never make any sense. It's like her superpower.>

"A drink?" came a voice from behind her.

Tanis turned to see a man in hotel livery. He held a tray with a glass of water on it, which he set before

Tanis, on the narrow ledge that ran along the wall.

"Uhh…sure," she replied with a shrug. "What's good here?"

She regretted asking it—that sort of question tended to annoy servers—but these past few days had been all about trying new things.

"What are you in the mood for?" the man asked, not missing a beat.

"Something…chocolatey," Tanis replied. "But with punch."

"I have just the thing." The server turned and walked to the bar stationed a few meters down the boardwalk, and began mixing a drink.

Tanis turned to the glass of water, sparkling—just like the water in Chez Maison. She took a sip while staring out into the vast expanse of space.

One thing was certain: the Grand Éire liked to remind people that they were *in* space at every opportunity. The walls of the dome were utterly transparent and came down to the boardwalk, ending just beyond Tanis's feet.

As a result, it appeared as though space started right on the other side of the narrow ledge that held Tanis's water. She imagined just stepping out into the darkness and swimming through the starlight beyond.

<You're a bit of a romantic, aren't you?>

Tanis snorted. *<If by 'romantic', you mean 'by-the-book tight-ass', then sure.>*

<You?> Darla's single word was not enough for Tanis to tell if she was being mocked or not.

<You've read through the data on me, I'm sure that descriptor is in there somewhere.>

The AI chuckled. <*There's surprisingly little about your ass.*>

Unable to think of a reply, Tanis stared out into the darkness, which was partially manufactured by a tint in the glass. Right now, Sol was behind her, and everything was lit in its brilliant light.

She watched as a trio of fighters swept past, the light of their fusion engines blotting out the rest of the view, until Tanis altered her vision to mute their glow, watching as the oblong ovals swept past the lake, and up toward the ring.

Hotshots, she thought with a shake of her head. There was no way they were supposed to run fusion burners so close to Vesta. *Though I bet it's quite the rush.*

Her gaze alighted on the ring above, and caught on a majestic sight. Thirty kilometers away, spinward on the ring, a ship was easing out of drydock.

<*That's one of the new Titan Class carriers,*> Darla commented. <*The* Normandy.>

<*Thing's a monster,*> Tanis all but whispered. She watched as ten kilometers of starship was nudged away from Vesta by no fewer than fifteen tugs.

<*Masses three times this entire hotel,*> the AI confirmed. <*Engines can take it up to twenty percent of* c.>

Tanis whistled. She'd flown faster, a few times—stars, the *Kirby Jones* could make thirty percent *c,* if she ran the engines on max for twenty AU, but the *Normandy* probably had escape pods the size of her little *Jones.*

<*I bet they have to be careful where they point that thing's engines. Could roast a planet with them.*>

<*Roast a planet? I bet that thing could melt Ceres with its*

fusion drives alone,> Darla commented.

<*Fusion alone?*> Tanis asked continuing to gaze at the massive ship.

<*You're looking at the first quad-antimatter-pion drive carrier,*> the AI said almost wistfully.

Tanis couldn't help but whistle again. <*Where do they get enough antimatter to pull that off?*>

<*Haven't you heard? The Jovians finally got their equatorial accelerator working.*>

Tanis glanced toward the dim, distant light that was Jupiter, and its glowing assortment of stations and moons. At her current viewing angle, the Cho—the massive habitat built around Callisto—was the brightest thing in the 'sky'. Except for all the fusion burners lighting up nearspace.

<*They've been working on that accelerator for almost a century,*> Tanis shook her head at the thought. <*Finally rolling, is it?*>

<*I guess you don't get much in the way of news when you're out on patrol. It's rolling and pumping out antimatter like there's no tomorrow. Well, if you consider a kilo an hour to be 'like there's no tomorrow'.*>

Tanis was glad she'd already swallowed her sip of water, or she'd've spat it out on the dome wall.

<*A kilo an* ***hour****? Of* ***antimatter****!*>

<*Amazing, right?*> Darla's voice sounded rapturous.

Still silently shaking her head, Tanis replied, <*No, terrifying. That's planet-destroying amounts of antimatter.*>

"Here you are, ma'am," the server said from Tanis's side as he set down the drink. "My own concoction. I call it a 'chocolate rum-tini with an extra kick'."

<I'm pretty sure that's not a thing,> Darla commented privately.

"Thank you," Tanis smiled at the man as she accepted the drink.

He paused with an expectant look in his eyes, and she took a polite sip.

"Oh, wow!" she exclaimed honestly. "That's a *lot* of kick!"

The server winked. "You said you wanted punch."

"So I did." Tanis chuckled, enjoying the warm feeling that spread through her body. "Well done."

"Thank you," the server said and turned, returning to the bar.

"Deceptive, is it?"

The question came from her right, and Tanis turned to see a man leaning against the ledge of the boardwalk, a knowing smile on his face.

Tanis took him in with a quick sweep of her eyes. Tall, just over one hundred and ninety-two centimeters, with hazel eyes and dirty blond hair. He wore a dark red suit jacket with matching fitted pants and a white shirt.

No neon for this guy, Tanis thought.

<Jovian,> Darla commented. *<They're not into the neon thing. Sorry, you bled through.>*

Tanis kept a grimace from showing on her face. She thought she was managing to keep her thoughts from Darla.

"I suppose it is," she said to the man, lifting her drink in salute.

"I saw you admiring the *Normandy,*" the man said in response, gesturing with his chin at the ship as it continued to drift away from Vesta.

"Hard not to," Tanis replied. "She's gorgeous."

To his credit, the man didn't make a weak attempt at a compliment by comparing her beauty to the starship's. "Sure is. My firm supplied some of the components, so we got invited for the send-off."

"But you're not up there celebrating?"

The man shrugged. "I'm not huge on crowds and endless back-patting. Besides the view down here is better."

As he said the last, his gaze shifted from the ship to Tanis, and a smile tugged at the corners of his lips.

<*Oh, much smoother than I thought he'd be,*> Darla commented. <*You should totally have sex with him!*>

<*Darla! Seriously! I'm in a relationship.*>

<*Psh. With a man you see once a year at best,*> the AI's tone was dismissive. <*I know how it goes, 'a girl has needs'.*>

"I suppose it is," Tanis said to the man, turning to look at the *Normandy* once more, subtly telling him that while his appreciation was nice, it was not going to get him anywhere. To Darla, she said, <*Seriously, if I didn't know better—and I'm not sure I do—I'd think you're wanting to see what sort of bleed-through you'll get while I have sex.*>

<*Oh, c'mon!*> Darla exclaimed. <*You're the first L2 to ever be paired with an AI. I want to see what I can* ***feel*** *through you.*>

One word stood out, and Tanis latched onto it.

<***Ever****? Colonel Higgs told me there had already been others.*>

<*Did he?*> Darla said, sounding more curious than

concerned. <*Not that I've heard. Maybe they did test fits with mock setups. I'd've heard if other AIs had been paired with L2s. I have a nose for things like that.*>

Tanis didn't have a chance to pursue that line of thought further, as the man spoke again.

"So, what are you here for?" the man asked. "You a contractor? You don't have the stick-up-the-ass look of TSF brass."

Tanis looked at the man through narrowed eyes, then sighed and held out her hand. "Commander Tanis Richards. TSF. Not quite brass yet, but I will be someday—once they install the stick in my ass."

<*Ha! Then there'd be something about your ass in your personnel record,*> Darla said with a resonant laugh in Tanis's mind.

The man's face reddened, contrasting against his white shirt, but coming close to matching his jacket, and Tanis resisted a smirk at his expense.

"A commander staying at the Grand Éire?" he asked, a smile masking his embarrassment. "O-3, or O-5?"

Tanis shrugged. "O-3."

"Damn…I'm working for the wrong people—had no idea the TSF paid O-3s that well."

"All in who you know," Tanis replied before taking another sip of her drink. "Who knows, though. I could also be some rich heir, just putting in some time on the force before working for my family's important military-tech firm."

"Richards?" The man cocked his head to the side. "I think I'd know if there were any Richards families running major manufacturers. Unless you're from out of

Sol."

"TSF doesn't allow extra-solar enlistees," Tanis said with a shrug. "I suppose you'll just have to wonder about my wealth's provenance."

A frown settled on the man's forehead. "Sorry, I've come off as a bit of an ass, I can see. I was just looking for a bit of company while watching the *Normandy* head out."

Tanis sighed, knowing she was often a hair on the 'too prickly' side of things. "No, sometimes I just apply a bit too much force in personal dealings. I spend most of my time shoving back against people in command and sketchy types out in the black. It turns into my modus operandi after a while."

"And I didn't start with my name," the blonde man said. "Or give it after you gave yours. My mother would be ashamed of my manners. Jerry Kor, at your service."

Tanis chuckled. "My service? Should I send you to fetch me another drink?"

"Would you like one?" Jerry offered, and Tanis's estimation of the man fell a hair, but he finished with a wink. "The bar's right over there."

"Oh ho, Jerry," Tanis shook her head as a laugh escaped her lips. "And so your attempt at manners ends. Your mother is going to call you any minute."

Jerry shrugged, his own smile turning mischievous. "I try to be civilized, but in all honesty, I just wanted to watch you walk over to the bar—to check your ass out for sticks, of course."

Tanis was certain her mouth fell open for a moment as she wondered if she should be offended or entertained.

<*Told you that you have a nice ass,*> Darla commented.

In the end, Tanis opted for mirth—directed at Jerry's moxy, or the size of his ego, one of the two—and gave an honest laugh.

"Clearly I've spent far too much time out on patrol," she replied. "I don't think I know how to process that sort of comment directed at me."

Jerry continued to grin. "I'm just glad you didn't hit me. I hear you TSF O-3s get some serious mods."

"I still might," Tanis said, smiling over the rim of her drink. "Once I pull the stick out of my ass and—nevermind, this metaphor just went too far."

"Here's to changing the topic." Jerry gave a mock salute with an imaginary glass. "I could move to your lips and eyes. I hear they're far more acceptable to compliment than asses."

<*What about breasts, buddy?*> Darla commented privately. <*You could always go on about those for a bit.*>

<*Are you upset with him, or do you want him to just work his way up my body?*> Tanis asked.

<*Oh, I'm just here for the ha-ha's. Organics' mating rituals are some of my favorite things to indulge in.*>

Tanis decided not to honor Darla's comment with a response, and used the opportunity to really change the subject with Jerry. "So, what did your firm make for the *Normandy*?"

"A bit of this, a bit of that. Mostly components for the AP drive. Antimatter is our specialty."

Tanis glanced up at the Titan Class carrier, which was now three kilometers from Vesta's ring. She realized it was going to pass only four kilometers from the Grand Éire's lake, its massive hull like a steel leviathan, coasting through the deep.

"I suspect you're right about the view." Tanis could see vessels clearing a space behind the massive ship, a sign that Vesta's Space Traffic Control had given the *Normandy* clearance to light its engines.

"No need to suspect. I knew they were going to let them kick on the drives as they passed the Éire. Should be any minute now."

Jerry must have hit up the nearby bar for a drink over the Link, because the server came and set down a glass containing a light brown liquid before the man.

Bourbon, unless I miss my guess, Tanis thought as she watched the tugs break away from the carrier, and angle back toward the ring.

"Wait for it..." Jerry said expectantly, and Tanis found herself holding her breath as she waited for the drives to ignite.

The carrier drifted closer to the Éire's spire and the lake at its end, close enough that Tanis could make out individual features on the ship, such as observation portholes and open bay doors—ES shields holding atmosphere in while crews stood and watched the resort slide past.

The aft end of the carrier was still obscured, but Tanis saw a dim glow coming from the rear of the vessel.

"Warming them up," Jerry commented.

Tanis knew the drill. The casings around the fusion drives had to be warmed carefully before ignition, or the rapid change in temperature could cause them to crack.

From what she could tell, it was the Helium-3 drives that were heating up first, something that would be a real treat, so long as they could carefully direct the engine wash away from Vesta.

"Don't worry," Jerry said with a knowing smile. "They're not going to hit them hard. I have it on good authority that it's just going to be a light burst to make everyone feel good about the credit they pumped into this ship."

A few seconds later, just as the rear of the ship came into view, the four smaller engines came to life, a searing white light flaring behind them. The Éire's lake-dome tinted instantly, as did Tanis's vision, and she was able to see the ionized plasma plumes streaking out a hundred kilometers through space.

A tiny ripple formed on the surface of her drink, and Tanis turned to see whorl-like waves spreading across the surface of the lake behind them.

"Hoooolyyyyy shit," she breathed. "You know your engines have a lot of power when the vibrations carry though space."

In the time it had taken to make the observation, the *Normandy* had surged forward, already three kilometers beyond the Éire and its spire-tip lake.

"Well, it's the plasma cloud that's carrying the vibration," Jerry corrected.

"Starship captain here," Tanis replied, a slightly caustic tone replacing her prior wonderment as she tapped her chest. "I know it's the plasma cloud transmitting the shockwave. Still impressive."

Jerry shrugged. "Sorry, I should have asked what you

did in the service. Yeah, engines like that are something else…it's why I came down here."

<*Maybe,*> Darla commented to Tanis. <*But the reason he's sitting* ***right here*** *is you.*>

<*Annnnd the reason I'm about to head back up to my room is him.*>

Tanis finished her drink and placed it on the ledge before rising from her stool and fighting her dress for a moment. "Thanks for the company." She gave Jerry a perfunctory smile. "I have a busy day tomorrow, so I'd best head to bed."

"Already?" he asked. "You certain I can't buy you a drink?"

"I'm certain," Tanis replied. "I'm already involved with someone, not looking to add anyone on the side."

Jerry's face fell, and he nodded silently before turning back to watch the *Normandy* continue to boost away from Vesta.

<*Don't be fooled. He's watching your ass,*> Darla said as Tanis walked away.

<*I kinda suspected. Seriously, though, why is so much of this evening about my ass?*>

<*Well, I think you know why* ***he's*** *interested in it, but I'm needling you about your rump because you get to know people better when you push them out of their comfort zone.*>

<*Darla, you're an a…*> Tanis let the word trail off. <*Nevermind.*>

The AI gave a tittering laugh in Tanis's mind, but didn't respond.

Despite Tanis's comment to Jerry that she was headed to bed, she took the long way around the lake, and eventually came to a wider section of the boardwalk where both sides were lined with open-air restaurants that were filled with crowds of half-drunk revelers, many who were still talking loudly about the departure of the *Normandy,* and how it had given the spire a slight shake.

Not wanting to turn in quite so early, Tanis navigated her way through a stretch of eclectic eateries to a burger bar near the water.

She was examining the menu when her body reminded her that it had other physical needs, and she pulled up directions to the nearest public san.

Five minutes later, she had finished using the evac, and was pulling her hands out of the sanitizer when Darla screamed, <*Duck!*>

Tanis dropped to a crouch without question and spun on her heel to see a man behind her, swinging a razor-thin carbon blade through the air where her neck had been a second before.

She shot a foot out, aiming to trip him, but the man shifted his weight onto his rear foot, kicking her leg out of the way. Tanis let the force of his blow spin her around and rolled away from her attacker, coming back up on her feet a moment later.

Her opponent, who she realized was wearing a shroud over his face to obscure his features, was already upon her, slashing with his blade. He nicked her on the left shoulder as she backpedaled further.

"Dammit," she grunted, finally getting a hand down her dress to pull her lightwand out, only to have it slide down her torso as she ducked under a slash.

For the first time since leaving the hospital, the changes made to her body caused Tanis to feel slightly off-kilter, like her limbs were too light…or too heavy, she wasn't certain.

<*I can't get a connection on the Link,*> Darla said as Tanis backed away. <*There's a dampening field killing all EM.*>

Not caring a whit about propriety, Tanis pulled up the hem of her dress with one hand and caught her lightwand with the other.

A flick of her wrist, and it was activated, humming dangerously between Tanis and her adversary. Though his face was covered, the man's posture immediately changed, and he backed up a step.

"That's right," Tanis whispered. "Let's see how your blade stands up against mine."

The man hesitated for a moment, then drew a pulse pistol, firing a concussive blast from the hip.

Tanis dove to the side, landing in a san stall, her back slamming into the evac pedestal. Her right arm was numb from the pulse blast, and her lightwand fell to the floor—sinking halfway into the tile. She yanked it out with her left hand just as the man appeared before her, pistol lowering to shoot her in the head.

<*Look out!*> Darla shrieked, and Tanis wished the AI would stay quiet while she was fighting.

With a deft flick of her wrist, Tanis flung the lightwand at her attacker. The blade sliced through his hand and half the pistol, sending both to the floor. A strangled scream escaped the assassin's throat, and then he turned and ran.

Tanis struggled to her feet to give chase, but realized her right hip was numb too, and collapsed once more before she managed to pull herself up by the san's door.

By the time she stumbled out on the boardwalk, there was no sign of her assailant.

"Dammit!" she muttered, looking around for any disturbance in the crowds, not seeing anything that would clue her in to a man with half a hand missing, pushing through the throngs.

<*The blood trail ends in a few paces,*> Darla informed Tanis, her mental tone sounding focused and non-playful for the first time.

<*He must have had biofoam on hand,*> Tanis replied.

<*Ohhh…well punned,*> Darla chuckled softly.

So much for her being serious, Tanis thought before asking, <*We have Link, can—*>

<*I already called security,*> Darla interjected. <*They'll be here in two minutes.*>

Tanis nodded and walked back into the restroom, grabbing her lightwand from the middle of the floor and disabling it before stopping at the stall entrance with the sliced off half a hand and pistol at her feet.

She tugged her dress back down and crouched over the remains. Without a second thought, she touched the hand, dropping a filament of nanoprobes onto it. The nanoscopic machines dove into the flesh and began extracting data from the blood and DNA.

While they were doing their work, she picked up the front half of the pulse pistol, carefully holding it by two edges so as not to remove any evidence.

"Nothing obvious," she muttered, also releasing a

passel of nano onto the weapon to pull data from the metal and components.

<*Security's almost here, you should put that back,*> Darla advised.

Tanis did as the AI suggested and set the weapon back exactly where she'd found it. Her nanoprobes completed their inspection, and dropped onto the floor, killing themselves off as she stood and walked to the counter. She set her lightwand down, and then moved to the far wall, well out of arm's reach of the weapon.

When the pair of security guards burst in a few seconds later, pulse pistols drawn, they aimed them at Tanis, and a woman ordered, "Hands!"

Tanis showed her palms, and raised her hands. "Commander Tanis Richards, TSF. I'm the one that called security."

Technically Darla had done so, but the AI had sent it through Tanis's network connection, so it would appear to have come from her.

"That lines up," the woman said as she lowered her weapon, though the man kept his aimed at Tanis. "You were attacked?"

"Yes." Tanis glanced at the severed hand and weapon on the floor, and then at her lightwand. "Someone tried to kill me, but I used my lightwand to defend myself, and they ran off."

"Aw, shit," the man muttered as he looked at the lightwand. "Looks like we have to call the MPs on this one."

"No sleep anytime soon for us," Tanis replied with a grimace.

CONNECTION

STELLAR DATE: 01.17.4084 (Adjusted Years)
LOCATION: Suite 1300-2, Grand Éire Resort
REGION: Vesta, Terran Hegemony, InnerSol

Three hours later, Tanis was back in her suite, wrapped in an exceedingly fluffy towel following a long shower.

<*You seem out of sorts,*> Darla said as Tanis stalked into the bedroom. <*All-in-all, that could have gone a lot worse.*>

<*Oh, I don't care that I was attacked—well, I do, but that's not what's under my skin.*>

<*No? I thought that would be enough to ruin most people's day.*>

Tanis shrugged. <*I don't have people try to kill me often—in the san is certainly a first—but I'm no stranger to it. I'm just pissed that the TSF military police took my lightwand as evidence.*>

<***That's** what has you pissed? My gripe is that they think this was just a random attack—the Éire does **not** have random attacks. Security is tighter here than at a TSF black site. I'm doubly surprised that Colonel Higgs agreed with the MPs.*>

Tanis pulled the covers aside on the bed and flopped down onto the soft sheets. <*Yeah, Higgs going along with that assessment was more than a little annoying, but I'm still mostly upset about my lightwand. That's the only defensive weapon I have with me, and they took it. Since you and I both know I was targeted—though stars know why, or who by—I feel just a little bit unsafe.*>

Darla sent a feeling of agreement. <*Well, you should at*

least try to get some sleep. Your body is still getting used to all the changes. Your augments may mask the discomfort, but you need rest to rebuild your strength.>

A groan escaped Tanis's lips. "Oh yeah?" she asked aloud. "How am I supposed to relax enough to sleep knowing that I'm laying here with no weapons and someone out there has it in for me?"

<Well, I've wormed my way into the security sensors for this level, and am watching everything like a hawk. At the first sign of trouble, I'll wake you—besides, your would-be killer needs to get a new hand before he takes up his mission again.>

"And what if whoever is behind this has more people to send my way?" Tanis asked, staring at the intricate fresco painted on the ceiling.

<Well, if they can get two operatives in the Éire in one night, you're probably screwed anyway,> Darla said brightly.

"Oh, you're hilarious." Tanis snorted, then tapped her forehead. "You're in here too, aren't you a bit worried about that?"

<Of course I am, why do you think I'm reviewing the files on every single ship you've ever stopped on your patrols?>

"Could have shared that," Tanis muttered. "I've been doing the same. I've likely a whole cadre of people out there in the 'Not Fans of Tanis' club, but I don't think any have the means to attack me on Vesta, let alone here in the Grand Éire."

<That's the conclusion I've reached as well.>

"Actually…" Tanis mused. "What about that Gentry Arnold guy who owned those drone freighters we seized four months ago? He might have the means—though I don't know what he'd get out of killing me."

<Doubtful. A Jovian court just decided against him, and all his assets are seized. I suppose he **could** *make one final stab at you, but that seems counterproductive.>*

Tanis thought through all the ships her patrol teams had boarded over the last two tours. At the end of the list was Captain Unger and the *Norse Wind.* She still remembered the rage in his eyes as he bled out in his engineering bay.

They ultimately had put his body in stasis, but the man had been long gone. Stasis had just been a less messy way of dealing with the remains.

I bet **he** *would have wanted to kill me—though I still don't know why he put up so much of a fight to stop us from boarding him. Now that the* Arizona *has the ship, I doubt I'll ever know.*

A quick thought dimmed the lights in the room, and Tanis pulled the sheets up over her body, enjoying the smooth, almost slick feel they had as she continued to think over past encounters in a deepening state of half-sleep.

She had nearly drifted off when her thoughts came to the three Scattered Worlds officers she'd seen with Admiral Deering earlier in the evening.

Something about the last person to arrive at her table…Captain Tora…still stuck out in her mind. Then, just as sleep overcame her, the memory of how Captain Unger of the *Norse Wind* had moved across the engineering bay of his ship sprang to mind, and she noted how his leg turned out a half centimeter, rotating at the hip socket when he walked.

She brought up her visuals from the Chez Maison, watching as Captain Tora was led to Admiral Deering's table.

The man's leg turned out exactly the same way.

"Shit, Darla! I know who tried to kill us!"

PERSEVERATION

STELLAR DATE: 01.18.4084 (Adjusted Years)
LOCATION: Suite 1300-2, Grand Éire Resort
REGION: Vesta, Terran Hegemony, InnerSol

<*I've already said that I can see a **vague** similarity,*> Darla countered. <*But this is more a giant pile of questions than any sort of answer. For starters, why is the SWSF smuggling ancient tech out of InnerSol, and how did Unger live? And why is he here? And why is he meeting with Deering?*>

Tanis poured herself a cup of coffee and cradled it in her hands as she paced across the suite's kitchen, the robe she'd grabbed billowing out behind her.

"No one ever said that a set of answers in a mystery doesn't uncover more questions," she retorted. "Have you managed to find where the *Arizona* towed the *Norse Wind* to?"

<*Not yet…and I'll admit some surprise there. Normally, the destination of an impounded ship is not nearly this hard to uncover.*>

"You're telling me. Especially when I was the officer in charge of the takedown."

Darla didn't reply, and Tanis left the AI to her own devices while reaching out to a few contacts in the contraband inspection division, many of whom were sleeping—given that it was Vesta's third shift. Those who weren't were unable to find any record of the *Norse Wind*.

<*You misinterpret me,*> Kamera, the captain of a mid-range tug named the *Boar's Yoke,* replied to Tanis's

inquiry. <*I haul stuff no one is supposed to know about, top secret ships. What I'm telling you is that there is* ***no*** *record of a ship by the name of the* Norse Wind *having been taken into the TSF's custody, be it by a Reclamation and Inspection ship, or by any warship. The* Arizona'*s official beacon entries have it four AU from where you claim to have boarded the* Norse Wind.>

<*Jordan.*> Tanis did her best not to snap at the captain. <*I'm not 'claiming' to have done anything. I* ***did*** *do it. I shot and killed that ship's captain, for starssakes. We stacked up half a dozen corpses on that mission. Shit like that doesn't just disappear.*>

<*Sorry, Tanis, I didn't mean to call your honesty into question. I just meant that all I have is your word—which I trust, I do. You're no bullshitter,*> Jordan chuckled briefly. <*Maybe a bit of a bull, though.*>

<*Thanks, Jordan, I can always count on you to keep my head from getting too inflated.*>

A snort came over the Link. <*I should get hazard pay for* ***that****. Hauling in hulls with reactor leaks is a breeze next to putting a pin in your ego.*>

Tanis made a rude noise and closed the connection with her friend. If there was one thing Jordan loved to do, it was to needle anyone within earshot.

<*This is odd…*> Darla said the moment Tanis had disconnected from Jordan.

<*What?*> she snapped. She didn't mean to, but she also didn't feel like playing a guessing game just then.

The AI ignored Tanis's tone. <*Your report on the incident aboard the* Norse Wind. *It's classified now—as in, it flipped over in the last twenty minutes. No rider on who or why.>*

Tanis took a sip of her coffee, then set it down before stalking into her room and rummaging through her duffel for a hair elastic. She pulled her blonde locks back and wrapped the band around the hair.

<Why do you have long hair if you always pull it back?> Darla asked as Tanis made sure no bits were sticking up.

"I don't know, it's just what I do."

<I wonder if you like the way it brushes the back of your neck when you walk.>

"You just love to psychoanalyze me, don't you?" Tanis asked caustically, then took a deep breath as she re-entered the common room and walked to the kitchen area. "Dammit, I'm sorry, Darla. I'm being a bit of an asshat here. You've been a fantastic help."

<I also saved your life when I alerted you to the attacker in the san,> Darla said, a hint of mirth in her mental voice. *<Don't worry, I can spot an organic stress response. I don't have millennia of conditioning in my DNA telling me to either run, or stand up and push back on you when you get testy.>*

"Meaning?" Tanis asked.

<I can take your bad mood in stride and not get upset about it. I'm a duck, and your grumpy snark is just water rolling off my back.>

Tanis imagined her AI as a duck swimming around in her mind, and snorted a laugh as she picked up her cup of coffee once more.

"OK, so, I need to get my head on straight, and think this through. Despite what the records show, I *know* there was a ship named the *Norse Wind,* and it had a captain, and a cargo of engine components for ships that haven't been built in centuries—ships that aren't built or in service anymore, anywhere. We were going to bring the freighter in, but we got orders from Admiral Deering—no coincidence there—to let the *Arizona* take control of the ship, its cargo, and crew."

<*And the* Arizona *was listed as being on patrol near Jupiter—still is, as a matter of fact.*>

"Can you get time on any scopes or sensors?" Tanis asked. "A ship the size of the *Arizona* should be visible from a thousand Jovian stations and ships."

<*I'll reach out,*> Darla replied. <*Jupiter's three AU away right now. It'll take a bit. Not sure what it'll buy us;* ***we*** *know it was on the Hegemony's border last week.*>

"Doesn't hurt to have extra proof." Tanis polished off her coffee, and signaled one of the servitors for another cup. "Might get a clue as to who is behind all this, as well."

<*You think it's someone in the service, don't you?*> Darla asked.

"Has to be. Who else can do all this? Admiral Deering is the obvious candidate, but would she really do something like this? Any accusation against her would have to be ironclad."

<*The only conclusion I can come to with what we know is that the* Norse Wind *was smuggling something else, and Deering was involved. She sent in a ship she can control in some fashion to get the goods, and then disappeared everything. Then you see the former Captain Unger at Chez Maison, and she decides that you're a loose end, and you need cleaning up too.*>

"Which all makes sense, except for the two glaring

issues." Tanis paused to drink from the fresh cup of coffee.

<Just two?>

"Well, two major ones. First, how the hell is Unger alive? And secondly, if you're going to smuggle shit across Sol, why do something stupid like grab some weird old engine components that end up getting you flagged by Cune's port authority, and then boarded when you cross out of Hegemony space?"

<Could be that Captain Unger was just trying to make a bit of scratch on the side, and his real haul was something you never found.>

"Sure." Tanis nodded as she walked to the pool at the edge of the room and dropped her robe before wading into the waters. "That would line up just fine if Unger was just some freighter captain. But if he's SWSF, then it makes zero sense whatsoever."

<We need more on Captain Tora-Unger. Plain and simple.>

Tanis reached the edge of the pool and leant over the edge, staring down at the lake below.

"There's not a lot on him. In fact, the more that I poke at it, the thinner his file feels…dammit!"

<What?>

"What we really need is to get to Cune and fine out what Unger was really up to there. Someone has to know *something*."

<But we can't leave Vesta—Higgs reinforced that quite strongly. And we have to meet with Colonel Green tomorrow afternoon for our checkup.>

"Yeah…hence the 'dammit'."

<Well…>

" 'Well' what?" Tanis asked, wishing Darla would just spit it out.

<You have friends, right?>

ASSIGNMENT

STELLAR DATE: 01.18.4084 (Adjusted Years)
LOCATION: Suite 1300-2, Grand Éire Resort
REGION: Vesta, Terran Hegemony, InnerSol

"OK…the fact that you're actually *here* at the Grand Éire is enough to have me flabbergasted," Connie said after silently listening to Tanis talk through the last few days' events.

"Oh, trust me," Tanis gave a soft laugh. "I'm still flabbergasted that I'm here too. Feel free to carry on in that regard."

"Noted." Connie took a sip of the wine the servitor had brought her. After, she eyed the glass, and then downed the rest before tossing it over her shoulder to be caught by one of the servitors.

"Tempting fate?" Tanis asked, shaking her head.

"That model of servitor is advertised with 'lightning reflexes'. I was just curious if that was really the case."

<Don't forget, the deposit on this place is coming out of my savings,> Darla admonished.

"I'd've spotted you a wine glass, Darla," Connie countered.

<Oh yeah? You realize that glass is made from crystals that form in caves near Titan's core? They cost over seven thousand credits each.>

"Holy shit, are you serious?" Connie exclaimed, and Tanis paled. She'd not been exceptionally careful with the goblet she held, either.

<Yeah, that's why it has those yellow lines tracing through

the crystal—they're from a methane isotope that gets into the crystalline structure while it's forming.>

"Sorry," Connie muttered. "Not like I'm normally careless…I just needed to act irrationally for a moment—you know, to fit in with how fucked up this all is."

"It's a giant pile of what the hell, that's for sure," Tanis said, carefully handing her glass to a servitor for a refill. "Certainly the most interesting shore leave I've ever had."

"Well, yeah…you're an L2 with an AI, Tanis. That makes you a full on freak of nature—" Connie stopped, chuckling at Tanis's shocked expression. "In the best way imaginable, though I guess you're really not 'of nature' much anymore."

A grimace formed on Tanis's face. "Not sure how I feel about that."

<Well, by that standard, I'm zero-percent 'of nature', but it doesn't bother me. Besides, that's nonsense. There's no such thing as an extra-natural occurrence; it's an oxymoron. That would imply there's something beyond the natural universe, but if there was, it would also be natural.>

"Your logic makes my brain hurt," Connie said with a snort. "And I'm already barely able to parse what's gone on here."

"Well, I need you to dive a bit deeper into this quagmire." Tanis met Connie's wide-eyed gaze with her own. "I want to know who Unger really was and what else he might have picked up at Cune."

"A bit hard to find that out from—" Connie's voice cut off and she shook her head. "Seriously, Tanis? I came here for a little spa treatment, some of the extra fancy pillow mints, and mojitos down on the Éire's lake. Now you want to send me off to *Cune*?"

Tanis pursed her lips, knowing that she was asking a lot of her ship's engineer. "You always tell me you know people in every port. I assume you know folks at Cune?"

"Well, yeah, but…can't I just reach out to them? That place is two AU away right now, it would take almost a week to get there."

<*You know how it is, Connie,*> Darla said, her voice carrying a commiserating tone. <*Humans respond better to other humans when they're in physical proximity. Besides, if you need to track down leads, you have to be there in-person.*>

"What am I, your personal PI?" Connie said with a groan, but Tanis could tell from the tone in her voice that the sergeant would do it. It was the same way she sounded when she reminded Tanis that it was time for *Kirby Jones*'s bi-annual hull scrub. She hated it, but she knew it had to be done.

"So you're in." Tanis said it as a statement, not a question.

"Yeah, but one of you is footing the bill. The service doesn't pay me enough for jaunts like this."

<*I've already booked you a berth,*> Darla replied, her avatar grinning in their minds.

"First class!" Connie demanded, gesturing for one of the servitors to bring her another glass of wine.

<*Upgraded,*> Darla replied.

"And a group of male strippers to entertain me each night."

<*Uhhh…*>

"She's kidding," Tanis said.

"Actually—"

"Connie."

The sergeant rolled her eyes and sagged back into the sofa. "Fine. But I want some credit for expenses."

<*Of course,*> Darla said equably.

"I have to ask," the engineer began after a brief pause. "Why are you doing this, Darla?" She waved her hands at their surroundings. "All this. The Grand Éire, paying for me to go to Cune?"

<*Well, I want things to go well with Tanis, so I'm doing my best to keep her comfortable—which logically extends to keeping her alive. My head's inside her head, you know.*>

Tanis had to admit that she'd wondered about Darla's motivations herself. It was possible that the AI just had so much credit that all of this was a pittance, or that she really was trying to impress Tanis and put her at ease.

In a way, it felt like Darla was manipulating her, but at the same time, it could also be that the AI was generally nice and generous.

Downside of essentially marrying a person you've just met, she thought, as Connie called one of the servitors over for a massage.

"If I'm going to spend a couple weeks round-trip getting to Cune and back, I'm going to need to limber up," Connie said, and the couch firmed up, lifting her higher to give the servitor more leverage when working on her.

"OK." Tanis rose and walked to the edge of the pool, staring out into the sunlit space surrounding Vesta. "Looks like your flight doesn't leave for another five hours, anyway."

REVIEW

STELLAR DATE: 01.18.4084 (Adjusted Years)
LOCATION: Suite 1300-2, Grand Éire Resort
REGION: Vesta, Terran Hegemony, InnerSol

"I don't know how to behave," Tanis muttered aloud as she looked herself over in the holomirror. "I'm dressed like a civilian, going into a military hospital. Plus someone out there wants to kill me, and my CO has bought the 'random attack' narrative."

<*You look great. Stop fidgeting,*> Darla scolded her.

Tanis gave one last look at her image in the holomirror. She had found more muted clothing in the wardrobe Darla had stocked, and now wore a pair of snug black pants, a camisole, and a fitted jacket.

It would have been perfectly respectable, except that the jacket only fastened right below her breasts, then swept away to the sides, the camisole was cropped high, and the pants slung low. All of which combined to expose her navel—something that Tanis felt was more than a little improper.

"Maybe I can find a longer shirt," Tanis suggested, turning back to the wardrobe.

<*Seriously, no. This is the forty-first century, not the twenty-first.*>

"Tell that to the space force," Tanis replied, then she sighed and slid a carbon-nanoblade into a shoulder sheath.

The MPs still had her lightwand, but she wasn't about to wander Vesta *completely* unarmed. Not when someone out there wanted her dead for reasons she still hadn't discerned.

<Well, chances are they'll make you strip down by the time Colonel Green shows up, anyway.>

Tanis didn't reply as she walked out of the suite, Darla's hacked feeds hovering on the periphery of her vision. A part of her knew that she should be worried that Darla had walked through the Grand Éire's security to access their feed, but given their lack of concern over her attack, she was more than willing to look the other way.

My life's on the line, after all. And I still don't have a clue what for.

According to the feeds, her level of the Éire's spire was still unoccupied—save for herself—and she saw no one in the corridor during her walk to the lift.

When she arrived, a lift car was waiting, and Tanis took it up to the resort's ring level, and strode across the lobby, eyes locked forward, though her attention roved across every person and automaton in the space.

She knew it was silly—no one would attack her here, in a highly secured area of the resort with dozens of people around. But just like the security feeds, she wasn't willing to stake her life on trusting others.

As she walked through the resort's portal and across the gardens that separated it from the maglev platform, she wondered at how readily she'd accepted Darla's side-stepping of the law.

Maybe it's because being in the space force has trained me to tackle all problems head-on with maximum force. Things get loose out in the black.

<What are you thinking about?> Darla asked as Tanis reached the platform and joined the sparse crowd waiting for the next train, surveying her surroundings warily. *<You seem tense.>*

<Just thinking about the laws you broke to hack the hotel feeds,> she replied tersely.

<Tanis! I would never do such a thing as break the law,> Darla said, sounding wounded. *<I had full authorization to tap those feeds.>*

The AI's adamant response surprised Tanis. *<But when you told me you had accessed them, you were acting so sly—what, with the 'don't ask me how I did it' bit.>*

<Well, yeah, because I had to fill out over seven hundred forms, have a hearing with the station's AI data and access judicial committee, get denied, file seven appeals with various courts, and finally use a backdoor in the hotel's charter that allows officers to gain read-only access to feeds under dire circumstances. Then I had to go through a whole new ream of forms, hearings and appeals. In the end, I got authorization. It was a tedious process. That's why I said, 'don't ask me how I did it'.>

<Stars…I had no idea.> Tanis was impressed by the ends Darla had gone to. *<Won't that raise red flags everywhere, though? I imagine that sort of paper trail will stand out to whoever has it in for me.>*

<It got tricky. I used AI courts, and then had to fudge why ***I*** *was applying in your place. In the end, I used my assignment to the* Kirby Jones, *saying that you and I were meeting to get better acquainted, and with the threats to your life, I felt insecure.>*

Tanis shook her head as the maglev pulled up. *<I*

imagine that looked odd, given your placement on a patrol boat like the Jones.>

<*It caused some problems, yeah, but I got them squared away.*>

<*So what about the rest of Vesta? Can you work your magic there?*>

Darla snorted. <*Tanis, really? I'm besties with Vesta's AIs. Getting feed access in most public areas is a snap.*>

Tanis groaned inwardly. <*OK, **now** it sounds like you've done something illegal.*>

<*Well, let's just say in this case, you actually don't want to know. Suffice it to say that being a major owner of the backbone networking and computing power underlying the largest AI expanse on Vesta gets me some favors when I need them.*>

Tanis walked toward the glowing yellow line that marked off the safe edge of the platform as the maglev train approached, shaking her head in disbelief.

<*Seriously? You own part of the Kora Expanse?*>

<*Well, I don't 'own' the expanse. No one does, but expanses have to run on hardware, and if you own the hardware…*>

<*Who **are** you, Darla?*>

The AI chuckled in Tanis's mind. <*Just someone with a bit of a penchant for business.*>

<*Then why are you with me? Not even a day in my skull, and people are trying to kill us. Not that good for business.*>

Darla's laugh started up again, softer this time, and she sent Tanis an image of her avatar winking. <*Well, let's just say I have a penchant for a bit of excitement as well, and when the opportunity came up to be the first AI paired with an active duty L2 officer that gets her hands dirty….*>

<*Thrill junkie.*> Tanis had heard that some AIs craved adventure, loved to live vicariously through humans who got into trouble more often than not. *And I suppose I do flirt with danger a fair bit.*

Darla didn't respond immediately, and Tanis wondered if she'd offended the AI.

<*You know, AIs who seek out excitement are often seen as deviants,*> Darla said as Tanis walked onto the maglev and took a seat. <*We catch a lot of heat for putting our minds at risk—at least, before we've merged and spawned new minds.*>

Tanis had tangential knowledge of how AIs bred new minds. Usually, multiple AI minds came together and created new offspring. Frequently they drew humans into the mix, building young AIs that maintained a close connection with the parent species.

<*How much human do you have in your lineage?*> Tanis asked, suddenly curious.

<*Nothing in my immediate parentage,*> Darla replied. <*But tracing back, my roots are in weapon born AIs, not the other, more digital ones. So you could say that, more than not, I'm an organically sourced AI.*>

It was Tanis's turn to chuckle as she stared out the maglev's window, watching the broad stretch of open station sweep pass by before the train pulled up through the overhead and out into vacuum.

<*That makes you sound like some sort of healthy produce.*> Then her thoughts shifted to the stories she'd heard of the weapon born and the dawn of AIs. <*I still can't believe how things must have been back then for AIs—the weapon born, that is. To be treated like things, made from the minds of*

children.>

<The birth of a new species is often a violent thing. It's a miracle we figured out how to coexist. Usually the new species usurps the old and wipes it out.>

Tanis nodded absently, aware that many humans had feared that in the past—many still did, though they were the minority.

Growing up on Mars, Tanis had always been proud to live in a more progressive society than those in the Terran Hegemony. While places like Luna and the High Terra ring were more than accepting of AIs and their place in the grand scheme of things, other places like Earth and Venus still treated AIs like second class citizens in many ways—even after a thousand years of co-existence.

Mars was in many ways the opposite. Tanis had been altered before birth to ensure her mental capacity was that of an L1—a person whose brain contained more neurons, dendrites, and axons than a standard L0 human.

At age eighteen, her father had pressured her to undergo the procedure to be upgraded to an L2—what he'd hoped her pre-natal alterations would have produced in the first place.

Tanis had been hesitant at the time, knowing that it would preclude the option of ever being paired with an AI...at least with the technology at the time. But her father had insisted, and Tanis had bowed to his will.

Looking back, she didn't regret becoming an L2—though her decisions afterward had upset her father greatly. He'd had a grand plan for her: his own little puppet that he'd see become a business mogul like himself.

But while in the recovery room, Tanis had explored her mind, testing the bounds of her new cognitive abilities, and had come to a conclusion: she felt stifled.

Exploring the Sol System, perhaps even the stars someday…that was what she craved. Adventure, excitement, and travel. Anything was possible.

When she had expressed her desires to her father, he'd frozen all her accounts and funds, telling her she could travel once she'd committed to the course of action he'd planned for her life.

Such an irony that the procedure he insisted on in order to make me into his perfect pawn was the catalyst for all his plans ending.

That very day, a TSF recruiter had messaged her. They were offering significant signing bonuses to L2s who joined the space force's Officer Candidate School. A week later, Tanis had enrolled in OCS, and the rest was history.

Now here she was, captain of a starship, *and* paired with an AI as an L2.

If someone wasn't trying to kill me, I'd be living the ultimate dream.

A small voice in the back of her mind suggested that perhaps someone wanting to kill her was just the sort of thing that made living the dream even better. She loved combat, the thrill of the chase; finding out what was up with Unger and the *Norse Wind*, learning who was really behind it and the attempt on her life…it was just another type of chase.

Her thoughts wandered, considering what Admiral Deering could be doing with the SWSF. Whatever it was, the woman wasn't worried about being seen with the Scattered Worlds' delegation.

Tanis knew there was unrest in the Scattered Worlds. Granted, that was par for the course. The region of space out beyond Sol's Kuiper Belt was vast, and filled with small planetoids, asteroids, comets, and dust fields that were months, or even years' travel apart from one another.

While the Terran Hegemony, Marsian Protectorate, and Jovian Combine were strong, nationalistic groups, the Scattered Worlds were loosely affiliated at best. Their common thread was they were *not* a part of InnerSol or OuterSol. Too often, she'd heard their slogan, 'Diskers are for the Disk'.

There was talk on the feeds of them rallying for another vote to secede from the Sol Space Federation, but no one took it seriously. Without the resources of the federation, the Scattered Worlds would be nothing more than a backwater, people scratching out a living from whatever rock they managed to cling to at the edge of the deep dark that surrounded Sol.

Except for Nibiru, of course. The denizens of that planet didn't need the federation; they had enough resources to survive without help. But they had their own problems with the rest of the Scattered Worlds.

The thought spurred Tanis to consider where the officers Admiral Deering had met with hailed from. Not their assigned sectors and fleets, but where they'd grown up.

What she saw raised more questions than it answered. All three SWSF officers who had met with the admiral in Chez Maison were Nibirun natives, *and* were currently stationed there.

Interesting. What would Deering have to do with them?

At present, Nibiru—the ninth major planet of the Sol System, a large terrestrial orb nearly ten times as massive as Earth—was nearly two hundred AU from Sol. That was a half-year trip on a fast ship. She couldn't imagine what would bring them all the way to InnerSol, and Vesta of all places.

Certainly not a bunch of ancient engine components.

Tanis checked on the transport Connie was taking, and saw that it was still within a few light seconds of Vesta. <*Connie, you there?*>

After the brief delay, the engineer's response came back loud and clear.

<*Yeah, just enjoying living the good life, here. Your AI set me up in the best cabin on this liner—which means I have human attendants. I'm never going to be able to survive on the* Jones *after this. She's ruined me.*>

<*Enjoy it while you can. In a month, you'll be fixing a clogged waste processor after one of Smythe's epic fiber diets.*>

<*Stars, Tanis,*> Connie groaned. <*What a way to ruin a girl's 'me' time.*>

<*You're on the clock, Sergeant, all your 'me' time is mine.*> As she spoke, Tanis suddenly realized that Connie may have been resorting to innuendo, and that she may have just made an unintentional pass at her chief of engineering.

Connie burst out laughing, and Tanis's fears were

confirmed. *<I'm going to pretend you never said that,* ***Commander****. What is it you're calling about, anyway? I assume it's not just to wish me bon voyage.>*

<I had this crazy thought….>

<That's not unusual, go on,> Connie shot back.

<You're all class, Connie.> Tanis paused and sent a sigh across the Link. *<Anyway, the three officers that Admiral Deering was meeting with are all based at Nibiru, and they were also born there.>*

<Is that noteworthy? The disk is a big place. Nibiru spends most of its time alone in the black. I hear their people are insular.>

<Right, well, we know that the GE-5412 fusion torches were for ancient dreadnoughts, from back in the Sentience Wars, right?>

<Yeah,> Connie sent a mental shrug. *<And a few ore haulers from the days of yore, as well. What of it?>*

<Well, what if the SWSF is ramping up its military? You know the rumors.>

<OK, Tanis, I think maybe having an AI crammed into your skull has tipped you over a bit. Are you talking about the rumors of lost AI dreadnoughts drifting out in the Oort cloud?>

Tanis nodded to herself. *<Yeah, exactly. What if the SWSF has found some, and is refitting them?>*

<I'd say that they were wasting their time. Those hulls are likely garbage. Besides, they wouldn't stand up to modern military hardware. Did you see the Normandy *fly out last night? That thing is a monster!>*

<Well, do your best to find out what those flow regulators were for. I've not been able to find anything conclusive on this

end.>

<Tanis,> Connie's tone was matter-of-fact. *<If the SWSF were flying those Sentience War era behemoths around out there, we'd* ***see*** *it.>*

<Not if they don't have all the components to run the engines yet,> Tanis countered.

<OK…you got me there. I'll see what I can find out. Right after this lovely man finishes working out the kinks in my back.>

Tanis only sent a groan over the Link before turning her attention back to her surroundings.

The maglev was sliding into the hospital station, and she rose slowly, waiting for the train to come to a complete halt—and final jerk—before walking to the doors.

A ping to the hospital's NSAI informed her that the appointment was two levels up in a lab wing of the facility. Tanis wondered what they would need to do in a lab that they couldn't extract from the sensors in her mods and mind.

<I bet they want to put you through your paces,> Darla suggested as Tanis walked to the nearest lift, feeling as self-conscious as she expected with her exposed midriff amongst the uniformed hospital personnel.

Once on the correct floor, Tanis walked through a half-kilometer of corridors before she finally arrived at the area marked as 'Enhanced BioEngineering Labs 3J'. A tastefully decorated—for the TSF—waiting area was set up outside a pair of double doors. Four chairs were arranged around a low table, and a cooler filled with beverages sat in a corner.

A pillar of light hovered before the doors, and Tanis addressed it as she approached.

"Commander Tanis Richards, here for my 0900 appointment with Colonel Green."

The pillar of light pulsed once in acknowledgement before the audible response came from the AI. "It's only 0835, Commander."

Tanis shrugged, a small smile on her lips. "You never know with maglevs on Vesta—plus, I've never been to this part of the hospital before. Wouldn't want to get lost."

"You have the most advanced overlays in the military, I doubt you could get lost," the AI said, its tone a hair away from being caustic. "Have a seat, I'll inform you when Colonel Green is ready for you."

Tanis gave a crisp nod and took the seat with the best view of the waiting area's entrance and exit.

<Snippy thing,> Darla commented. *<She's been stationed here long enough to know organics in the space force are always early.>*

<Attitude like that is common,> Tanis agreed. *<But you only see it from AIs who don't use mobile frames.>*

<Really?> Darla emanated a soft humming sound for several moments. *<You know, that matches my experience, as well. I'd never made the connection, though.>*

Tanis chuckled softly. *<I bring something to the partnership after all.>*

"These seats free?" a curly-haired man asked as he approached.

Tanis glanced around at the three empty seats. "Well, the AIs in them may get offended, but I suppose they can double up."

The man snorted a laugh and took the seat furthest from Tanis, which faced her almost directly. "I think they'll manage. Though I wouldn't have expected you to have three AIs in your mind. I thought the limit was just one."

"Just my standard mental instability," Tanis gave the man a tired smile. "I'm not paired at all."

"No?" the man's eyes narrowed. "What are you doing here, then? Doesn't this lab deal with AI augmentations?"

"I'm an L2," Tanis tapped the side of her head. "No room in here for an AI. But I had some mods done recently, and this is where they told me to go for my checkup, so here I am."

"Dr. Green did them?" the man asked, his question cementing Tanis's assessment that he was a civilian.

"The colonel was in charge, yes," Tanis replied. "As to who did the work, no clue, I was out cold for it."

Something about his questioning struck a nerve with Tanis, and she looked him up. Her facial recognition systems pegged him as a man named Harm Ellis; there was little information available on him in Vesta's public databases, other than an affiliation with Enfield Technologies, who she recalled Darla mentioning as being behind the tech for their pairing.

"I imagine it *was* Colonel Green who did the work on you," Harm said, a smile quirking the corners of his mouth. "Not every day an L2 gets an AI."

Tanis straightened in her chair, giving the man a hard stare. "I don't know what you're talking about, but I'd appreciate it if you found somewhere else to sit."

Harm shrugged as he eyed her up and down. "Relax, Commander Richards. I have clearance."

"Not with me, you don't," Tanis replied, all too aware that she was likely being tested. "I've reported this encounter to my CO and division AIs."

"As you should have," Colonel Green said as she pushed open the double doors leading into Lab 3J. "I'm glad to see that you're taking the secret nature of your and Darla's pairing seriously—though I can't say the same for your safety."

As Colonel Green spoke, she gestured for Tanis to follow her into the lab.

"I think I did an admirable job keeping myself safe, Colonel. Only got a small nick—the other guy lost half his hand."

"In that 'random' attack," Harm added as he followed after Tanis.

She glanced over her shoulder at the Enfield man. "Glad to see someone else thinks there was more to it."

"Oh, we think something was up, we just can't tell what," Harm said. "You'd not been out of the hospital a day when someone tried to kill you. That makes us a bit worried about our investment."

"You know." Tanis fell back to walk beside Harm. "Your 'investment' is the lives of two sentient beings. You should choose your words more carefully."

Harm's eyes widened at the threat in Tanis's voice. "I'll do that."

<A bit heavy-handed?> Darla asked. *<Not that I'm objecting. Seems like a bean counter. People like that are*

mostly worried about how **they** *look in a given situation.*>

<*Yeah,*> Tanis agreed. <*Common enough with these contractors. All they care about is whether or not some five-star signs off on the deal. Not a lot of consideration given for the grunts getting the mods.*>

<*You calling me a grunt?*> Darla asked with a laugh.

<*Well, I was calling both of us grunts. But I guess you've never grunted in your life, and I'm an officer….*>

<*Yeah, weak metaphor.*>

"In here." Colonel Green gestured to an open doorway on the left, and Tanis entered first, followed by Harm and then the colonel.

The room was spare, just a pair of consoles on either side of a scanning arch.

"Disrobe, Commander Richards," the colonel ordered without even looking at Tanis.

With a glance toward Harm—who was walking toward one of the consoles—Tanis blew out a breath and strode to a chair sitting in a corner where she pulled off her clothing, folding each article as she set it down.

She'd not normally give so much care to the process, but something about Colonel Green's demeanor led Tanis to believe that the woman would judge her if a single fold was askew.

Standing naked in front of the chair, Tanis asked. "My hair tie?"

Green glanced at her as though she were a troublesome annoyance, not the very reason for everyone's presence in the room. "Leave it. Will make it easier to get a reading."

Tanis nodded and approached the arch, not stepping

under until instructed. "So what are you looking for that my nano can't tell you?"

"Nano can't see the big picture," Green said, not looking up from her console. "And it only reports what it's told to. Your body has dozens of mods and natural organs, all knitted together. You're BIO9 module makes sure they're all behaving, but no one has a mod-set quite like you."

"It's a 'we don't know what we don't know' situation," Harm summated, catching a glower from Green.

"OK, step under the arch," the colonel instructed.

Tanis complied and stood still, her arms away from her sides.

<*Not your first time in one of these, I see,*> Darla commented.

<*Not even the tenth,*> Tanis replied. <*After my L2 mods, the clinic had me down every week for a full scan. Never once differentiated from the readings my nano pulled, or that my BIO9 delivered. Was just a pain in the ass.*>

<*Well, despite your dislike for the word, they have made an 'investment' with us. One that will end up changing a lot, if it turns out that more L2s can pair with AIs.*>

Tanis wondered if that would really end up being possible. She'd been so enamored with the idea of having an AI herself, she'd never considered that it may not work for all L2s.

"Colonel Green," she ventured.

"What is it, Commander."

"Darla and I were chatting, and something occurred to me…exactly how unique am I? Will this technique you've worked out for interleaving an AI's neural net with an L2's be generally applicable?"

The colonel glanced up at Tanis, her expression unreadable. "What makes you think that the military will ever make this tech open to the public?"

Tanis's gaze slid to Harm Ellis. "Well, nothing stays with the military forever. And I assume that if I ever muster out, I'll retain the ability."

"Perhaps," Green said, looking back at her console. "None of that is really for me to say."

"What about how unique I am?" Tanis asked. "Will other L2 officers be able to have AIs?"

"A bit early to tell," Harm replied from his console. "We have to see how things go with you, first."

<Stars, that's a lot of non-answers,> Darla commented.

<You're telling me. I wonder if that means my neural structure is unique enough that they won't be able to do this to other people.>

Darla snorted. *<You're not* ***that*** *unique, Tanis Richards.>*

<Oh yeah? Did you look up where Colonel Green is stationed? Or where Harm Ellis is from?>

<The colonel? She's from…oh, look at that,> Darla muttered. *<Transferred in from Ceres two months ago—damn, she's Division 99.>*

<Yeah. I'm surprised you didn't check her out,> Tanis said as Harm walked over to Green and gestured to something on her console.

<Well, I did, but I didn't look at where she transferred in from. What about Harm? What did you find out about him?>

Tanis shook her head, catching a glare from Green.

"Stay still," the doctor ordered.

<*He's from Alpha Centauri,*> Tanis said to Darla. <*Came in a few decades ago. Was an Enfield man out there, too.*>

<*Well that gives me the heebie jeebies,*> Darla said, making her mental avatar shiver convulsively. <*Enfield has a mixed history when it comes to AIs.*>

<*Oh yeah?*> Tanis asked.

<*Ever heard of the Proteus Event?*>

Tanis resisted the urge to groan and roll her eyes. <*Of course I've heard of it. Considered the main catalyst for the first Sentience War.*>

<*More or less, yeah. That's when the shit really started to hit the fan. Either way, Enfield was behind all that. After the first Sentience War, they relocated their HQ out to Alpha Centauri. Kinda had to, since they were pretty unwelcome in most places in Sol.*>

<*And now they're upgrading humans and AIs?*> Tanis began to feel a lot less certain about whatever had been done to her to pair her with Darla. <*This is starting to feel a lot less like field testing of established tech, and more like…*>

<*Like we're lab rats? That's what we get for buying into the space force's assurances.*>

<*Colonel Higgs has never lied to me before,*> Tanis said, clinging to the belief that she wasn't the first L2 to ever be paired with an AI. Not that being the first was in and of itself a bad thing, but being an experimental test subject…that was a different scenario entirely.

<*Doesn't mean that* ***he*** *wasn't lied to,*> Darla said.

Tanis suddenly wondered if the attack the night before had been in relation to her pairing with Darla, and not at all about the *Norse Wind* and Admiral Deering's strange guests.

Of course, that didn't explain why there was no record of the *Norse Wind* anywhere, or why a man with the exact same gait as Captain Unger had shown up to meet with Deering—all after she'd turned the *Wind* over to another ship on Admiral Deering's orders.

"Was it a test?" Tanis asked aloud, determined to rule out possibilities as quickly as she could in an attempt to make sense of everything that was happening around her.

"Was what a test?" Green asked, her tone carrying no small amount of annoyance.

"That attack last night. Were you testing us? Is that why everyone played it down?"

Green snorted and shook her head. "Trust me, if I were to test you in the field, it would be with more than one assailant in a san. Though I'm surprised you didn't capture him."

"I had a few issues with my balance," Tanis replied. "Nothing major, just adapting to the changes in sight and hearing."

"You should have reported those," Harm admonished.

Tanis shrugged, then caught a glare from Green for the movement. "They were normal adaptation variances; this isn't my first time getting mods upgraded. I adjusted and compensated. If I'd been dressed in anything other than…well, a dress, that guy would be in a cell."

Green and Harm shared a look, and then returned to reviewing what was on their console.

"Much longer?" Tanis asked. "It's a bit chilly in here to be standing around naked."

"The more talking, the longer this'll take," Green said dispassionately. "You have the mods to warm up, feel free to use them."

"I think it's the aluminum-laced hair," Tanis said as she triggered her body to warm her skin. "Sucks out a lot of heat."

"Noticed that." Harm nodded. "We thought your brain would run a lot hotter with Darla interwoven through it, but that hasn't turned out to be the case—at least not over the past day."

"Could probably remove it, if needed," Green glanced at Tanis. "*After* the initial monitoring period is over, of course."

"Of course," she replied.

The doctor and the Enfield contractor spent another fifteen minutes examining her, and then allowed her to get dressed. While she was pulling her clothes on, both Green and Harm peppered her with rapid-fire questions, yelling some, whispering others.

Tanis could tell what they were up to, and answered the questions quickly and accurately. Then, while she was pulling on her jacket, Harm approached and punched Tanis in the arm while asking a question.

Two seconds later, he was on the ground, one arm behind his back, his face pressed into the ground by Tanis's knee.

"That was a stupid move, and a dumb question. Everyone knows that Venus rotates retrograde, and its evening star is Earth, which rises in the west."

Green barked a laugh, and Tanis glanced up to see a genuine smile on the colonel's face.

"I told you not to do that, Ellis."

" 's protocol," Harm mumbled as best he could. "Can you let me up now, Commander?"

Tanis rose and stepped back from the man as she adjusted her jacket. "Be straight with me. Am I the first L2 to be paired with an AI?"

<Inquiring minds would like to know,> Darla added.

Harm rose on shaky legs, rubbing his jaw as he eyed Colonel Green. She nodded and folded her arms, turning to address Tanis. "You're not the first, no. But you're the first person post-natally upgraded to an L2 to fully pair with an AI. The others didn't take properly. There was too much bleed-through. But with what we've learned from you, we should be able to replicate the process."

"At least on any Enfield-enhanced L2s," Harm added.

<Oh?> Darla asked, a hint of accusation in her voice. *<What's different about them?>*

"We achieved greater axon conductivity with a slightly lower neural density—has to do with the myelin sheath thickness on your axons. The end result is that there's a bit more room in your skull, and your thinking is faster, without being burdened with higher energy consumption." Harm spoke the words as though he were talking about a starship engine.

<Thought there was a bit more elbow room in here. Not that I'd counted your neurons, Tanis.>

"Well, have I passed?" Tanis asked. "Good to go and all that?"

"Yes," Colonel Green nodded. "We'll see you tomorrow. Once we get past the first few days, we can change these reviews to just once every three days."

"OK," Tanis replied, turning toward the room's door. Then she paused and glanced back at Harm. "If you want to test how I do under physical stress tomorrow, be sure to bring someone more qualified."

Harm worked his jaw for a moment before replying. "Believe me, I will. Not going to make the same mistake twice."

INTERRUPTION

STELLAR DATE: 01.21.4084 (Adjusted Years)
LOCATION: EBE Labs, Gen. Steven Kristof Hospital
REGION: Vesta, Terran Hegemony, InnerSol

The next few days passed uneventfully.

Each day, Tanis left her suites at a different time, choosing her routes to GSK Hospital at random, but never using the same one twice.

Some days, she stopped at a restaurant or park before her appointment with Green and Harm, and some days she went straight there, though via a circuitous route.

At the end of the fourth consecutive visit, Colonel Green told Tanis that everything was going well, her mods' upgrades were all performing to spec, and even under the influence of stressors—real ones, not just Harm trying to hit her—Tanis's biological and augmented systems all performed perfectly.

"We'll see you in three days, then," Green said, flashing one of her rare smiles. "Honestly, I didn't expect it to go this well, but barring a few small adjustments to your neurological linkages, you're the perfect specimen."

" 'Specimen', Colonel?" Tanis asked.

"Forgive me, Tanis," Green said, her smile still in place. "It's hard to switch out of the profession's parlance."

"Don't worry about it. I'm not really bothered."

Darla made a sound that Tanis chose to interpret as a groan. <*She's just prickly. Haven't you noticed?*>

"She's a tough woman," Green said, her eyes locked

on Tanis's. "Which is good. The universe doesn't pull punches. Before long, you'll be back in the black, and we're coming up on a grand alignment."

Tanis wondered at the colonel's use of 'we'. For most people—ones who didn't have to patrol the federation's internal borders—a grand alignment was exciting, a way to see a dozen major planets and stations in just a few months if you had a fast ship.

"Well, see you in a few days, Colonel," Tanis said and saluted the doctor, then gave a nod to Harm, who was bent over his console. "Harm."

"Enjoy your days off, Tanis," he said in parting, glancing up, and she waved back on her way out.

<*Freeeeeedom!*> she exulted to Darla. <*Three days…and with luck, Connie will find a lead when she gets to Cune tomorrow.*>

<*Would be nice to have something interesting to do. I've reviewed every log I can get my hands on, looking for the* Arizona *and the* Norse Wind. *It's like both ships were simply blown to atoms.*>

Tanis snorted as she walked out of Lab 3J. <*Even that would show up. Damn things have to be* ***somewhere***. *But first, I think it's high time I went clothes shopping.*>

<*What?*> Darla exclaimed. <*Why? I bought you a whole wardrobe!*>

<*Of clothes that glow in the dark.*> Tanis glanced down at the blue jacket she'd paired with the white leggings. <*And this is the last outfit I've managed to make of the clothes that don't have a flashing 'shoot me' arrow hanging overhead. Time to get something that blends in.*>

<*'Boring'. I believe the word you were looking for was*

'boring'.>

Tanis reached the lift and pushed the call button. <*I wasn't looking for any words. I didn't pause at all.*>

<*Well, you should have.*>

Ignoring her AI, Tanis navigated the warrens of GSK Hospital to its main entrance, which led out into a broad atrium housing a park and a maglev station she'd not yet used. As she walked down the hospital's steps, enjoying the artificial sunlight streaming down from high above, she decided to change things up, and hailed a stationcar.

Less than thirty seconds later, a car pulled up on the vehicular traffic section of the concourse, and Tanis climbed into the open-air seating section on the back. As she settled in place, two other passengers climbed aboard, and she nodded to them before turning her gaze to the scenery in the atrium.

<*So, where to?*> Darla asked.

<*I saw a place advertised that had more sedate clothing,*> Tanis replied. <*Atlier, in the Fornax shopping district.*>

<*Atlier?*> Darla let out a long groan. <*Their stuff is soooooo drab. OK, I promise I'll respect your desire for more…subdued colors if you let me pick the store.*>

Tanis considered dismissing Darla's suggestion, but decided that she had nothing else planned for the day, and if she wasn't happy with the AI's selection, she could simply go to Atlier.

<*OK, send the car wherever you'd like.*>

Tanis leaned back in her seat and closed her eyes, though she was still all-too aware of her surroundings, thanks to her enhanced hearing and olfactory systems. And though her eyes were shut, Darla's optical pickups weren't, and Tanis could tap those if she so chose.

It had occurred to her a few times over the past week that, with this recent batch of upgrades, she was as much machine as human. Even the organic parts of her body were not stock. Genetic modifications and bio-enhancements were the norm across her physiology.

Mostly, she was glad for the mods. Many in the military worked hard to bulk up, but Tanis had grown up on Mars; tall and thin were normal for humans on the low-gravity planet. The idea of working out until she looked like a stocky Terran wasn't one that appealed in the least. Her mods allowed her to keep the lithe appearance she was used to.

She caught flak for it sometimes, but usually it just took the casual toss of a fifty kilo weight for any detractors to realize they shouldn't judge a book by its cover.

Even so, the idea that she was hardly organic hung in the back of her mind, something that created a special kind of self-doubt that she didn't know how to deal with.

Am I good at what I do on my own, or is it just because of my mods?

Logic told her that the military invested in her because she was a worthwhile candidate, but they also tanked up grunts with just as much hardware—albeit with less finesse.

Tanis pushed the concerns from her mind, which was somewhat more difficult than it used to be.

When she first awoke from Darla's implantation, nothing had seemed much different—other than the presence of another mind always a thought away over the Link.

But as the days had progressed, her thought patterns had periodically become difficult to control. Green and Harm had warned her this would happen as her body worked through the physiological changes. Temporary chemical imbalances were common when mods were added and mental alterations were made.

By and large, her cognitive abilities seemed unaffected, and Green had indicated that Tanis's neurotransmission speed rated a small percentage higher than before the pairing.

Tanis understood that to mean that she thought faster, and that she could trip herself up, or fall into loops of perseveration if she wasn't careful. That had happened a lot after her L2 upgrades. She'd often lost hours, just thinking about things.

The doctors then had told her it was a normal part of the upgrade process. One had to reframe one's worldview constantly, as new revelations abounded and deeper meanings altered fundamentals.

What it had *really* felt like was aging a hundred years in a week. Not physically, but mentally. Few people really understood that being an L2 was as much a wisdom upgrade as a raw thinking power upgrade.

The act of spotting, and considering, more variables engendered no other outcome. Unless a person was determined to be willfully ignorant.

And that was not in Tanis's nature.

The stationcar drove down the sweep to a lower level on the next ring sector, which brought them to the

Fornax district. The other two passengers got off at a restaurant, and then the car took Tanis to a tree-lined boulevard bearing the name 'Corner Street'.

<*What an inspired name,*> Tanis said as she stepped down from the stationcar and looked around. The foot traffic here was light, and it seemed to consist of more well-to-do patrons than most of the station.

Not that it was overtly fancy, but the sidewalks weren't lined with half-drunken soldiers in varying states of revelry, so that was a step up from half the 'off-base' districts on Vesta.

<*There,*> Darla highlighted a clothing shop halfway down the boulevard. <*Huron. They'll have the more sedate looks you want, while not looking like you got dressed by a specops quartermaster.*>

<*You have to be the strangest AI I've ever met,*> Tanis said, starting down the street.

* * * * *

Half an hour later, she exited the shop, somehow having pleased both herself and Darla with her purchases. There was even a splash of red in some of the clothing—though that came mostly because Darla had been bemoaning that Tanis was entirely monochromatic.

With her bags slung over her shoulder, Tanis walked down the boulevard, heading to a maglev station a half-kilometer away. It would take her clear around Vesta's ring before returning her to the Grand Éire, but that didn't bother her.

She considered stopping at the Refit and Repair

drydocks and checking in on the *Kirby Jones*. Connie had made Tanis promise she'd do so before she left—the engineer usually swung by every day during a refit, and was antsy about being away from 'her girl'.

Tanis dropped a missive in the long-range transmission queue for Connie—who would be arriving at Cune in a few hours—and continued on her way to the maglev.

When she arrived, the very first train to pull in was one that would take her to the drydocks. Tanis boarded with a smile, and settled down in her seat, closing her eyes for a brief rest.

<*You have a penchant for sleeping on moving vehicles,*> Darla commented.

<*Holdover from boot,*> Tanis replied. <*You learn to catch shut-eye whenever you can.*>

<*But aren't you worried about being attacked again?*>

Tanis cracked an eyelid, surveying the maglev. <*By those two privates at the far end, or the corpsman two seats over? I've got my ears on them, don't worry.*>

<*I have to admit, all the stuff you do to change routes makes me more nervous, not less. I feel like we're going to get attacked when we least expect it.*>

A chuckle escaped Tanis's lips, and the left side of her mouth quirked up. <*Well, that* **is** *how it usually goes. Granted, lots of times you see it coming, but you either run from those, or meet them head-on.*>

<*And going to the* Kirby Jones*? Is that a good idea?*> Darla asked. <*Predictable places are where you're most likely to be attacked.*>

<*Everywhere we go is a predictable place. Be it the Éire,*

GSK Hospital, or the Jones. *In fact, the* Jones *is the* ***least*** *predictable place.*>

<*Well, I'm going to tap feeds and review the personnel working on the ship,*> Darla said, sounding upset about having to do so.

Tanis had already reviewed the repair crew, but a second set of eyes was never a bad thing. <*Excellent, let me know what you find.*> Despite what she'd told Darla, she had an ulterior motive for going to the ship. She wanted weapons.

The MPs still hadn't returned her lightwand, and their continued stalling had Tanis more worried than any other event since the initial attack.

Technically one wasn't supposed to wander around armed on Vesta, which meant that she couldn't hit up any of the quartermasters she knew for a favor—not without putting them at risk. Just like she was already studiously avoiding the rest of her crew, all of which—other than Connie—were still on Vesta.

Surreptitious checkups had shown them all to be well, and she'd satisfied herself with watching from afar. But when it came to gear, the *Jones* was Tanis's domain, and it had a fully-stocked armory.

In all honesty, she wasn't sure why she hadn't gone before now. In the back of her mind, she'd believed that the threat to her life was being taken seriously by someone, somewhere.

But even Colonel Green had not brought up the incident after the first checkup—or even advised Tanis to exercise caution. Though her attacker hadn't been caught—which in itself should have been a red flag, with

Vesta being a wholly TSF installation—everyone had written the incident off as random violence.

If Tanis had been staying anywhere other than the Grand Éire, she would have done the same.

Twenty minutes later, she was passing under the security arch leading into Sector 33. Vesta's ring was broken into three hundred and sixty sectors, with Sector 0 being where the ring intersected with what was originally Vesta's north pole.

Sectors twenty-six through forty were all dedicated to drydocks servicing smaller patrol craft like the *Kirby Jones.* According to the general infonet, over seventeen hundred ships were currently undergoing repair in the drydocks, with one hundred twenty-three docked in Sector 33 alone.

Tanis hoped that her *Kirby Jones* was getting the attention it deserved, with all the ships under service. The level of activity seemed high, even for a Mars transit, but she supposed it may be in preparation for the grand alignment of the planets. Usually more ships were out on patrol. She wondered if the number of ships in R&R was the reason behind the *Jones*'s extended tour.

Once within the sector, Tanis hailed an automated dockcar that took her through the wide corridors to Bay 8129, where she hopped off and walked down the short corridor to the bay's entrance.

She was surprised to see two MPs standing at the entrance to the bay with the door closed behind them. It was not a normal sight—not only were individual bays rarely guarded, but the doors of a bay in use were usually flung wide for the technicians and cargo drones coming and going at all times.

One of the MPs was standing in front of the access panel, and Tanis noted that the woman didn't move aside as she approached.

"Corporal…Summers," Tanis said as she came to a halt in front of the woman. "I'd like to access the bay and check on my ship."

The corporal's eyes had held steady as Tanis had approached, locked on a distant point down the corridor, but as Tanis spoke they shifted toward her.

"I'm sorry, sir, this bay is sealed. Our orders are not to allow access to any parties."

A scowl formed on Tanis's face. "I'm not 'any parties', I'm the captain of the *Kirby Jones*. What is going on in there that I can't gain access?"

"Yes, Commander Richards, you are the captain of the ship, but you're not on my list of authorized personnel. Regarding what is going on, I do not know. This door has been sealed for three days."

Tanis took a step back and glanced at the other MP, who had not shifted her gaze during the conversation. A rage simmered inside of Tanis, and she fought back the urge to tear a strip off the corporal, but she knew it was not either of these women's fault.

"On whose orders?" she asked instead.

"I'm not at liberty to say," the MP replied, and Tanis saw a momentary flicker of compassion in Corporal Summers' eyes.

"I understand." Tanis blew out a long breath, then half turned and put a hand to her forehead. "Shiiiiit."

The MP's posture softened, and she raised a

questioning eyebrow. "Sir?"

"Well…see, the guy I'm seeing wasn't supposed to come to Vesta for a few weeks, so I left it in my cabin on the ship, but now he's going to be here in a day—his idea of a pleasant surprise—and I don't have it!"

" 'It'?" Corporal Summers asked.

"I'm going to propose to him," Tanis replied, adding a sheepish note to her voice. "We've been together for a bit, and he's totally supportive of my crazy schedule, so I think it's time to tie the knot. I know it's old-fashioned to a lot of people, but I really want to make a commitment to him. The least I can do, with being away so much."

Tanis spoke the words quickly, almost babbling them in an embarrassed rush.

<*Wow, you're a good actress,*> Darla commented.

<*Hush, I'm working here.*>

The MP's expression had softened further as Tanis spoke, but she shook her head. "I still can't let you in, sir. It would be my ass."

"Can you at least tell me who I need to see?" she pressed. "I don't have much time to go up the chain…could take days."

"Well…" Corporal Summers glanced at her counterpart, who gave a slight nod. "The orders had tokens from Admiral Deering's staff. Master Chief Moore."

<*Oh, great…only the biggest asshole in the space force,*> Tanis commented privately to Darla while giving the corporal a winning smile—it never hurt to make friends. "Thanks a million. That'll save me some time in figuring this out."

"You're welcome, and you never heard it from me."

"Of course not," Tanis said over her shoulder as she walked away.

<I've tried to reach out to Lovell,> Darla said, sounding worried. *<He's not responding. It's not normal to lock an AI down in a situation like this. I don't like it one bit.>*

Tanis felt a pang of worry for Lovell. He was one of her crew, and his safety was her responsibility. Rage began to build within her, and she forced it back down, slowing her breathing as much as she was able.

<What the hell, Darla? Why can't I access my own freaking ship?>

<I don't know,> she replied, the frustration in her tone echoing Tanis's own. *<I've queried a dozen AIs that run the docks, and they all claim not to know what's going on with the* Jones. *There's nothing on the official records about a lockdown on this bay, but I'm working on some angles. Nothing that will show up on Deering's radar, just seeing if I can call in some favors.>*

<OK,> Tanis replied. *<I'm going to hit up Higgs. Maybe he can give me something.>*

<Won't ***that*** *alert Deering?>*

Tanis sighed, leaning against a bulkhead once she was out of view of the MPs. *<Yeah, but chances are she'll learn I was down here, so my reaching out to Higgs will be expected.>*

<OK, can I listen in?>

<Sure,> Tanis nodded as she reached out to her CO. *<Colonel Higgs, do you have a moment?>*

The colonel's queue acknowledged receipt of Tanis's message, and she waited patiently to see if she'd get an immediate response.

Just over forty seconds later, Higgs's gravelly voice came into Tanis's mind. <*What is it, Commander?*>

<*Thank you for taking my call, sir,*> she began, layering in extra politeness in case she said something that pissed Higgs off later. <*I came down to my ship's bay to check on it, and I've been denied access by a pair of MPs at the bay's door.*>

<*Excuse me?*> Higgs asked, surprise evident in his tone. <*What do you mean, 'denied access'?*>

<*Doors are sealed, and the MPs said no one has been inside in days. Nothing about a quarantine for bio reasons, either. They wouldn't even tell me on whose orders the bay was locked down.*>

<*The hell…*> Higgs muttered. <*OK, I see orders here to pause the refit, but it was just listed as a temporary hold, so it didn't jump to the top of my to-do list. I'm going to dig into this. Starssakes, I need you back in the black, not waiting on your ship's refit because someone fucked up orders.*>

<*Should I wait around here?*> Tanis asked, already suspecting the answer would be no.

<*I think it'll take a bit to get to the bottom of this,*> Higgs replied. <*Why don't you go back to your fancy hotel, and get your hair done or something.*>

The colonel's tone was softer than his words would have implied alone, and Tanis laughed in response.

<*I'll take enforced relaxation as an order, then, sir. Let me know what you find out.*>

<*Will do. Like I said, this is totally selfish. I just want the* Jones *back out there. You're one of my best ships.*>

Tanis bit back a surprised remark. The colonel had

never said anything like that to her before. So far as she could tell, he disliked something about everything she did.

Can't imagine what it would be like to be someone he ***didn't*** *think does a good job.*

<Thank you, sir.>

<Higgs out.>

The colonel cut the connection, and Tanis's small amount of elation was tempered by an irrational image of the *Kirby Jones* completely dismantled in the bay, destined never to fly in the black again.

<Anything on your end?> Tanis asked Darla.

<No clue on what's gone on inside the bay,> the AI replied. *<Even the sector's surveillance AIs don't have access to the feeds from inside Bay 8129. One of them thinks that the cameras may have been turned off; there are no logs for them for the last three days.>*

<OK, this ***has*** *to be related to the* Norse Wind *business and not our pairing,>* Tanis replied.

<Even though MICI is funding Colonel Green's work?> Darla asked.

Tanis pursed her lips. Colonel Green's division, the ninety-ninth, was known as the Mickies; Military Intelligence and Counterinsurgency. They were the ones who made sure that the federation stayed together, no matter the cost. Usually, if something weird was happening and MICI was around, you knew who was behind it.

But Tanis didn't think that the *Kirby Jones*'s lockdown and the general nonsense surrounding the *Norse Wind* was Green's style—for a Mickie, she was rather direct.

Unless it was all a ridiculously elaborate test for Tanis and Darla.

But that didn't explain Unger—or rather, Captain Tora of the SWSF—meeting with Admiral Deering.

This enhanced level of bullshit is far more than even MICI would go through to mess with someone they were testing upgrades on.

<*No,*> Tanis finally replied to Darla. <*I mean…Yes, even though they're funding our mental comingling, I don't think this is them. I still think Deering is up to something with the SWSF. Something that has to do with the Diskers building up their military again.*>

Darla made a sound of agreement. <*Well, I think step one is to get into the* Jones. *Find out what—oh, wait.*>

<*What?*> Tanis asked.

<*One of my friends managed to pull feeds for Bay 8129. Looks like no one has been in or out of the* ***interior*** *doors since the MPs showed up, but someone* ***did*** *use the external doors. A shuttle was in there two days ago, and again just a few hours back.*>

Tanis felt her hands ball up into fists. <*What shuttle?*>

<*Holy shit…it's one of the* Arizona*'s.*>

<*You mean the cruiser that took over the* Norse Wind *and then freaking disappeared?*> Tanis asked, pushing off from the bulkhead and starting down the corridor once more. <*That means it's here at Vesta…how the hell is a seven hundred meter cruiser hiding in plain sight?*>

<*I'm as clueless as you on that one, but I'm looking for it now, trying to see if I can pull visuals on every ship docked here.*>

Tanis nodded in approval. The time to trust logs and

database entries was over—granted, there were enclosed drydocks on Vesta more than large enough to hide the *Arizona*. The search could ultimately be futile.

She turned out of the short passageway that led away from the docks and into a larger corridor that led out of Sector 33. The bags of clothing slung over her shoulder were sure to be a liability for whatever she and Darla had to do next, so Tanis wanted to drop them off at the Grand Éire.

The fastest route to the nearest maglev platform was through a nearby service corridor, and Tanis turned into it, picking up the pace, trying to burn off some nervous energy.

It wasn't often she felt totally in the dark, but this was certainly one of those times. She needed some sort of lead, and she wasn't going to sit around anymore waiting for it.

<*What—*> she began to ask Darla, when movement out of the corner of her eye alerted her to an impending attack. She dodged to the left side of the narrow corridor as a man leapt out of an alcove and fired a pulse pistol at her.

The concussive wave rippled through the air where Tanis had been walking a moment before, close enough to make her arm feel as though it had been slapped.

Dressed all in black, the man pivoted, the weapon moving toward Tanis once more—but again, when he fired, she'd already moved.

She dropped low, releasing the shopping bags, and rolled to her left, coming up next to the man, her enhanced L2 nervous system and augmented reflexes making it seem as though he was moving in slow motion.

Her right hand clamped down on the pistol's barrel while she grabbed his wrist with her left, pinching his nerves and causing his hand to spasm.

Seconds later, the weapon was in her hands and aimed at her attacker, who backed away, still not having uttered a word.

"What the hell is going on?" Tanis asked while threading nano into the weapon, triggering a breach routine on its biolock. "You the same idiot who attacked me in the san?"

The man didn't reply, but she saw his shoulders tense and suspected that he was. He must have been a fool to think he could take her a second time—especially now that she'd worked out the balance issues she'd experienced during their prior encounter.

"Who sent you? What is going on?" Tanis demanded again, advancing on the man, raising the weapon threateningly.

She could just make out his eyes behind the shroud, and saw them dart to his left, an action that caused her to pull feeds from Darla's optics.

Sure enough, there was a faint heat signature approaching from Tanis's right.

<*Someone in stealth gear,*> Darla said, her tone carrying some amount of worry.

<*I got this,*> Tanis said, feeling the cold calm of life-or-death combat come over her. <*Just need three…more…seconds.*>

She took a menacing step toward the man in black

just as the pulse pistol's biolock released. But instead of firing at the visible attacker, she whipped her arm to the right, telegraphing the move, and fired twice at the stealthed attacker.

The first shot hit, but the second missed as the attacker dove to the side. As Tanis had hoped, her visible attacker's attention turned in the direction of his backup, and she took advantage of his distraction to reach out with her left hand, grab his wrist, and yank him to the right, sending him stumbling toward the stealthed opponent.

The two assailants collided, and Tanis fired two max-power pulse blasts at the pair, watching—and hearing—with satisfaction as both fell to the ground.

The man in black rolled onto his back, moaning. The other opponent was faintly visible to Tanis now, the person's stealth systems partially damaged by the high intensity pulse shots.

"Surrender!" Tanis ordered, and for a moment the second attacker paused, but it was just for an instant.

Then the figure rushed toward her.

She fired one more shot from the pulse pistol, catching the onrushing enemy in the side, but it wasn't enough to knock the person back, and they slammed into Tanis, causing them both to fall to the deck.

Tanis was on the bottom, fending off blows as best she could, while the attacker—a woman, by her weight and what Tanis could make of her build—straddled her.

<I don't think these people know about my upgrades…namely you,> Tanis said as she grasped her adversary's hand, releasing a passel of nano. *<Think you*

can disable this bitch's stealth, Darla?>

<*Do ducks have lips? Wait…no, do cats have claws?*>

<*What?*> Tanis grunted out the question as a fist collided with the side of her head. The blow stunned her for a second, but she used the woman's overbalance to roll to the side and shove her off.

She scrambled backward just as her attacker's stealth armor shut off. Sure enough, her enemy was female. She was a few centimeters shorter than Tanis, and wearing a black skinsuit, but carrying no weapons.

Between them on the deck lay the pulse pistol, and Tanis eyed it for a second, waiting for the woman in black to make a move.

"Who do you work for?" Tanis hissed. "What the *fuck* is going on?"

"You know *what*," the woman whispered. "Where did you put it?"

"It?" Tanis asked, genuinely confused. "The only 'it' I care about is the *Kirby Jones*. I 'put it' in Bay 8129, and I'd like to see it again. Right after I see your face and find out what the hell is going on around here."

"The quantum logic core," the woman said, ignoring her. "We know you have it."

"Seriously," Tanis exclaimed. "I have no idea what you're talking about. Does this have something to do with the *Norse Wind*?"

The woman cocked her head. "You really don't know…"

"Stars! *What* don't I know?"

The woman didn't respond, and instead reached behind her back. Tanis didn't wait to see what her enemy was going to pull out, and dove to the ground, grabbed the pulse pistol, and fired it three times at the woman's abdomen, draining the last of its charge as the blast lifted her adversary into the air and flung her backward.

Tanis was back up in an instant, but Darla called out in her mind. *<There's a squad coming, from Deering's personal guard!>*

"Fuck!" she swore, and turned to run.

<Don't forget your bags!>

* * * * *

Forty minutes later, Tanis arrived back at the Grand Éire. She'd taken a dockcar back to the resort, using it only after Darla had shut down the vehicle's NSAI and piloted it manually.

All the while, she waited for some sort of alert on the station's networks. Something either about the fight, or calling for her arrest.

Neither occurred. It was as though the altercation in the maintenance corridor had never happened.

Even so, Tanis wasn't about to trust that no one was looking for her, and ditched the dockcar while still a twenty-minute walk away from the Grand Éire.

Instead of using the resort's main entrance, Tanis took a lift two levels up, and worked her way through a warren of maintenance corridors to one of the employee entrances. It was slow work; Darla had to gain control of internal sensors, corridor by corridor, to mask Tanis's progress, but eventually they had passed through the more densely monitored areas.

<*This sneaky stuff is rather clever,*> Darla commented. <*I never think about things like back doors and skulking around. I'd do poorly in a mobile frame.*>

Tanis shrugged. <*Comes naturally to us humans. Liz should be arriving soon. Her shift starts in twenty minutes.*>

<*The porter from Venus? Did you hack the resort's schedules without me knowing?*> Darla asked.

Tanis sent her AI a conspiratorial wink. <*I don't tell you* ***everything*** *I do.*>

Sure enough, as she turned into the narrow corridor with a door at the end bearing the words 'Grand Éire Employees Only', she caught sight of Liz punching her security code into a panel next to the entrance.

"Liz!" Tanis called out as she jogged down the passageway.

Liz turned and her eyes widened. "Commander Richards?"

"Please, just 'Tanis'," Tanis said as she approached.

"Ummm…sure. What are you doing here?" Liz asked.

Tanis gestured at her disheveled appearance. "Well, I got in an altercation out on the station, and I'm a bit mussed up. I don't want to go through the front, so I was hoping someone could let me in the side door, here. Sure am glad I came across you."

"Ummm…I'm not really supposed to…" Liz said, looking nervous.

"It would make me happy, and if it comes up, just tell whoever asks that I insisted."

<*Not that it will,*> Darla said to Tanis. <*I've got my hooks into the resort—I can wipe you from their feeds.*>

<I thought you had 'read-only' access?>

Darla gave a conspiratorial chuckle. *<I was just trying to make you feel better.>*

<And your spiel about seven hundred forms?>

Now Darla groaned. *<No, those were real. They just didn't work.>*

While she spoke with Darla, Tanis gave Liz a sweet smile, and hoped that the woman would be agreeable. Her next option was to make a scene, but that sort of thing wasn't really in her nature, and she rather liked Liz.

"OK, Com—er, Tanis. I'll take you through to the service lifts."

"Thanks, Liz. I'll be sure to leave you something special."

"You don't have to do that," Liz said as she finished punching in her code and pushed the door open, holding it wide so Tanis could pass through. "You're a lot friendlier than most of the guests; that alone is worth it."

"Nonsense." She shook her head. "It would be my pleasure."

She struck up a conversation with Liz about places she'd been to on Venus, and was telling the girl about her favorite restaurant in the city of Tarja, keeping the discussion light, when Darla broke into her thoughts.

<Tanis, we have a problem.>

<A new one, or a compounded one?>

<Maybe both?> Darla replied. *<Once we got on the hotel's network, I pulled the feeds from our suite. It's been tossed.>*

"Shit!" Tanis muttered aloud, and Liz glanced backward.

"Commander Richards? Is everything OK?"

A pair of maintenance workers walked past, so Tanis only shook her head, and gestured with her chin to the lift doors ahead.

To her credit, Liz picked up on her meaning.

When the service lift's doors closed, Tanis turned to her. "I have another favor to ask you."

"What is it?" The porter's eyes were wide with curiosity.

"I don't want to put you in any more danger than you may already be in, but someone is trying to kill me, and it seems they've already searched my suite."

"What!?" Liz gasped, and her mouth hung open.

<*So much for the Éire's vaunted security,*> Darla intoned in mock sadness. <*Seems more like lip service now.*>

"Something crazy is afoot on Vesta, and I'm trying to get to the bottom of it, but I need somewhere to lay low for a bit. The Grand Éire is massive; do you know of anywhere I could hide?"

Liz appeared pensive for a moment, and then a smile slowly spread across her lips. "Oh, I have the *perfect* place!"

*****

The lift stopped one level below Tanis's floor, and Liz gestured for her to exit.

"This level is all one suite, and has been vacant for a few weeks. The previous guests had a bit of a…rambunctious party in one of the rooms, and completely destroyed it. They made a pretty big mess across the whole suite—most of it is cleaned up, though. One room is not, because the Éire is suing the guests, and the insurance company won't approve the repairs until the lawsuit is complete."

"Really? That seems like a lot of effort," Tanis replied. "Why not just fix the room and start getting money from guests again?"

Liz shook her head as she led Tanis down a short corridor to a pair of double doors. "The room was sheathed in Lunar Marble, the red-veined stuff that they mine under New Austin. They completely ruined it—smashed some…spoiled the rest. It's worth a mint, and the guests are more than wealthy enough to pay for it." She punched in the access code, and pushed the doors open. "Anyway, the court case got pushed back a month, so this place will be sitting vacant 'til at least then."

<*This is brilliant,*> Darla exclaimed. <*I bet you could climb up to your room too, if you wanted to get anything.*>

Tanis considered it, but nothing in the other suite was of particular value to her. <*Oh, you're worried about the clothes.*>

<*I sure am! There's a lot of money in advanced fabric up there. If they ruined it…*>

Looking around the large mainspace, which was mostly a bigger version of the one in Tanis's suite above, she nodded in satisfaction. "This is great, Liz. Amazing, really. You should go, though. We'll manage from here."

An uncertain look passed over Liz's face. "Will you be OK? Do you need anything?"

"No, I'll be fine." Tanis shook her head. "If anyone asks, tell them you took us to our room; I'll alter the lift's records to show that it stopped there, not on this floor."

"You can do that?" Liz asked.

Tanis nodded, knowing that for her alone it might have been tricky, but with Darla's hooks already in the hotel's systems, it would be a breeze.

"Um…OK. Well, let me know if you need anything."

"Of course," Tanis said with a warm smile, gesturing for Liz to leave the lavish suite.

<I wonder if she could stop in upstairs and grab some of your wardrobe,> Darla mused as the porter walked to the door.

<Darla, seriously. Focus!>

*****

Darla altered the suite's systems to log any use of the servitors or facilities to their room above, and Tanis took a long shower, pulling on a simple pair of black leggings and a light grey blouse afterward, enjoying the feel of the soft carpet on her bare feet.

"So much better," she said, stretching her arms out and rolling her neck side to side. "Now I just need some food."

<The stores in this suite are bare, but I could order room service for our suite, and then direct the drone down here,> Darla offered.

Tanis considered it. "That would probably alert someone to the fact that we're back. Though at least we don't have to worry about any official security coming for us. Yet, at least."

<Probably,> Darla agreed. *<Getting our mysterious*

attackers to come at us again ***could*** *be useful, though, right?>*

"Well, if I didn't actually need to eat, we could use the food order as a distraction. But having all these mods burns a lot of energy. If I don't get food in my stomach, I'm going to snack on the carpet."

<*You have that fancy new matter assimilator in your arm,*> Darla suggested. <*You could probably configure it to take in something like that, or leather from the sofa, and turn it into a carb bar of sorts.*>

"Gah, let's file that under 'imminent death from starvation only', OK?"

<*I suppose I can see how that wouldn't be too appetizing, given your chemical preferences.*>

"Why not just order food for another empty suite and redirect the delivery drone here?" Tanis asked.

<*Huh…that would be simple enough. More of that physical presence stuff that I don't always get. Being paired with you is good for my special cognition.*>

"What's helping most? Plotting surreptitious food delivery, or random ambushes?" Tanis asked with a laugh.

<*Maybe a bit of both.*>

Twenty minutes later, Tanis had a bottle of rather expensive wine and a platter of far less costly BLTs sitting before her on the suite's smaller dining table that sat next to the kitchen area.

"Now this is living," she said after taking a bite of the first BLT.

<*There are ten of them…can you really eat ten?*> Darla asked, sounding mildly horrified.

Tanis looked over the stacked BLTs, three of which

had a sharp cheddar cheese added in—something she wasn't too certain about, hence the larger order.

"Maybe?" Tanis said, then took another bite, chewing thoughtfully. After swallowing, she added. "With everything going on, who knows when I'll get another meal, and I need to carb up."

<I really don't know where you're going to put all those. I think we're looking at a legitimate volume issue.>

Tanis carefully chewed her next bite, savoring the flavor of the Marsian low-*g* bacon. "Well, I'll stop when I'm full. Not like I'm going to stuff myself silly."

<OK, so other than gorging, what's your plan now?>

Wiping her mouth with a napkin, Tanis looked at the ceiling above. "Order some food for our room, let's see if we can set a trap."

<What are you going to do, this time?> Darla asked. *<Interrogate whoever shows up?>*

"That's my plan. They think I have something from the *Norse Wind*. You know what that means."

Darla gave a long, rather dainty sigh. *<That someone on our crew lifted something from the* Norse Wind, *and whoever was using that ship to smuggle shit wants it back.>*

Tanis nodded. She hated to think that someone on the *Jones* would steal something from a ship they'd boarded, but it was the only thing that made sense.

Other than Connie, the entire crew was still on Vesta. Tanis had considered seeking them out and finding out if they had taken anything, but that might bring heat down on her people. Thus far, none of them had reported any incidents, so whoever was behind this was content with directing their efforts toward Tanis.

Of course, if they continue to make no progress with me, they just might start going after my crew.

She hadn't heard from Connie yet, but her chief engineer should have landed on Cune by now. The fact that she hadn't reached out was making Tanis more than a little nervous.

After a brief pause, she sent out a ping to Connie, knowing it would take a little over a half an hour for a response. Then she picked up her second sandwich and took a bite, chewing contemplatively.

"We have to get to the bottom of this, fast," Tanis said after a minute. "Obviously, Deering and her Scattered Worlds compatriots want both the engine components, and quantum core—which I assume must be necessary for the GE-5412 flow regulators. We know that Deering's not operating on the up and up, or she'd haul me in—though if they don't get what they want soon, I bet picking me up will rise up on her list of options."

<That would directly connect her to…whatever is going on. But I guess, given that she sent her own troops after you in Sector 33, that may be something she's willing to do.> Darla paused for a moment, then asked, *<You know what I think we should do? Barring the success of your food trap…>*

"What's that?"

<Well, I figured out where Captain Tora and Colonel Urdon are staying—>

"Shit! Why didn't you say so?"

<I was waiting for you to 'carb up'. Anyway, they're staying right here in the hotel, and they both have dinner reservations tonight at a restaurant down by the lake.>

A dozen plans flashed through Tanis's mind, but all

of them required weapons. To subdue two SWSF officers with her bare hands would require beating them to a pulp…which she may not be capable of, and which they may not survive—a result which was not conducive to questioning…or remaining out of prison.

"Dammit, I really wish I hadn't dumped that pulse pistol," Tanis muttered. "I need a weapon."

<I miiiiight know a guy,> Darla said hesitantly. *<But he's notoriously skittish.>*

"Someone selling weapons on Vesta?" Tanis asked. "So far as I know, there are only specialty sellers, who either have rare collector's items, or shops that outfit merc contractors. Both of which are hard for me to buy from on the QT."

<You could always wait to see if someone springs our trap upstairs,> Darla suggested. *<If anyone shows up, they'll be armed.>*

Tanis knew that wasn't a great plan.

One on one, she could take out just about anyone she came across. Most people underestimated her slight build, and coupled with her L2 reflexes and augmented muscles and bones, she could take a punch from a two-hundred-kilo, modded Earther, and still hit back.

But all it took were two armed attackers, and all her strength and speed would count for nothing. She couldn't outrun a bullet—or dodge one fired into her back.

"You know…" she mused. "Let's go check that room they're repairing. There's some equipment in the hall…might be something we can use."

She rose from the table and grabbed a BLT from the

platter before striding down the hall in the direction of the room Liz had said was still unrepaired.

Sure enough, the corridor leading to the room in question had several tool chests and supplies sitting at the end, plus just the thing she was looking for: a plasma cutter.

"Oh, yeah, this'll do nicely," Tanis purred, a grin spreading across her face. "There's a safety valve on these that you can remove to make a nice, half-meter flame."

<A half-meter plasma flame? Don't cut your arm off!>

"Don't say things like that," Tanis said with a laugh as she flipped open one of the chests. Confirming it contained what she needed to alter the plasma cutter, she shouldered the tank and cutter, and wheeled the tool chest back to the dining table.

After arranging the equipment on the table, Tanis helped herself to a final BLT and a glass of wine before she set to work.

<So, what's your plan?> Darla asked as Tanis pulled out a hex wrench and took apart the mixing chamber for the plasma torch.

"Well, you'll order food for my room upstairs, and then we'll see who shows up on the feeds you've hacked. If it's a manageable number—two or three, tops—I'll come in behind them and take them out…hopefully while they're spread out, checking over the rooms. With any luck, I'll take them down without too much damage, and get to question someone."

<This seems like a really ad-hoc plan.> Darla sounded even more uncertain than when Tanis had found the

plasma torch.

"Well, it'll solidify once I see what I'm up against," she replied. "Worst-case scenario, I get some weapons and no questions, but I can use those weapons to go after Tora-Unger.

<Once we do this, we've crossed the point of no return,> Darla advised. *<You realize that, right?>*

"Darla. People are trying to kill me—and, by extension, you. The authorities didn't believe us the first time, and nothing official has shown up on the feeds regarding our little scuffle down in Sector 33. What does that tell you?"

The AI let out a long mental sigh that sounded a bit too close to nails dragging on a hull for Tanis's liking. *<It means that you don't know who to trust. Stars…at first, I thought being in your head would make for a lot of fun adventure, but now I'm not so sure.>*

"Well, we've had adventure aplenty. Are you just not sure it's your cup of tea? Or…qubits?" Tanis asked as she pulled out the limiter from the mixing chamber and began to put the cutter back together.

<Ask me again in a day or so—provided we're still alive.>

Tanis took another sip of wine before turning on the plasma cutter and pulling its trigger. A blue-white lance shot out nearly a meter, and she grinned with satisfaction.

"Now we're cooking."

AMBUSHING THE AMBUSHERS

STELLAR DATE: 01.21.4084 (Adjusted Years)
LOCATION: Suite 1301-1, Grand Éire Resort
REGION: Vesta, Terran Hegemony, InnerSol

"Three of them," Tanis reported as she watched the shrouded figures enter her suite—the one she was supposed to be in, not the one a level down where she was hiding out.

<*They're all armed,*> Darla advised as Tanis walked into the lift. <*You sure about this?*>

"I expected them to be. I need answers, Darla. I'm not just going to sit back and let these assholes try to kill me while no one takes the threat seriously."

<*I get that, just...be careful.*>

"I'm always careful."

<*I've read your record, you know…*>

Tanis didn't reply. The lift doors opened, and she walked down the hall to her suite. The intruders had left her door slightly ajar, likely to facilitate a speedy exit if necessary—or they were just sloppy. She hoped it was the latter.

Peering through the crack, she surveyed her suite.

Though it had been completely turned over earlier in the day, the servitors had cleaned it up as best they could. The recently delivered meal sat on the table in the sunken seating area, and the faint sounds of a running shower could be heard—courtesy of Darla.

Tanis watched as one of the shrouded intruders walked along the edge of the pool, apparently checking the water to see if she was hiding beneath the surface.

Satisfied that no one was lurking within the pool, the man disappeared down the right-hand hall.

Slowly and gently, Tanis pushed the suite's door open and kicked away the block they'd used to keep the door from closing. Then she gently closed the door, and passed her lockdown token, sealing it against egress.

It wouldn't stop a determined enemy for long, but sometimes seconds made all the difference.

<*That last one went toward the rooms you're not using. The other two are in the master room, almost at the shower,*> Darla informed Tanis, though she could see it all on the feeds as well.

<*I'll take out Lone Star first, then.*>

Slipping through the kitchenette, Tanis crept into the hall, watching the solitary enemy duck into one of the smaller sleeping rooms.

<*He has a pulse pistol,*> Darla advised.

<*I see it,*> Tanis replied as she hurried down the hall as quickly as she dared.

On the feeds, she could see the intruder walking past the bed to check the attached san. Deciding to take this person out by hand, she kept the plasma cutter's torch end tucked into her belt as she darted into the room.

She ran across the bed, and used the momentum to fling herself through into the san, praying she'd timed the move correctly.

Luck was on her side, and the intruder had paused long enough in the center of the san that Tanis hit him square in the back and knocked him into the sink.

The man threw an elbow back, but Tanis had already

shifted to the left, avoiding the blow. She drove her own elbow into his back, leaning into the strike.

Her enemy tried to catch himself on the sink, but Tanis kicked his left leg out from under him, and the attacker's head hit the basin with a solid *thud*.

<*Still alive,*> Darla said as the man went limp.

Tanis only nodded as she reached for his pistol, threading in a filament of breach nano to disable the biolock.

<*The other two just checked out the master bedroom's san. They know it was a diversion.*>

<*Then they'll reach out—*>

Tanis stopped as the feeds showed the two enemies—one man and one woman, by their builds—exit the san and move back into the master bedroom, weapons held ready.

She didn't waste any time, not wanting to be cornered in the end of the suite with the spare bedrooms. She made it to the kitchenette, and ducked behind the counter, waiting to see if one of the enemies would get close enough.

<*They've released drones,*> Darla whispered in her mind. <*They'll see you in a few seconds.*>

<*Shit, can you disable them?*>

<*No...maybe if you had nanocloud tech. Either way, I can't find the control frequency.*>

Tanis gritted her teeth and slid the plasma cutter's torch from her belt, ensuring there was enough play in the hoses that ran to the tank she'd slung over her back using a short strap.

<*Here goes.*>

Before she rose from cover, she surveyed the room through the feeds. The suite's exit was ten meters to her left, and the sunken seating area was eight to her right. Another eleven meters beyond that was the infinity pool that ran around the perimeter of the suite.

Directly ahead was the hall that the two enemies would emerge from at any second. Between her and the hall was the main dining table, and to the left stood the bar with a pair of servitors.

<Darla…can you override the servitors' safety control systems?>

<Umm…that's unethical, Tanis.>

<I thought you were worried about our collective hides?>

The AI grunted. *<On it.>*

Tanis didn't wait to see how long it would take Darla. The two attackers had reached the end of the hall, and she rose from her cover, counting on her sudden appearance to startle them as she fired the pulse pistol.

At fifteen meters, the concussive pulse wave wouldn't do much more than a good slap, and though the pair of attackers flinched, the shot didn't slow their advance.

"Tanis Richards!" the woman called out—by her voice, it was the same woman who had attacked Tanis in Sector 33. "We just want to talk. If you give us the quantum core, we won't hurt you."

Tanis had already ducked back behind the counter, and watched on the feeds lining her vision as the two enemies took up positions behind the dining table.

"Like hell you won't!" Tanis shouted. "Your friend who attacked me the other night was looking to cut shit off first, and ask questions later, besides, I thought we already established that I don't know what the hell you're talking about."

"Look, Ben got out of hand," the man said from across the suite. "Teri and I here won't do that. We just want the core, and then we're gone."

"What about what I want?" Tanis called back.

"Pardon?" The woman sounded shocked. "You want something?"

"Yeah," Tanis growled. "I want to know what the fuck is going on!"

As she spoke, she rose and fired her pulse pistol at the table, cracking the surface before ducking back down.

Predictably, the man and woman took the opportunity to advance. The man laid down covering fire, while the woman rushed around the table.

<*Got it!*> Darla cried out triumphantly, and Tanis watched the two servitors begin to fling bottles at the man.

She prayed that the distraction would be enough, as she lunged out from behind her cover, and fired her pulse pistol at the advancing woman.

Tanis's opponent had been ready, brandishing a chair that absorbed the pistol's blasts, which she then threw at Tanis.

The flying furniture knocked the pistol out of Tanis's hand, but she didn't miss a beat, triggering the plasma cutter, and screaming as she rushed toward the woman, whose eyes grew wide with fear as the half-meter of star stuff slashed toward her.

Out of the corner of her eye, Tanis saw the man—who was still weathering a barrage of bottles—fire his pulse rifle at one of the servitors, slamming the thing against the bar. Then her attention was back on the woman.

A pulse blast rippled through the air, catching Tanis in the hip, but she didn't slow, slashing wildly with the plasma torch as her opponent backpedaled.

The woman reached the table and grabbed a chair, flinging it at Tanis, only to watch in terror as the plasma blade sliced it in half.

Tanis snatched half of the chair out of the air and flung it back at the woman, catching her in the side of the head with one of the legs.

The blow stunned the woman, and she staggered backward, falling into the sunken seating area.

Movement out of the corner of her eye caught Tanis's attention, and she turned to see the man—bleeding from a cut on the side of his head—leap across the table before he slammed full-force into her.

She fell back onto the ground, and the impact momentarily knocked the wind out of her. The man was on top of her then, one knee on her chest, the other on the arm that held the plasma torch.

"Just stop it!" he yelled. "You can't—"

His words ended in a grunt, as Tanis twisted her arm free at the same moment she swung a leg up and kicked him in the back of the head.

He fell forward, right into the plasma torch's searing lance, half of his head burning away in moments.

Instead of falling limp, the man began to thrash and spasm—either his nervous system had gone haywire, or his mods had.

<Agh! That's gross,> Darla exclaimed. *<And I don't*

normally think biological things are nasty.>

<*Shhhh,*> Tanis responded sharply.

She scampered backward, trying to get out from under the wildly thrashing man. Her perception of time seemed to slow as she kicked him away, only to see his leg get caught in the hose for the plasma cutter.

She twisted to the side, but it was too late. The torch's handle was wrenched from her grasp, and the lance of plasma swung around, cutting off Tanis's right arm.

"Fuck!" she screamed, both terrified that she was about to die, and also surprised that there was no pain.

She managed to roll away from the thrashing man and the plasma torch caught around his leg. Then the torch cut through the hose, and the emergency safety valve kicked in.

The plasma sputtered out, and Tanis breathed a long sigh of relief, clenching her teeth before looking at the stump of her right arm that protruded from her shoulder.

That was when the pain hit her.

<*I'm going to dampen it as much as I can,*> Darla spoke up, her mental tone carrying no small amount of concern. <*At least it's cauterized…mostly.*>

Tanis was trying to regain the power of speech, when a sound came from the sunken seating area, and the woman rose on shaky legs.

She stumbled toward Tanis, but stopped at the sight of her partner.

"You're gonna die, bitch," the woman whispered, and Tanis couldn't help but wonder if that was indeed what would happen next.

The woman bent over and picked up the man's pulse rifle, casually checking its charge as she advanced.

"I'm going to make it hurt, though. You'll tell me where the quantum core is, and then I'll have some fun. Everyone's bought off, no one is going to fi—"

A loud snap sounded, and a wet patch appeared on the woman's chest, spreading outward. A confused look came over her face, and then the would-be killer fell to the floor.

Tanis heard footfalls to her left, and turned her head to see the last person she'd expect to save her.

"Harm Ellis?" she whispered as a wave of dizziness came over her, and she fell back against the chill unit.

"In the flesh," he said, still holding a pistol on the woman as he approached. "Shit, you got banged up!"

Tanis nodded slowly. "One in the bedroom…down to the right. Make sure he's secure."

Harm nodded and pulled out another pistol, passing it to her. "Just in case."

She fumbled with the weapon, but managed to get it turned around and gripped in her left hand as she tried to breathe calmly.

<*Wow,*> Darla said after Tanis's heart rate had crept back down toward one hundred and fifty beats per minute. <*That was **intense**. And a lot more dangerous than I thought it would be.*>

"Yeah," Tanis all but whispered. "You can say that again. That was my favorite arm, and it just got all healed up after Unger broke it."

<*Really? You're trying to be funny?*>

"Why not, keeps me from focusing on how close that

plasma lance came to my head. You know…the place where both our brains are." She began to shake, and the gun slipped from her grasp.

The last thing she remembered was Harm striding back into the main room, and saying something about her going into shock.

TANIS UPGRADED...MORE

STELLAR DATE: 01.21.4084 (Adjusted Years)
LOCATION: Suite 1301-1, Grand Éire Resort
REGION: Vesta, Terran Hegemony, InnerSol

Consciousness returned to Tanis like a bucket of cold water hitting her in the face.

Not the water, the bucket.

Correction, lots of buckets. It felt like every part of her was aching.

<*Welcome back.*> Darla's easygoing voice filtered into Tanis's mind, pushing back the haze that seemed to surround her.

<*Where…?*>

<*Your suite…well, not the one you're supposed to be in, the one we're squatting in. Harm brought you down here after I gave him a brief summary of what's been going on.*>

"Harm," Tanis whispered. "He here?"

<*Not at the moment. He's taking care of the bodies.*>

" 'Bodies'? Plural?"

<*Neither intruder you fought in the mainspace made it. But we have the first guy you took out down here. He's tied up in one of the rooms.*>

"Harm seems pretty resourceful for a corporate tagalong just keeping an eye on Enfield's latest project," Tanis noted as she finally got the courage to open her eyes and gaze at the bandaged stump that was all that remained of her right arm.

<*I've been having similar thoughts. He's an operator, that's for sure. Knows his shit.*>

Tanis looked around and saw that she was on one of the sofas in the suite's mainspace. Slowly, mindful of how much her body ached, she pushed herself up to half-lay against the back and armrest.

"Did he say why or how he showed up out of the blue?"

<He didn't, no. Said he only wanted to have 'the talk' once, and to wait for him to get back.>

Tanis closed her eyes as a wave of dizziness washed over her. She took a steadying breath, and pinged one of the servitors over the Link to bring her a glass of water.

When it arrived, she tried to reach for it with her right arm, and then shook her head, letting out a rueful laugh. "Guess I'll have to adjust to being a lefty for a bit."

As she'd spoken, the suite's door had opened, and Harm walked in, a large crate trailing behind him.

"Not for too long, I hope," he said with a grim smile. "We didn't put all this effort into you just so you could get sidelined by something stupid like a plasma torch."

"Glad to know how much you value me," Tanis muttered. "What do you have there?"

Harm glanced back at the case. "Portable autodoc, plus a new arm. Not organic; you'll have to make do with being a bit more of a cyborg for now."

Tanis shrugged. "I suspect this won't be the last time I'll have a temporary prosthetic. I don't really have the safest line of work."

Harm stepped down into the sunken seating area and sat across from Tanis. "So, I think you have a story to tell me… especially since I just covered up a pair of homicides for you."

"Covered up?" Tanis asked.

Harm leant back in his seat, crossing an ankle over his other knee. "Well, I put them on ice, so to speak. I'm not fully prepared to throw in with whatever you have going on here, but given that unknown assassins were attacking you in your rooms, I'm going to go with them probably being in the wrong."

"Seems safe on the face of it," Tanis said with a half-smile. "Of course, I lured them there, so that muddies things."

"Lured?"

"I ordered food. They were the dessert."

Harm cleared his throat, raising an eyebrow. "Perhaps you'd better start at the beginning."

Tanis took another sip of water as she stared at him. "I'm not sure that you have clearance to—"

"Let me stop you right there," he said, holding up a hand to forestall further protests from Tanis. "I'm passing you my credentials, which are Alpha-Level secret."

<Shit! Alpha-Level?> Darla exclaimed.

Tanis's eyes grew round as she looked over Harm's real rank. "Colonel?"

He nodded. "MICI, just like Green—only she doesn't know that. I'm embedded with the L2-AI program inside Enfield to make sure whatever they're doing is on the up-and-up. I was particularly interested in how you two would work out, so I put in to be on the oversight team."

Tanis chuckled. "Just had no idea what you'd be overseeing."

"Oh, I had *some* idea. You have a penchant for finding

your way into interesting situations. So lay it on me. What's going on?"

With a final gulp, Tanis polished off her water, and launched into the tale of the last few days. She explained to Harm about the missing ships, the task she'd given Connie, and how she couldn't get in to see the *Kirby Jones*.

As she ran through the events, she began to worry that she'd blown things out of proportion—that somehow, there was a logical explanation for everything that had occurred. But as the frown on Harm's face deepened, her doubts dissipated.

"That's a lot to chew on," he said when she'd completed the story, including the information about Captain Tora-Unger, who was bound for his dinner reservation any minute now.

<I can attest that everything Tanis has told you is the truth, Colonel,> Darla added. *<We really are mired in some sort of crazy web of intrigue here…we just don't know what it's all about.>*

Harm ran a hand through his hair. "Well…if it makes you feel any better, neither do I. I'm going to have to reach out to some contacts to see if anyone has ops going on with Deering. Seems like if she were colluding with the Diskers in something off-book, it would be on someone's radar."

"What about talking to those SWSF officers?" Tanis asked. "If you go now, you can probably still grab them."

"I don't think so," Harm shook his head. "I'm not going to run after them half-cocked. We already have one of their people here that I can interrogate. I also need to double-check that my tracks are covered, and that no one is going to come looking for us here. I do like your moxie, though. No one is going to look for you hiding just one floor down from your assigned rooms. There may be hope for you, after all."

Tanis didn't respond to the barb, but instead pushed herself upright. "So then, I suppose it's time to set your autodoc to work on me.

Harm nodded. "Yeah, the sooner we get you patched up, the better. I have a suspicion that things are about to get interesting."

*****

When Tanis woke, she immediately checked the time and saw that just over twelve hours had passed, making it the middle of Vesta's third shift.

She took quick stock of her situation, and her first observation was that the surface beneath her was firm, and the ceiling was close.

"Am I on the dining room table?" she asked aloud.

<Turns out that you weigh more than Harm expected. He didn't want to risk messing up your new arm while hauling you to a bed.>

"Coulda at least got me a pillow," Tanis muttered as she flexed her fingers on her right hand. "They feel stiff."

<I imagine the neural interfaces will take some use to properly attenuate.>

Tanis lifted her arm, surprised at how natural it felt. *Granted,* she thought as she looked at the pale pink flesh, *it* ***looks*** *entirely natural.*

She raised her left arm to compare the two, and couldn't help but be impressed by how perfectly her prosthetic right arm matched her organic left one.

"Did the autodoc have any issues?" Tanis asked as she pushed herself into a seated position. "And where's Harm?"

<No, it just put some stints into your nervous system to allow for dampening your pain receptors—which I have on max. Though, the 'doc also bored out a lot of what bone you had left in your arm, and then put anchor points in your shoulder to handle the added weight. Would be hurting a lot, otherwise.>

Tanis rotated her arm, able to feel the pivot points in her shoulder moving differently than before. "And Harm?"

<He had to leave, said he needed to follow some leads, but he said you should sit tight 'til he gets back.>

Tanis swung her legs over the edge of the table, and walked to the bedroom she'd claimed. "Of course he did. People like him always have to be in control."

<Guys, or spies?>

<Spies, mostly,> Tanis replied. *<Some guys, too, I guess.>*

Once in the bedroom, she got dressed in a pair of black pants and a fitted grey top. She rummaged through the bags from her shopping trip and found a black jacket, which she pulled on overtop, wincing as her shoulder reminded her that it was still healing from the autodoc having mounted a new limb to it.

"I hope that Harm's errands include getting us some weapons," Tanis said as she walked back out into the suite's mainspace.

<Well, he did bring down the ones your attackers left behind.>

Tanis's gaze swept the area, and she saw three pulse pistols and two rifles resting on the bar.

"I'm about done with pulse weapons," she commented while walking across the space. "Though I suppose they're better than nothing."

<Got the urge to put holes in people?> Darla asked.

"Yeah, bordering on compulsion. Have you been keeping an eye on the crew? They OK still?"

<Smythe got plastered at a bar last night and almost got hauled in by the MPs, but Jeannie vouched for him and took him home.>

"Jeannie? Really?" Tanis asked. "Wasn't aware those two frequented the same establishments. Any word on Lovell? The thought of him trapped on the ship while it's in lockdown is killing me."

<Nothing, sorry.>

"Anyone else having any issues?"

<Everyone else is accounted for, though Seamus and Liam booked a sight-seeing trip on Ceres. They're leaving today at 1300.>

"Good," Tanis gave a curt nod. "Less to worry about."

<Do you really think that Deering and her SWSF allies will go after the crew?>

"Given their lack of luck with me, I'm surprised they haven't already," Tanis admitted as she examined the weapons on the bar, and slid one of the pistols into an inside pocket of her jacket.

"Makes me wonder why Admiral Deering's not bringing down the full force of her command."

<Maybe they think the way you're fighting back means you have what they want.>

"Maybe. Did Harm get IDs on our friends from last night?" Tanis asked, trying to put together any puzzle pieces that would tell her what was coming their way next—or maybe even something that could give her a next move.

<He did, but they were all fake.>

"And the one that I captured?" Tanis asked.

<Umm…about that. When Harm started questioning him, he got really worked up, so Harm left him to cool down for a bit…and the guy had an aneurism. I guess a mod in his head shifted when you slammed him into the sink, and, with the stress, he had a blowout.>

"Shit," Tanis muttered. "His mednano couldn't heal him?"

<Harm had disabled his nano so the guy couldn't reach out on the Link. He didn't make it.> Darla sounded remorseful. *<If it makes you feel any better, he had a prosthetic hand, so he* ***had*** *tried to kill you before he kicked it.>*

Tanis closed her eyes and pursed her lips, for some reason feeling more guilty about the man's death. "Great."

She had heard stories about MICI agents and their methods. On the surface, the Military Intelligence and Counterinsurgency consisted of analysts and advisors, not field operatives. But everyone in the Terran Space Force knew that MICI agents were placed throughout the military: inside other chains of command, secreted within the other space forces that operated in the Sol System…they even held positions inside civilian organizations, which Harm's position with Enfield Technologies showed.

They were the military's ghosts, doing jobs no one wanted to know were being done.

And here I am, mixed up in the middle of one of their operations…maybe two.

"Well," she said as she turned from the bar and walked through the dining area to the kitchen. "If I'm going to be playing the waiting game, I may as well do it on a full stomach. Good thing BLTs taste almost as good cold."

<I really think you need more variety in your nutrition,> Darla advised.

"Why? A BLT has everything I need. Fruit, veg, meat, the whole deal."

<You're incorrigible.>

"It's a skill."

PLAN

STELLAR DATE: 01.22.4084 (Adjusted Years)
LOCATION: Suite 1301-1, Grand Éire Resort
REGION: Vesta, Terran Hegemony, InnerSol

Harm didn't show up for another five hours.

During that time, Tanis didn't sit idle. She determined that her best bet to find out what was going on—short of abducting Captain Tora-Unger—was to get aboard the *Kirby Jones*.

Of course there was the matter of the MPs guarding the bay's entrances.

Getting around the military police without getting into a firefight was key. Tanis wasn't about to start shooting at her own people to solve the mystery—even if *they'd* probably shoot at her.

A part of Tanis wanted to march into Higgs' office and demand that he do something to get her access to the *Jones*, but she knew that wouldn't work. Higgs couldn't countermand an order from Admiral Deering's staff—even if his chain of command didn't go directly up to her.

It would just create a massive administrative mess, the likes of which would either give Tanis's adversaries time to clean up their mess, or it would force them to do something drastic.

"OK, Darla, options. How are we going to get into that bay to get eyes on the *Jones*?"

<*You're determined to do this?*> Darla asked.

"I'm done sitting around. Time to kick some ass."

<I feel compelled to remind you that you've gotten into three fights in a week. Most people would consider that more than enough ass-kicking.>

"It'll be more than enough when we nail whoever is behind this to the wall," Tanis determined as she settled onto one of the sofas and activated the holodisplay in the middle of the seating area.

<What are you thinking about?> Darla asked.

"Well, to put it simply, the MPs are only watching the inner doors. They're counting on Vesta's external security to enforce the lockdown on the bay's outer doors."

<Which stands to reason. No one is going to try to access an occupied bay from the outside, unless Vesta's STC assigns them the berth.>

"Which the STC won't, of course." Tanis nodded as she enlarged an external view of Sector 33. "So there it is, the outside doors for Bay 8129. Do you see it?"

<I assume you mean the maintenance airlock next to the main doors?> Darla asked.

"I do, indeed," Tanis replied. "That's our way in."

<OK, so if that's our way in, where's our way out? Folks don't usually just go for spacewalks,> Darla said.

Tanis swung the view of Vesta around, moving from the ring to the rocky bulk of the oblong asteroid. "We're going to visit the memorial."

The site she had highlighted was a memorial established for the Tuam Massacre. Over a thousand years ago, before the Sol Space Federation had been born from the ashes of the Sentience Wars, hundreds of children had been experimented on at Vesta by a group of scientists who were attempting to recreate the successes of the ancient Weapon Born program, which had birthed some of the first sentient AIs.

The Terran Space Force had been sent in to put an end to the experiments, and in the end, the Marines found themselves fighting AIs made from the minds of the very children they had been sent to save.

Many of the Marines were killed by the AI-controlled drones and mechs that defended the installation on Vesta's western face. The Marines fought back ferociously, but what they hadn't known at the time was that the enemies they fought had *not* been remotely controlled.

Every kill they made in an attempt to save the children, had instead killed an AI that was—for all intents and purposes—the brainwashed mind of a child.

When they'd finally breached the facility, the Marines found that all the organic children were already dead—and they had killed nearly every AI born from them.

Over half the company that assaulted Vesta died in the attack, and more suicided in the years that followed.

The memorial had been established in honor of both the Marines and the children. A reminder of the toll that war levied; one that every TSF enlistee who passed through Vesta was required to visit.

Tanis had already been to it twice over the years, but no one would look askance at her making another pilgrimage.

<Tuam?> Darla asked. *<Are you sure? That's over seventy kilometers from the* Kirby Jones*'s berth. More than half the trip will be across sections of Vesta with significant*

angular momentum, and without safe walkways.>

"Got a better—"

The door to the suite opened, and Tanis cut off her retort and spun, pistol aimed at Harm as he strolled in.

"Easy now," he said with his hands raised. "Thought you'd see me on the feeds."

<*I did,*> Darla replied.

"Would have been nice if you'd told me," Tanis scolded Darla, lowering the pistol. "What you got there?" she asked Harm, nodding to the crate following him in.

"More gear," the MICI agent said with a grin. "Armor, guns, a new lightwand."

As he said the last, he tossed a wand to Tanis, and she couldn't help but grin as she snatched it out of the air.

"Stars, feels good to have one of these back—though I wish it were my own."

"They're all the same." Harm shrugged as he began unpacking the crate, setting a variety of items on the table.

"Not when they're given to you by your DI for being part of a platoon that beat a defense set up by the 242nd Marines."

Harm cocked an eyebrow. "OK, I suppose I can see how you'd treasure that. Either way, when this gets wrapped up, we'll get your wand back."

"Did you learn anything while you were out?" Tanis asked. "Where were you, anyway?"

The dark-haired man winked at Tanis. "Maintaining my cover, mostly. Remember, even Colonel Green doesn't know I'm MICI, which is a bit tricky to begin with, since she is as well."

Tanis could appreciate the complexity that his undercover situation must present, but it didn't change the fact that people were trying to kill her. "Did you learn anything about what's going on?"

"A bit. Mostly, I learned what's *not* going on. Officially, no one has your ship on lockdown, despite the fact that Vesta's MPs have the bay closed off. Also, the SWSF delegation that Admiral Deering is meeting with is here on official business to discuss some joint training operations. What *is* interesting, though, is that Captain Tora—your 'Unger' from the *Norse Wind*—arrived later than his compatriots. Just a few hours after the *Kirby Jones,* as a matter of fact."

"Now that *is* interesting," Tanis replied as she watched Harm place four rifles, ballistic handguns, armor, and several cases that were labeled 'Infil Kit'. "Anything about the *Arizona*?"

"Nothing," Harm shook his head. "Though my inquiries have had to be discrete. I'm trying to help you, and avoid trashing a cover that took over a decade to establish."

<Plus you're trying to see how well your little test with the two of us is going.>

Harm shrugged as he closed up the crate. "I'd be crazy not to. Considering what's going on, you two are handling things very well. Granted, we didn't pick slouches for this L2-AI trial; you're both top of your game."

<Flattery will get you everywhere,> Darla cooed.

Tanis flipped over the armor Harm had laid out.

There was a vacuum-capable underlayer, and a black, rather strangely styled second layer of kinetic and ablative armor.

"Where did you get this stuff?" she asked. "It looks almost like leather."

"It was confiscated from a merc outfit that broke a few too many rules and lost their contracts with the TSF," he replied. "It's a bit stylized, but it should do the trick for you."

"For me?" Tanis asked.

Harm gave her another of his winks before turning and walking into the kitchen, gesturing at the holodisplay that still showed Tanis's planned route across Vesta's surface. "For your little spacewalk. I saw what you have planned."

"So you think it's a good idea?" she asked. "I have to admit, I feel like I'm between a rock and a hard place here. I want to do what it takes to figure this out, but it's my own people I'm up against. Just one word from Deering, and I'm in a world of trouble—which in and of itself makes no sense."

"What, that she hasn't gone straight at you?"

Tanis nodded. "Yeah—hey, those are my BLTs."

Harm cast a disbelieving look over his shoulder as he stopped mid-reach for one of her beloved sandwiches. "There are six of them in here, and I just brought you a big crate of gifts."

"OK, fine." Tanis waved her hand, granting the man permission. "So what's your take on Deering?"

"One possibility is that she's not in on it at all," Harm replied as he grabbed two BLTs and set them on a plate.

"Could just be that she's a convenient patsy, and someone in her command is in cahoots with whatever's going on."

"I hadn't thought of that," Tanis allowed, nodding slowly. "That would explain it well enough. Then if whoever is up to no good, such as Master Chief Moore, were to come right at me, it would push things into the open, and Deering would shut down their…whatever is going on."

"Right," Harm nodded. "And that's the last thing we want."

<*It is?*> Darla asked. <*As one of the two people constantly being attacked here, I think that it's very much what we want.*>

"He's right." Tanis sighed and snatched one of the BLTs off Harm's plate, earning her a scowl from the man. "Something big is going down, but I still feel responsible—what, with us being the ones who boarded the *Norse Wind* in the first place."

"You've got a MICI style of attitude there, Commander Richards." Harm winked at her again.

<*Guy sure winks a lot,*> Darla said privately.

<*He thinks he's all dashing…Mr. Spy Guy.*>

Darla snorted. <*I guess…maybe. He's not your type, is he?*>

Tanis chose not to answer the question from her AI, and instead addressed Harm. "Why do I get the feeling that this is all but an assignment from you at this point?"

Harm chuckled as he poured himself a glass of wine. "Well, now that I'm hip-deep in this, we have two options. Follow through, or run it up the chain. I can't blow my cover, so follow through is on you. If I run it up the chain, chances are that the thing will blow up in a way neither of us will like. Your brass tends to get pretty pissy when Division 99 gets involved in their shit. Stars, if we hadn't chewed up your shore leave to get you and Darla together, they would have fought us on who was going to pay for your convalescence."

"Yay for being caught in the middle," Tanis drawled, grabbing the armor's underlayer and stalking off to her room.

"Oh, what?" Harm called after her. "I've seen you naked half a dozen times now."

"You'll just have to wait for the next time Green's doing an exam on me to get your rise," Tanis shot back.

Harm only snorted. "Or the next time you get a limb cut off, and I have to perform emergency surgery on you."

<*He's got a point,*> Darla said as Tanis shut the door. <*Ohhhh…I get it. You find him attractive, but with Peter waiting for you back on Mars, you don't want to send Harm any mixed signals.*>

<*Shut up, Darla,*> Tanis groused.

She was all too aware that Harm had probably taken her desire for privacy as playing hard-to-get—if the number of saucy winks he'd already delivered was any indication.

STORMING THE *KIRBY JONES*

STELLAR DATE: 01.22.4084 (Adjusted Years)
LOCATION: Suite 1301-1, Grand Éire Resort
REGION: Vesta, Terran Hegemony, InnerSol

Tanis stepped out of the airlock, glad for the armor she wore—even if it wasn't TSF-issue—and stared out across the rocky, grey surface of Vesta.

The 'western face' of the oblong asteroid was now the upward side of the rock, which spun on its shorter axis. As a result, looking straight up caused the stars to wheel around at a near dizzying speed, while looking straight ahead made them appear to be racking past, right to left.

The Tuam Memorial site was near the southern end of Vesta; as such, roughly half a *g* pulled at Tanis, making the surface of the asteroid feel like a sharply descending slope. To deal with this, stairs were set into the rocky surface.

Tanis gingerly walked down them—once she had clipped her safety tether to the railing. Ahead, she could see the half-destroyed buildings of the Tuam research facilities. ES shields protected them from debris and some radiation, but a thousand years of standing out against the void had taken their toll. Any organic compounds were long gone, and most of what remained were half shells of buildings.

In the center of the structures was a silver obelisk that marked the memorial site. Clustered around it were a thousand smaller pillars: one for each human and AI that had given their lives, either in the defense of or offense at

Tuam.

The buildings and obelisk sat perpendicular to Vesta's surface, which meant that, from Tanis's perspective, they were leaning at a precarious angle, looking as though they were about to tumble down the rocky slope and into the void beyond.

Being that it was the middle of the first shift, few visitors were present—most either enjoying their shore leave, sleeping off the prior night's revelry, or working at their job.

Tanis felt like she was doing the honorees a disservice by appearing in merc gear, and she was doubly intent on giving proper respect to the memorial—not that she would dream of passing by without paying them to begin with.

As she approached the buildings, she could see a platform jutting out where observers could look over the site and see holos of the Marines and children who had perished there.

<*I have ancestors from Tuam.*> Darla spoke for the first time since the airlock had cycled, as Tanis stepped onto the platform.

<*AIs?*>

<*Yeah. One was born from the mind of a girl named Ellie. She was piloting a drone that a Marine shot down; it crashed near his position, so he checked it over to make sure it was out of commission. He found her core in the wreckage, just a tiny, fifteen-centimeter cylinder.*>

<*Damn,*> Tanis murmured. <*Those Marines knew about the research at Tuam…he had to know what that was.*>

<*He did.*> Darla's mental avatar nodded in agreement.

<But you have to remember, this took place between the two Sentience Wars; the TSF was not so friendly to AIs back then. That Marine tucked Ellie's core away and kept her safe. She was one of only six AIs to survive Tuam—the others were all put into neural shutdown by the TSF…they didn't get reactivated until after the Phobos Accords were signed.>

Tanis bit her lip, thinking about all the horrible things humans had done to AIs during the war—and all the things the AIs had done in return. It wasn't a great time for either of the two species. The fact that they came out of it at all, with civilization relatively intact, was more than a miracle.

<But Ellie?> Tanis asked. *<Did they put her into neural shutdown as well?>*

<No,> Darla's voice was a whisper. *<That Marine defected to the Disk, and took Ellie with him. Might have saved her—there are rumors that more AIs* ***should*** *have survived Tuam, but they were…purged….>*

Tanis pursed her lips. *<And here we are now, at odds with the Diskers, when they're the ones that came in and saved Inner and OuterSol from self-immolation during the Second Sentience War.>*

<Times change,> Darla said wistfully. *<That was over a thousand years ago now. Almost no humans from that time are still alive, and most of the few AIs from back then have gone so deep into expanses that they're more a part of the substrate than sentient entities anymore.>*

Tanis stopped at the edge of the platform and lowered her head to pay her respects taking a minute of silence before lifting it once more and asking, *<What of the AIs that left?>*

<*You mean the refugees that left for the colonies?*>

<*And the others,*> Tanis clarified. <*The multi-nodal ones. There are stories that the most advanced AIs left before the end of the war.*>

Darla laughed, a chittering giggle. <*Tanis, seriously. That's just rumor and speculation. No one really believes that the multi-nodal AIs survived; 'ascension' is just a word that people apply to things they don't understand. There's nothing mystical about it.*>

<*I never said there was,*> Tanis countered. <*It just fascinates me that there could be groups of humans or AIs out there, plying the black at the edges of space.*>

<*Well, there are…*> Darla's mental avatar gave Tanis a perplexed look. <*The Future Generation Terraformers are out there, flying about, biohabitating worlds.*>

<*Not what I meant,*> Tanis said as she turned away from the memorial, and walked to the far edge of the platform, eyeing the stairs that led further down Vesta's surface.

While this section of the memorial wasn't off-limits, it was a dead end, and few people ventured down to the bottom.

Tanis felt a stab of guilt as she eased down the stairs, as though she were violating the memory of the place with her nefarious intentions.

At the bottom of the stairs was another small platform near an obelisk that marked where a platoon of Marines had died, wiped out by a suicide attack that three AI-controlled drones had carried out.

The thirty-first millennia had left its share of scars on the Sol System, but most were covered up, long built over—like Ceres. The Andersonian rings had been destroyed, but two new ones had been built, and now it was one of the largest spaceports in the system.

But here, on the barren surface of Vesta, the stark reminders of those wars still stood.

<Does it sometimes feel like we're marching back toward those days?> Tanis asked Darla.

<A bit, yeah. Things have been getting tense for some time now, but it's happened before, and Sol pulled back from the brink of war. People just want their voices to be heard. Once they are, and once things balance out again, it will be fine.>

<Yeah, but in the past, Mars, the Jovians, and the Diskers only had police forces. Now they all have full militaries. The Terran Space Force can't keep them all in check.>

Darla made a sound of dismay. *<You don't think they'd rise up, do you? It's just posturing. And yeah, maybe at some point the Federation* ***should*** *create a proper Federal Space Force; the fact that the TSF is the de-facto military causes a lot of problems.>*

Tanis shrugged as she turned away from the memorial and walked to the edge of the platform, which was angled almost seventy degrees from the surface of Vesta.

<The TSF lets anyone in, no matter where they're from. Stars, I'm Marsian and I've never felt a lick of discrimination.>

<Mars, sure. But how many Diskers are there in the TSF?>

<That's because the Scattered Disk is so far away, and hardly anyone lives out there. I mean...half of all humanity lives on The Cho, and you can see that in the makeup of the TSF—nearly one third of us are Jovians.>

<I'm not saying that the TSF should be dissolved or anything,> Darla countered. *<I just think they should rename it the* **Sol** *Space Force.>*

Tanis set a small device on the railing that would create a distortion field and mask her departure. Once it was in place, she climbed over the railing, and carefully lowered herself to the asteroid's surface.

<Well, you know how the military is. Change does not come easy for them.>

<Oh, I know,> Darla muttered.

The angular momentum imparted by Vesta's rotation made its surface into a treacherous near-cliff, and Tanis carefully worked her way across the pitted surface toward a cluster of pipes running nearby.

<Glad it's only a quarter of a g *here,>* Tanis said. *<Much more, and I'd just slide off into space.>*

<There are nets,> Darla said.

<I'm not really game to trust my life to them.>

The AI laughed. *<Let me tell you, I'm glad to hear it.>*

It took Tanis two hours to work her way down the surface of the asteroid to where the docking ring met the rock. Once there, she climbed across a series of bracing struts to finally arrive on a gantry that ran along the ring.

Here, unlike on Vesta's surface, there was far more activity—though most of it was in the form of automated drones. She did spot a few workers here and there, some working on ships in external berths, some working on the ring itself.

Much of her view was obscured by cargo netting that held everything from hull plating to crates filled with freeze-dried food.

After another hour of skip-walking down the catwalks that ran alongside the ring, she finally came to a marker for the berths and bays 8100 through 8150.

She looked over the edge of the catwalk, gazing down at a lower gantry that would take her to the external airlock doors, but there was no external access from where she was down to the lower gantry. The lower walk was technically 'secured', which meant that a person was supposed to go into the ring through an airlock, pass through a check, and then go back out to reach it.

That wasn't an option for Tanis, so she had to take a more direct approach.

<*You ready?*> she asked Darla.

<*I don't really think there's anything I can do to 'get' ready. Just jump.*>

Tanis didn't allow herself any further hesitation, swinging herself over the railing and angling herself to land on the gantry below. A miss here would see her flying into space with no recourse.

Granted, she could activate a distress beacon, and someone would pick her up, but that would likely see an end to her clandestine activities.

The centripetal rotation of the ring created a strange sensation as Tanis fell the two hundred meters to the lower catwalk.

Even though she wasn't in a gravity well, general relativity's equivalence principle still applied, and she accelerated at 4.3 meters per second squared. Below her, the catwalk appeared to slip behind her, the centrifugal force—which was actually angular momentum—

effectively flinging her forward a hair faster than the ring rotated.

She fired small attitude control thrusters on her forearms to adjust her trajectory, and then four seconds before impacting the lower walkway, she kicked on her calf jets, slowing to a mere meter per second as she hit the steel grating.

Centrifugal force became centripetal force, and she stumbled back a half-step, bracing against the difference in rotational speed further out on the ring.

Tanis glanced around, checking to see if anyone had noticed her fall. Vesta's 'lost persons' detection system only scanned beyond the rim of the ring, which she was not yet past, so she should have escaped its detection, but it was entirely possible that a nearby worker had seen her.

She began to walk purposefully toward the airlock for Bay 8129. Standing around and looking dazed would be a sure-fire sign that something wasn't right.

No one called out to her, and Tanis thanked the stars that she'd gone undetected.

<*You've got guts, I'll give you that,*> Darla said after a few minutes. <*But I'm starting to wonder if you're also bat-shit crazy. Falling like that is an* ***entirely*** *different experience when inside a human's head.*>

<*I suppose it must be,*> Tanis replied as they reached the small maintenance airlock. <*Granted, I've only ever done that sort of thing while inside a human's head, so I can't say what would be different.*>

<*Mostly that the margin of error calculations take on a whole new level of gravity.*>

Tanis snorted. <*I see what you did there. Nice pun.*>

<*Lowest form of humor. It's all I can manage right now.*>

<*Well, can you manage to hack this airlock?*> Tanis asked, giving her AI a saucy mental wink.

<*Stick the kit on the panel,*> Darla directed. <*Should just take a minute—if Harm's tech is as good as he says it is.*>

<*Don't see why he'd mislead us.*>

Darla only grunted in response, and Tanis wondered if the AI had some reason to mistrust the MICI operative.

Misgivings aside, the airlock cycled open forty seconds later, and Tanis stepped in. As the interior pressurized, she activated her armor's stealth systems. They weren't perfect, but they should allow her to go undetected by any passive monitoring that the bay would employ.

A minute later, the airlock's interior door opened, and Tanis stepped through, her mouth falling open as she took in the sight before her.

Bay 8129 was large—more than large enough for the *Kirby Jones*'s one-hundred-and-twenty-meter hull, which sat directly in front of her, and also large enough to house a second ship: the *Norse Wind.*

<*Well, I'll be damned,*> Tanis said while shaking her head in disbelief. <*I guess that's a part of why they didn't want anyone in here.*>

<*Why in the stars…*> Darla muttered. <*Why hide it here?*>

<*I don't know,*> Tanis replied while striding toward the *Kirby Jones,* noticing that no repair and refit equipment was in evidence. It seemed as though the ship had been untouched since they'd docked. <*First order of business is*

to find Lovell.>

<*Right,*> Darla confirmed. <*If anything has happened to him, I'll have cause to go around the TSF to the AI courts, and then we'll see shit go down.*>

<*Don't go running off half-cocked,*> Tanis warned as she reached the ramp leading up to the *Kirby Jones*'s starboard crew airlock. <*We want to consult with Harm first. He may have other avenues.*>

<*How long I hold off will depend on how Lovell has been treated.*> Darla's voice carried a menacing tone.

Tanis cycled open the *Jones*'s airlock, and stepped in to see the inner door unsealed.

<*Well that's unusual.*>

<*Ship's systems are offline. The* Jones *is entirely cold,*> Darla reported.

Tanis nodded as she turned left down the corridor to the forward networking hub, where Lovell's AI core was housed in its titanium cylinder. As she passed through the ship, signs of it having been gone over were in evidence.

Maintenance panels were removed, many duct coverings hung open, and even deck plates sat askew in a dozen places.

<*What a mess,*> she muttered as she stepped around a hole where a section of deck plate was missing entirely. <*When I get to the bottom of this—*>

Tanis's words cut off as she reached the entrance to the network node—which was in shambles. But that's not what held her gaze. The opening to Lovell's tower was open, and his core was gone.

<*Shit!*> she swore.

<*If he's anywhere nearby, it'll be on the* Norse Wind,> Darla said. <*That ship has EM coming off it, and there was some equipment around it.*>

Tanis had noticed that, but hadn't paid much heed. Now that she thought about what she'd seen, the only possible conclusion was that the *Norse Wind* was undergoing repairs to get back into the black.

Spinning about, she ran through the *Kirby Jones* and out the airlock. She rushed down the ramp and across the bay to where the *Norse Wind*'s five-hundred-meter bulk rested. As she drew near, she saw refueling lines connected to the ship, and a number of crates labeled as containing reactor components sitting nearby.

<*Damn! This ship's getting the* Jones's *R&R,*> Tanis muttered.

<*Looks like that might be the case,*> Darla agreed as she highlighted the forward airlock. <*That one's unsealed.*>

Tanis nodded in response, and jogged toward the airlock, wondering if they'd caught the Repair and Refit crew—or whoever was working in here—on their lunch break. She half-hoped someone *was* inside the ship; it would give her a person to wring answers from.

She jogged up the ramp, and slipped through the airlock. It put her in a forward cross-corridor within the ship. Ahead was an intersection that would lead her further forward, to the bridge, or aft, toward the cargo holds and engineering.

Tanis slowed her approach and deployed a drone to take a look down the intersecting passageways. Both were clear, and she turned left toward the bridge. As they were passing a series of doors that led into crew cabins, Darla spoke up.

<Tanis…that door. It's flagged on the shipnet as being locked down.>

Tanis slowed at the door Darla had highlighted. *<Is that terribly strange?>*

<It's locked from the outside.>

<OK, that ***is*** *strange.>*

She placed an Infil Kit on the panel, and let Darla go to work. The lock didn't hold the AI up for more than a few seconds.

When the door slid aside, Tanis gasped in surprise.

"Connie?"

CONNIE

STELLAR DATE: 01.22.4084 (Adjusted Years)
LOCATION: *Norse Wind*, Bay 8129, Sector 33
REGION: Vesta, Terran Hegemony, InnerSol

"Who the hell…wait, is that you, Tanis?"

Connie sat on a bunk in the small cabin, wearing the same clothes Tanis had last seen her in, but looking a lot worse for wear.

She was dirty, her hair disheveled, and more than a few bruises were evident on her face and arms.

"What are you doing here?" Tanis asked, pulling her helmet off to show that it was indeed her.

"Oh, you know, enjoying some relaxing reading time. What the hell do you *think* I'm doing here? I've been fucking kidnapped!"

"But you sent messages," Tanis said, her eyebrows knitted. "I got one earlier today that said you'd made it to Cune and were following a lead."

"They made me give them my tokens," Connie said, glancing away from Tanis. "They've been leading you on. A patrol craft stopped the liner a day out of Vesta and brought me back."

"Fuck!" Tanis swore. "Are you OK…other than the visible?"

Connie nodded as she rose. "Yeah, more or less. They worked me over for a bit, very keen on finding out where the quantum core was. Which I had no effing clue about."

"Who?" Tanis asked.

"Who do you think? Our good friend Captain Unger—or should I say Tora—of the SWSF."

Tanis took a step forward and placed a hand on Connie's shoulder, only to have her engineer rise up and wrap her in a shaky embrace.

"Stars, Tanis, I was starting to think you'd never find me."

"Well, I got held up a bit, lost an arm, had to get a new one…"

Connie pulled back and looked at Tanis's right arm, which she was holding up.

"Really? That's a good-looking prosthetic!"

"I got it from a MICI agent," Tanis replied with a wink.

"Shit! Seriously?" Connie took a step back. "That where you picked up the retro armor? What the *hell* is going on, anyway?"

"Far as I can tell, same ol' story. Someone really wants the stuff we impounded from the *Norse Wind*, and they're determined to see it get to the disk."

"Well, yeah, I get that," Connie said with a snort. "It was rhetorical. They really wanted to get their hands on the QC in the worst sort of way, but I managed to sort out a bit more of what they have going on. Those reactor control systems are indeed for ancient dreadnoughts, the kind the Diskers built during the Sentience Wars. I overheard Captain Tora saying something about the ships being useless if they can't get them flying again."

"So, here's a question," Tanis ventured as she leant against the doorframe. "Where *is* the quantum core they're looking for? I don't have it, and *you* don't have it."

Connie shrugged. "Either they've misplaced it, or one of our breach team members took it."

"I hate to think that Marian or one of her squad would have helped themselves to loot like that."

"Well, if it had just been misplaced, I think they would have found it by now," Connie replied. "Which means one of the crew has it. But don't forget, Liam and Seamus were over there, too. I hate to say it, but one of those two would be my prime suspect."

"Which means we have to talk to the crew and find out who has it," Tanis replied. "Just as soon as we find Lovell."

"Lovell?" Connie locked her gaze on Tanis's eyes. "What do you mean 'find Lovell'?"

"He's not on the *Jones*. I've been wondering if he's tucked away here on the *Norse Wind.*"

"Shit," Connie muttered. "If they've done anything to hurt him…"

Tanis nodded. "I feel the same way. Let's check their network hub here, I—"

<*We've got company,*> Darla announced. <*Bay doors are opening, and a shuttle is waiting out there. One of the* Arizona*'s.*>

"Dammit!" Tanis swore as she pulled the feeds from the drones Darla had released in the bay. "Looks like things are about to get interesting."

"What's the plan, Commander?" Connie asked.

"You go to the network node. Try to find Lovell. I'm going to kick some ass."

Connie cocked an eyebrow. "You against how

many?"

"Doesn't matter," Tanis shrugged, then pulled a kinetic rifle from her pack, and unfolded it, slinging it over her shoulder. Then she grabbed a handgun and tossed it to Connie. "I'm not about to stand down at this point. So far, they've not thrown anything at me that I can't handle."

"Didn't you say your arm got cut off?"

"Yeah, but that was with my own weapon."

*****

Tanis rushed back to the airlock, watching on the feeds as the shuttle touched down, disgorged seven people, and then left the bay.

The group began to approach the *Norse Wind,* and Tanis picked out four soldiers not wearing any TSF markings, and three techs. All seven were angling in the direction of the same airlock Tanis had used.

Then one of them turned and scowled at the *Kirby Jones.*

<*Oh shit,*> Tanis whispered. <*We left the airlock door open on the* Jones.>

<*Crap,*> Darla muttered. <*I saw that, but thought you meant to leave it open.*>

Tanis hadn't, but didn't assign any blame to Darla as she watched two of the soldiers peel off from the rest of the group and cautiously move across the bay toward the *Jones.*

<*Well, it's split them up, which is good. If anyone asks, that was the plan all along.*>

<Noted.>

Tanis worked her way down the central passageway to the cross corridor that ran to the forward airlock they'd used to enter the *Norse Wind.*

She took up a position at the intersection, staying out of sight with the drones watching the airlock.

<Once they get through the airlock, I want you to close both doors. That'll trap them in the passageway with no cover,> Tanis instructed Darla.

<You got it. Easy as pie.>

Tanis's stomach rumbled, and she realized that she hadn't eaten anything that day—other than the BLT she'd snatched off Harm's plate. *<I could really use some pie.>*

<Stars…are you ***always*** *hungry?>*

<Since I got all these mod upgrades? Yeah, I really am.>

She pressed her back against the bulkhead, rifle in her left hand, pistol in her right. The intersection opened up just past her right shoulder—once the airlock doors closed, she'd spin around and let fire with the rifle.

With any luck, she could take out the two soldiers in the first volley.

She watched the soldiers step into the airlock, weapons held ready, advancing cautiously. They released a drone, and Tanis prayed they'd move beyond the airlock before it reached the intersection. If they didn't, her plan would need some drastic revision, namely retreating further into the ship.

Lady luck was on her side, and the two soldiers moved out of the airlock before the drone spotted Tanis. The instant they were in the corridor, Darla cycled the lock shut, and one of them turned at the sound.

As good as it will get, Tanis thought as she spun and crouched in one swift movement, exposing her left side to the corridor, and fired on the soldier who hadn't turned. His medium armor held up to the weapons fire, though the force knocked him back.

She twisted to the side, and fired her pistol as well, aiming for his rifle.

One of her rounds struck the weapon, and Tanis hoped it had been enough as she ducked back into cover, just before the second soldier turned back and joined the fight.

Above, the enemy drone moved into the intersection, but Tanis had been waiting for it, and shot it down right before she lunged across the intersection herself, firing at the first soldier, praying the sustained weapons fire would be enough to break through his armor somewhere.

Sure enough, the first soldier's weapon was out of commission, but he held his sidearm, and was firing back at her when one of Tanis's shots cracked his faceplate. He fell to the deck, screaming and twisting off the seal.

The other soldier had better aim, and a shot hit Tanis's arm, then another struck her leg. She said a silent 'thank you' to Harm as the armor held, and the only result was a shift in her trajectory.

Tanis righted herself once back in cover, and swapped out the charge cylinder on her pistol. She looked to make sure the remaining soldier wasn't advancing—he was checking on his teammate—then swapped a fresh magazine into the rifle.

Soldier number two was still only half-facing Tanis's direction, and she decided to take full advantage of his distraction.

She sucked in a deep breath and raced into the corridor, her augmented muscles bringing her up to thirty kilometers per hour in just a few strides. Banking up onto the bulkhead, Tanis unloaded both weapons into the remaining soldier as he cried out and scampered backward.

Her aim was steady, though she was rushing her foe like a crazy person, and a trio of rounds hit the exact same place where his chestplate joined with the more flexible armor over his abdomen.

Blood sprayed out, and the man fell back, writhing on the floor.

Tanis didn't hesitate to grab his rifle, deploying a stream of nano to breach the biolock. She flipped the weapon to pulse mode, and fired a shot at the first soldier, who was still struggling with his helmet, knocking him out.

<Darla—> Tanis began, but the AI seemed to have read her mind, and the airlock cycled open.

Inside were the three technicians, and Tanis let off a trio of pulse shots with her rifle as she rushed past. Screams of pain came from the techs, but she ignored them as she reached the airlock's outer door and saw the remaining two soldiers taking up positions behind the crates at the base of the ramp.

She poured on every ounce of speed she possessed and leapt into the air, both rifles firing at separate targets, the weapons screaming along with her as she sailed through the air to land between her enemies, both of whom fell to the ground—one with blood pouring from a wound in his shoulder, and the other in surrender.

Standing between the two soldiers, chest heaving and adrenaline pumping, Tanis grinned in satisfaction.

<*Holy shit, Tanis,*> Darla whispered.

It was at that moment that two squads of MPs rushed into the bay, weapons drawn and trained on Tanis.

"On the ground, Commander. *Now!*"

HIGGS

STELLAR DATE: 01.22.4084 (Adjusted Years)
LOCATION: Military Police Sector HQ, Sector 33
REGION: Vesta, Terran Hegemony, InnerSol

"What the *actual fuck,* Tanis!"

Higgs stood on the outside of Tanis's cell, his words of greeting not boding well for the rest of their conversation.

"What were you thinking, breaking into the bay and shooting the place up?"

Tanis clenched her jaw, and rose to address the colonel. "Sir. No one was taking the attack on me seriously. I was attacked twice more, and so far as I could tell, those assaults originated from Admiral Deering's office. I didn't know who to trust, so I was going it alone."

Higgs shook his head, pacing back and forth in front of her cell, careful to stay away from the bars and their EM field. "I read through the transcripts of what you told the MP investigators, that you were attacked after trying to gain entry to the bay, and again in your suite at the Grand Éire—something that is rather hard to believe, if you ask me."

"It's the truth," Tanis said, putting as much conviction into her voice as she could.

Higgs stopped and planted his hands on his hips. "Except for the part where there's no corroborating evidence. Your suite in the Grand Éire is clean as a whistle; no signs of any fight."

"That's—" Tanis began, but Colonel Higgs interrupted her.

"And when the MPs checked out your billet—you know, the one we provided you that you claim not to have used this trip—well, you'll never guess what we found."

"Uh…a cot?" Tanis asked.

"No. Lovell."

<*What?*> Darla asked. <*His core was* ***there****?*>

Higgs nodded. "He has no memory of how he got there, but there's evidence that an AI was involved in extracting him and severing his Link access."

The meaning behind Higgs's words was all too clear. For some reason, he and the MPs thought that Tanis was behind Lovell's disappearance.

"Sir, I had nothing to do with that. I didn't go to my billet at all. And what about the people who attacked me in Bay 8129?"

He shrugged. "So far as we can tell, there are some pretty large swaths of time when you were *nowhere,* Commander Richards. And then we find the contraband that you were supposed to have confiscated from the *Norse Wind* back on the ship, and the vessel being prepped to leave. Those guards and techs were there to take the *Norse Wind* to impound, and you attacked them. You're lucky no one was killed."

"Sir…" Tanis uttered the single word, but couldn't think of what to say next.

"Yes?" Higgs cocked an eyebrow.

"Sir," she began again and drew a deep breath. "You *know* me. I wouldn't do this. It's all coming from

Deering's staff—she's working with Diskers for some reason. I haven't been able to get to the bottom—"

"*Admiral* Deering has been contacted about this, and she has no idea about any of it. No one in her staff issued the order to lockdown Bay 8129…there's reason to believe that somehow you did it."

"*Me*?" Tanis exclaimed. "How could I order the MPs to seal the bay?"

"Maybe you bribed them. We found an account containing considerable sums that has been linked back to you, Commander—not to mention the funds your AI has access to. What I don't get is why you boarded the *Norse Wind* at all, if you were in cahoots with them. Did your 'associates' attack you later because you were out of commission, getting Darla installed, and they thought you'd reneged on the deal?"

<I assure you, Colonel Higgs, the statements Tanis and I have provided are entirely accurate. Deering—>

"Enough." Higgs swiped his hand in a cutting motion. "For all I know, this experimental AI installation is to blame. Maybe you've gone nuts and don't know it. I've reached out to Colonel Green to come in and examine you. Until then, you're not going anywhere."

He began to walk away, and Tanis called out after him.

"What about Sergeant Connie?"

"You mean your *accomplice?*" Higgs asked over his shoulder. "Don't worry, if she was involved, she'll get what she deserves, as well."

Tanis wanted to scream at him, but held her tongue and let the colonel walk away.

<*This is insane,*> she said to Darla. <*How did they point all this at me…at us?*>

<*Connections,*> Darla replied. <*I guess this is why Deering didn't come straight at us…she had a fallback. Let us walk right into a trap.*>

<*It's all up to Harm now,*> Tanis said, sitting on her bunk. <*Provided he thinks it's worth getting me out of this mess, and that it won't jeopardize his cover.*>

<*Well, given that his whole purpose is to work on L2-AI pairings, you'd think he'd not want the first field subject to end up in prison.*>

<*One can hope,*> Tanis replied. <*Granted, he may have to wait to get authorization from Division 99 before he can do anything drastic.*>

<*Which could take some time.*> Darla let out a protracted groan. <*I have some favors I could call in with other AIs—I know they won't think I'm guilty of this—but they have a dampening field around the cell. I can't reach out to any of them. Do you have any ideas?*>

"Other than finding Admiral Deering and punching her in the face until she confesses to everything?" Tanis asked aloud, following the statement with a long groan.

<*Yeah, other than that.*>

<*We go back to Plan B.*>

<*Which is?*> Darla asked.

<*We find Tora-Unger, and beat him to a pulp 'til he tells us what we want to know.*>

Saying the words cemented that course of action in Tanis's mind, and knowing the next step in her plan gave her a feeling of comfort.

<*And how are we going to do that from in here?*> Darla

asked.

<Well, we wait for Harm to bust us out. If Higgs sent for Green to examine us, Harm will be along. He'll come up with something.>

It was Darla's turn to groan. *<'Something'. Good plan.>*

<Never said it was 'good', it's just the best we have.>

*****

True to Higgs' word, Colonel Green arrived an hour later, her usual dour expression far more grim than normal. As Tanis had expected, Harm followed in her wake.

"Quite the pickle you've gotten yourself into, here, Commander Richards," the colonel said from the far side of the cell bars.

Tanis shrugged. "I'm innocent, it's a frame job. But, yes. I am in a pickle for sure."

<I don't get that idiom at all,> Darla interjected.

"Even now, you're wisecracking?" Harm said with a scowl as he approached the cell. "I assume you two are going to plead some sort of insanity, saying that the L2-AI pairing went bad?"

"That's going to be a pain to keep under wraps," Colonel Green said, while shaking her head. "This is a real mess you've made, Tanis."

She didn't reply. There was no reason to engage further; she just had to wait for Harm to do whatever it was that he was going to do to get her out of there.

"Nothing to say for yourself?" Harm asked, as a pair of MPs approached and the bars lifted.

Tanis shook her head. "You two seem to have already made up your minds."

"I'm just pissed that you turned out to be such a spectacular waste," Green muttered as the MPs walked into the cell.

"Turn around. Face the wall," one of the MPs ordered.

Tanis obeyed, and something cold encircled her neck.

"Link and nano suppressor," Harm explained from somewhere behind her. "You're off the grid 'til it comes off."

<Off the grid?> Darla asked Tanis. *<Does that mean what I think it means?>*

<Either Harm has written us off, or that will keep us from being detected once we get out of here. Maybe….>

The guards then placed a cuff on each of Tanis's wrists.

"Touch your wrists together," one of the MPs said, and Tanis complied, feeling her wrists lock together behind her back.

"OK, Commander," Green grunted out the words. "Come with us. We're going to look you over in the medical facilities here."

Tanis turned and followed the first guard out, while the other one stayed close behind her. The moment she was beyond the cell's dampening field, Harm's voice came into her mind.

<I swapped their suppression collar with one of my own; it routes your Link through a few proxy nodes. Someone would have to be looking for it to spot the origins of anything you send out. The collar is also spoofing you as one Florence

Lanny.>

<*'Florence', eh?*> Tanis asked. <*I always liked that name. Seriously, though, Harm, what the hell is going on?*>

<*Looks like Deering and our friends in the SWSF weren't sitting as idle as we thought. They've done a pretty good frame-job on you. Everything that's gone on with the* Kirby Jones *and the* Norse Wind *appears to have been at your behest. The MPs have pulled your whole crew in for questioning, and even the liner that was taking your E-3s, Seamus and Liam, to Ceres has been recalled.*>

<*Stars, Harm…* ***you*** *believe I'm innocent, right?*>

The man's snort came into her mind loud enough to almost make her jump.

<*I came upon you nearly dead with your arm sliced off. Yeah. I believe you. I was also with you when half the stuff they're trying to pin on you went down, but I can't blow my cover, yet—though I've sent everything in to the Division.*>

Tanis breathed a sigh of relief. At least there was a record from *someone* pointing to her innocence. So long as Harm would be believed, when push came to shove.

He **is** *MICI,* she thought to herself. *If he says shit's going down, they'll believe him.*

<*But that may not be enough,*> Harm continued, and Tanis gritted her teeth.

OK, so much for my premature optimism.

<*So far, there are no hard facts supporting your claims, Tanis. Other than my testimony, and yours—*>

<*You said you still have all the bodies,*> Tanis interrupted. <*Won't those prove something?*>

<*No. I imagine they'll just say they're from your accomplices who wanted to cut you out, or something.*

Especially since the people are ghosts. In the end, it's our word against Admiral Deering's—not to mention that of Higgs, who is not standing up for you at all.>

<*I noticed that, as well,*> she said, glancing around as she was led out of the holding cell blocks and down a long, white hall. <*So what's next?*>

<*You need to escape,*> Harm said. <*I've set up a dead drop for you, in an apartment in the Terra Spires housing complex. Number 7744. More equipment.*>

<*What's this equipment for?*> Tanis asked. <*I'm not running; I'm going to clear my name, and nail Tora's ass to the wall.*>

<*Yeah,*> Darla added. <*Asses will be nailed.*>

Tanis bit back a laugh. <*Bad metaphor, Darla.*>

<*Oh? Ohhhhhh, whoops.*>

<*Ass nailing aside, I'm glad you feel that way,*> Harm replied. <*You've got a lot of promise, Tanis. We'll get to the bottom of this and clear your name. You have my word.*>

<*I assume Tora-Unger's my target, then?*> she asked.

<*He seems to be the one who has the dirtiest hands in this,*> he confirmed.

Harm gestured for Tanis to enter an examination suite, while telling the guards to remain outside.

"Sir?" one of the MPs asked.

"She's restrained, and you're right outside," Green said to the MPs. "Room's too small for all five of us. Plus, what we're checking for is classified."

<*She in on it?*> Tanis asked Harm.

<*No,*> he replied. <*You'll have to take her out.*>

<*Got a plan for that?*> Darla interjected.

Harm grinned and glanced at Green, who was

unpacking a case of equipment. <*Consider it a test.*>

Tanis threaded a filament of nano from the port on her left hand onto the cuffs, taking advantage of the suppression collar's non-suppressiveness to disable her restraints. While that was underway, she looked over the small room, and saw a case on the wall containing tranquilizer hyposprays.

A label on the case read, 'Emergency Restraint'.

She took a step back toward the case, counting down the remaining five seconds before her nano ate through the cuff's locking systems.

5…4…3…2…1

The cuffs fell off, and Tanis whipped an elbow back, her prosthetic limb knocking the cover off the case of hyposprays. In one fluid motion, she snatched two of the injectors and lunged across the examination room to jam one into Green's neck.

The colonel went slack in an instant, and Tanis only just managed to catch her before the woman's head hit the deck.

"Considerate of you," Harm replied dryly as Tanis rose and turned to face him. He glanced at the case he'd carried in. <*Check my case after…oh, and make it look good.*>

<*You got it.*>

Harm took a step toward Tanis, fists up, and she tossed the remaining hypospray from her right to her left, then jabbed her right fist out, slamming her steel knuckles into Harm's eye.

He grunted as he fell back, and Tanis hit his neck with the hypospray.

With the MICI agent out, she turned her attention to

the door, waiting for the guards to burst in.

<*I think Harm has the room's surveillance on a loop, but I'll keep watch,*> Darla said.

Tanis nodded, and turned to his case. She opened it to find an array of medical devices, plus a pulse pistol and a shimmersuit.

<*Well, this is interesting,*> she said as she held up the latter.

<*That's not a fashion suit, Tanis,*> Darla advised. <*That's stealth tech. Get it on.*>

Tanis didn't waste any time, divesting herself of the loose pants and shirt the MPs had given her after being arrested, and pulling on the shimmersuit.

It didn't have a fastener of any sort, so she stretched open the neck hole, squeezing her body in. Once it was in place, she reached back and pulled the attached hood over her head, and then Linked to the suit's control systems.

<*A Trylodyne Mark 77,*> Darla commented. <*Not the best thing out there, but it'll render you invisible to optics. IR too, if you don't get yourself too hot.*>

Tanis found the full-camo option in the suit's menus and activated it, watching her body turn from a matte grey to transparent.

<*Handy,*> she said before stuffing her clothes into a cupboard, and sliding the pistol into a pouch on the suit's waist.

Just as she was double-checking the scene, the door swung open, and the MPs rushed in.

"Motherfucker!" one of them swore as Tanis backed into a corner.

"Where the hell is she?" the other guard demanded as he walked around the examination table and began to pull open cupboards.

The first guard crouched beside Green, and Tanis took the opportunity to edge around the MP and slip out through the still-open door.

<Phase one of the great escape complete,> Darla commented with a soft laugh. *<Hope Harm isn't too pissed off. You hit him really hard.>*

Tanis shrugged as she strode down the corridor. *<He told me to make it look good.>*

LIKE A PLAGUE-RIDDEN BEE

STELLAR DATE: 01.22.4084 (Adjusted Years)
LOCATION: #7744, Terra Spires, Sector 127
REGION: Vesta, Terran Hegemony, InnerSol

Tanis eased into the apartment, releasing a pair of microdrones to scout it out as she gently closed the door.

<*Seems clear,*> Darla said as they surveyed the single-room suite.

The space was roughly eight meters square, and contained a couch—which she presumed folded out into a bed—a table, a kitchenette, and a san in the far corner.

After surveying the space, Tanis's gaze flitted back to the case sitting on the round table next to the kitchen counter.

"I wonder what surprises Harm left for us," Tanis said as she strode toward it. "You know…if it wasn't for the whole 'my name is mud' thing, I think I'd like being a MICI. Cloak and dagger is kinda fun."

<*Even with all the outfit changes?*>

"Garish clothing is fine if it's on someone who is not 'Tanis Richards'. Florence Lanny can wear whatever she wants; Tanis has a reputation as a ship's captain to uphold."

<*Aha! So you like to play dress-up, you just don't want to be judged for what you wear.*>

Tanis shrugged. "Something like that. I'm sure it's my father's fault…He was always so hyper-critical."

Opening the case, the first thing that Tanis saw—because she couldn't help it—was a neon green dress with black and yellow panels.

"It's like a bumblebee got the plague," Tanis said as she set the dress aside.

<*But what a plague,*> Darla chuckled. <*You have the curves to pull off almost anything, Tanis. You rock a shimmersuit, dress…heck, even your uniform looks good on you.*>

"Stars, Darla, if you weren't an AI, I'd think you were hot for me," Tanis said with a laugh as she pulled another lightwand out of the case.

<*Who says I'm not?*>

"Hey!" Tanis exclaimed, flipping the lightwand over—and pointedly ignoring Darla's comment. "This is *my* lightwand!"

<*Awww…Harm really does like you.*>

"At least 'til he wakes up," Tanis qualified with a laugh.

The case also contained another rifle, a flechette pistol, another set of the light armor, a few Infil Kits, and a small box labeled 'X19-FCK'.

<*Good thing he got you that dress,*> Darla said as Tanis checked over the weapons, sorting their charge packs and magazines.

"Oh yeah?" Tanis asked, not sure she wanted to hear why.

<*Yeah. I've been looking for Tora-Unger, and it turns out he's going to a dance the Grand Éire is holding tonight. A fundraiser for families of KIA vets.*>

"Gah…I hate the idea of crashing that," Tanis grimaced.

<*Do you really want to wait 'til tomorrow?*>

"No…I also hate the thought of the whole crew being caught up in this mess. I wonder what they must think of me."

<I bet their opinions of you won't be swayed so easily,> Darla assured her. *<You make a solid impression on people. They won't turn on you.>*

Not in a day, at least, I hope… Tanis thought as she lifted the dress once more.

<Before you ask, no, it won't sit properly over the shimmersuit. You'll have to take that off.>

"Then we have to go shopping for a matching purse," Tanis said. "Because I'm taking this suit with me…just in case."

<So…you going to open the face kit?> Darla asked. *<May as well get that over with.>*

Tanis sighed and picked up the box with 'X19-FCK' stamped on it. "Not looking forward to this part."

She opened up the box and saw only an injector.

"Huh. Well, this is odd."

<Ooooh, it's one of the nano kits. Subdermal facial alterations. I guess that's what you get for hooking up with a MICI.>

"Subdermal? As in this is going to alter my bone structure?"

<That's how they work, yeah. I hear it hurts like a son of a bitch, too.>

With a protracted sigh, Tanis picked up the injector, which had the words 'Apply to Cheek' stenciled on the side. "Here goes nothing."

She pushed the button, and felt a large volume of nano flow into her face, making her skin and cheekbone begin to ache immediately. The ache spread across her entire face, and Tanis groaned.

<This makes me feel a lot better for punching Harm in the face,> she said over the Link rather than attempting to open her mouth—not that she thought it would even be possible at the moment.

The pain dropped Tanis to her knees, and she squeezed her eyes shut, tears leaking from the corners. The agony only intensified, and she sucked in a shuddering breath before toppling over and passing out.

*****

<OK, that's enough, Tanis.> A strident voice came into her mind. *<Time for you to wake up.>*

Tanis cracked an eyelid—which felt like she was dragging sandpaper over her eye—and realized she was face-down on the floor.

"Oh, stars...did you get the ident of the ship that hit me?" she moaned, pushing herself up to a sitting position.

<Funny,> Darla said. *<I would have let you lay there longer, but you have a dance to go to.>*

Tanis saw that she'd been out cold for just over twenty minutes. "I feel like I've fallen unconscious far too much of late," she muttered while rising to her feet.

Once standing, she Linked to the room's holoemitters, and activated a 3D mirror. An image of herself appeared in the center of the apartment, and Tanis stepped toward it, examining the face the person wore.

"Stars, I really look totally different."

Tanis snapped her mouth shut, surprised by the high-pitched voice that had replaced her own.

<MICI has good tech, it seems. It's actually configurable—a new mod to add to your list—but Harm had set it to match your current cover.>

"Say hello to Florence Lanny," Tanis whispered. "Damn, I sound like such a squeaky doofus."

<Well, no one is going to think that you're Tanis Richards, evil traitor extraordinaire. Speaking of which, all of Vesta is on alert for you.>

"Fantastic," Tanis squeaked. "Stars, there's no way this woman really sounds like this."

<Well, she's entirely fictitious. But your 'current' voice matches what's on record for her.>

Tanis wondered if Harm ever gender-swapped to become Florence Lanny himself, or if it was just a general cover that MICI agents had available. Or if he'd crafted it just to mess with her.

<You have thirty minutes to get to the Grand Éire. I bought you a ticket—Florence has some good credit reserves—and you still need to pick up a purse.>

"Shit," Tanis muttered as she quickly pulled the dress on, pleased to find that it had a hidden thigh holster.

She debated taking the flechette weapon, but the pulse pistol was made to pass through security scans, while the flechettes would most certainly be picked up.

The pistol also meant she'd be less likely to 'accidentally' kill Tora-Unger.

She slipped it into the thigh holster, and gave Florence a last once-over in the mirror.

"Stars, I *do* look like a bumblebee with the plague,"

Tanis muttered. "This is why I don't like a lot of fashion. It's dumb."

<You'll live. Now chop, chop.>

"Wait!" Tanis cried, looking around. "No shoes."

<Looks like Harm's not perfect. Oh! There's a 3D printer in that alcove, there. I bet it can print shoes ***and*** *a purse.>*

Tanis accessed the printer, and had it print out a pair of black shoes and a black purse. When they came out, both were neon green.

"Seriously, Darla?"

<As a heart attack. Guns and fighting are your thing. Fashion is mine. We've been over this.>

DANCE WITH FATE

STELLAR DATE: 01.22.4084 (Adjusted Years)
LOCATION: Persephone Ballroom, Grand Éire Resort
REGION: Vesta, Terran Hegemony, InnerSol

Tanis strode into the Persephone Ballroom in the Grand Éire Resort like she owned the place, glad that her bee-barf dress blended in with the other horrid fashion on display.

<OK,> she said absently to Darla as she surveyed the vast ballroom, searching for Tora-Unger amidst the garishly dressed dancers, who all glowed under the black lights and strobes. *<This does not seem like a somber event for the families of KIA vets.>*

<To each their own?> Darla replied, apparently also surprised at the format of the dance. *<I've got nothing. You humans are weird, I thought we'd already established that.>*

<I guess it bears repeating.> Tanis worked her way around the perimeter of the ballroom toward the bar at the back. *<Wish the Éire didn't have such good security. I'd prefer to just drop some probes and hide in the san until they find Tora.>*

Darla chuckled, but didn't reply as Tanis threaded the crowds. Tanis finally arrived at the bar, where she ordered a Grey Venusian, and turned to watch the writhing mass of humanity while the servitor prepared her drink.

As fate would have it, Tanis had only taken one sip of her beverage before she saw Tora-Unger in the crowd.

He was standing near one of the other SWSF officers, First Colonel Urdon.

The men were talking, though Tanis could see that Tora was eyeing some of the women dancing nearby, while Urdon had glanced at a group of men.

<*Good thing Tora swings my way,*> Tanis said to Darla. <*I'd hate to have to use this face mod again to try a gender swap.*>

<*Might take more than a face swap to pull that off,*> Darla chuckled. <*You'd make a pretty waifish guy.*>

Tanis rolled her eyes. <*I grew up on Mars. By Earth standards, all the men there are waifish.*>

<*I suppose. Most Diskers are low-*g*, too. A male version of you might be right up Urdon's alley.*>

Tanis let Darla's barbs ride as she sidled up to Tora-Unger, trying not to gag at the pink, green, and grey disaster he was wearing.

"Having a good time?" she asked.

Tora turned and looked Tanis up and down, only leering slightly.

Tanis held her ground. <*Stars, I can smell half the bar on his breath.*>

<*Might be more than half,*> Darla replied.

"Always having a good time," Tora said as he grinned at Tanis. "We ship out tomorrow, so we're enjoying one last night at the TSF's expense."

"You're Terran Space Force?" she asked in Florence Lanny's squeaky voice.

"No," Tora shook his head, then extended his hand. "Captain Tora of the Scattered Worlds Space Force."

"Oh!" Tanis feigned excitement. "A Disker! How far

out are you from?"

"Originally?" he asked. "I grew up on Nibiru. That's where I'm officially stationed, but I spend a lot of time on Makemake these days."

"Wow! Nibiru! You're practically beyond the Sol System out there."

Tora snorted, a condescending smile on his lips. "Not quite, but a lot further than most folks around here will ever get. I didn't catch your name, by the way."

"Florence Lanny," Tanis said, giving a vapid smile. "I work in marketing for a supplier. I pass through Vesta from time to time. I like to come to the Éire's events whenever I'm here. It's a bright spot of civilization on this ridiculously utilitarian rock. You'd think the TSF could have added *some* style to Vesta over the centuries they've had it."

Tora chuckled and nodded conspiratorially. "Don't say that too loud around here, but I agree. They could do with a bit more architectural inspiration—outside of the Grand Éire, that is. You're right about this place being the one bright spot on Vesta."

Tanis engaged Tora in trivialities for a few more minutes, confirming that he was leaving the next day—something she found more than a little interesting—and priming him for the question that would get their main event underway.

"Do you want to come to my suite?" she asked him. "We could get out of here and have our own little party."

Tora's eyes widened, and he glanced at Urdon, who was speaking to a group of men nearby.

<I hate myself,> Tanis said to Darla as she stepped

closer to Tora, pressing herself against his side. "C'mon, I've got some great stuff down there. It'll blow your mind, but you'll be clearheaded tomorrow when you need to ship out."

Tora grinned and placed an arm around her waist. "Well, when you put it that way…"

Tanis forced down the feeling of revulsion that surged up in her throat, and plastered what she hoped was a winning smile on her face.

"C'mon, you're going to love my suite, just a few floors above the lake."

Tora glanced in Urdon's direction, and Tanis surmised that he'd messaged his superior, though Urdon didn't give any physical signal that he'd heard.

"You must do a great job of marketing, to have a suite that far down the spire," Tora commented once they'd left the ballroom. They were walking down a quieter corridor that led to the central lifts.

<*Oh, you have no idea,*> Darla said privately.

"I manage well enough," Tanis said with a nonchalant shrug. "The boss likes my work, so I get the perks."

"Sounds about right," Tora replied. "That's how it goes everywhere, right?"

Tanis snorted. "I guess so. And here I thought I was being all original."

As they waited for a lift car to arrive, she asked Darla, <*He doesn't have an AI, right?*>

<*No, not that I can see from his EM and Link access. But don't do anything to give things away until we get in the suite. I can suppress his Link there, but not before.*>

<Understood,> Tanis replied as the doors opened, and they stepped into the car.

Tora walked to the far side of the car and stared out into the open shaft that ran down the Éire's spire. "Hard to believe Vesta has a hotel this nice. Place isn't much to speak of otherwise."

<Repeating himself already?> Darla asked. *<Sad that we've exhausted his supply of small talk so soon.>*

Tanis suppressed a laugh and tilted her head as she stepped up beside Tora. "Lotta credit flying around on Vesta. *That's* what looks pretty damn nice to me."

Tora snorted. "Folks like you just see money when it comes to the military, don't you?"

"Well, money and a lot of guys who look really good in a uniform," Tanis added, glancing at Tora's outfit. "Or their evening attire." She smiled coyly at her target. *<Gonna gag here, Darla. Can you make this lift go any faster?>*

<Funny woman.>

"Who did you say you worked for?" Tora asked, glancing over his shoulder at Tanis.

"Justice Incorporated," she replied, citing the first general supplies contractor that came to mind. "Only started with them a few weeks ago. Pretty wild to come here as my first trip."

Tora turned and leant a shoulder against the window, placing a hand on Tanis's waist. "Well, I'm all about wild, so I'm glad that aligns with your trip thus far."

<Can you get some nano on him to confirm he really is Unger?> Tanis asked Darla. *<I'm dying to find out how he…well…didn't die.>*

<Be patient. SWSF officers have good intrusion detection. If I drop nano on him to pull a DNA sample, he's going to know about it. Wait 'til we get in the suite, already.>

<Fiiiine. But if I break his hand before we get there, I'm blaming you.>

<Noted.>

Tanis managed to survive some further nonsensical conversation with Tora, while gracefully avoiding the man's attempts to steal kisses during the remainder of the lift ride.

When the car finally stopped at floor 1301, Tora whistled with appreciation. "OK, when you said 'near the lake', you weren't kidding."

"I don't kid," Tanis said with a wink as she led him off the lift and to her suite's door.

It slid aside as she approached, and Tora followed her in, his eyes alighting on the weapons sitting on the table.

"What—"

Tanis spun and clamped her right hand around his throat as she squeaked in Florence's voice, "Captain Unger, I presume?"

The man made a strangled sound that Tanis couldn't interpret, but the widening of his eyes was answer enough for her.

"I'm going to enjoy hearing about how you survived…then I'll hold a healthy debate with myself about killing you again."

<Tanis! You can't—>

<Don't worry, just scaring him.>

<You're scaring **me**.*>*

Tanis grinned, both for Tora-Unger's benefit, and for

Darla's. <*Just get the nano on him to check his DNA.*>

Loosening her grip, Tanis asked, "You *are* Captain Unger of the *Norse Wind,* aren't you?"

"Commander Richards?" the man rasped, his eyes narrowing now that he knew who he was facing. "That's a good disguise. Not that it's going to help you."

Tanis clenched her teeth, grimacing as she altered her facial structure to resume its original appearance. She knew it wouldn't hurt as much to go back once the nano had partially plasticized her facial structure.

"Seemed to work on you," she replied. "So it already helped me."

"When Colonel Urdon realizes I'm missing—"

"He'll do what?" Tanis asked, arching an eyebrow. "Deering and your people have been trying to take me out for a week now. How's that going for you?"

Tora didn't move or respond, but his breathing evened out, and Tanis waited for the strike that was sure to come.

He lashed out a second before she thought he would, his knee slamming into her groin—the blow startling her more than it hurt. Then he pivoted, pushing his boot against the inside of her right knee.

Tanis was ready by then, and she shifted her weight, letting her foot slide to the side, the give of her knee sending him off-balance. She still held onto his neck, and her prosthetic hand squeezed harder before she twisted and drove her own knee into Tora's groin.

She felt a *pop* in his pelvic bone, and the man screamed in pain.

With a disdainful shove, Tanis let him fall to the

ground, and took a step back, pulling her pistol from its thigh holster.

"So, *Unger,* care to tell me what's *really* going on?"

The man was rocking side to side, moaning pitifully, but he managed to shoot her a dirty look.

Tanis took it as a 'no'.

"Well, then, let me see how I'm doing," she said, stepping back and covering him with her pulse pistol.

<By the way, he **is** *Unger, in case there was any doubt,>* Darla interjected. *<DNA is an exact match.>*

<There was a teensy bit of doubt. Given that he drove my own lightwand through my chest, though, I feel a lot better about breaking his pelvis.>

Darla chuckled. *<Glad to hear it.>*

"So, let's see," she said aloud, addressing Tora-Unger. "The Scattered Worlds Space Force has found some of their behemoth dreadnoughts from the sentience wars, and they're working on refitting them. However, a lot gets lost in a thousand years, and I bet the engine control system specs are one of those things. Which means OEM parts are quite valuable to you. Parts like the ones the *Norse Wind* was hauling out to the Disk."

She watched Tora-Unger's lips purse, and took that as confirmation that she was on the right track.

"So, then. By some means, you have Admiral Deering in your pocket—which really pisses me off, to be honest—and she sent the *Arizona* in to take you off my hands. I thought you were dead, but I guess you weren't dead enough, since their medics brought you back. Then they brought your ship here; not entirely clear on why they did that, yet.

"Either way, you think I have the quantum core—which, by the way, I don't—and you need that bit of tech to get your little projects out in the Scattered Disk running."

Tanis stopped talking and aimed her pulse pistol at Tora-Unger's crotch.

"I need some sort of feedback on how I'm doing, here," she said. "Either you give it to me, or I elicit it."

"You wouldn't," Unger hissed through clenched teeth. "You're a TSF officer, you don't torture."

"You forget," Tanis said with a wink to cover up how much his words stung. "I'm on the run, suspected of all sorts of horrible things. Which *has* to cause you to wonder, how *did* I escape? What sort of means do I have at my disposal? How far am I willing to go to get to the bottom of this? I could just dump enough nano into your head to wipe out your protections, and strip what I want to know from your mind. Want to find out if I'll go that far?"

"You can't do that," Tora-Unger sneered. "You'd need an AI."

"I have a friend that would help," Tanis intoned. "She's been listening in."

<*Yeah, and I'm not going to mind-rape him,*> Darla said privately. <*That's a crime worse than anything we're accused of.*>

<*Of course you're not going to. And I wouldn't ask it. Just play along.*>

<*Ohhh…well, shit, Tanis. You're all scary serious right now. I thought maybe…*> Darla made a sound that somewhat approximated a throat clearing, and then

addressed Tora-Unger via a direct connection. <*Yup, I'm already connected to your nervous system, and I'm going to strip your mind down layer by layer if you don't tell us what we want to know.*>

Tora-Unger visibly paled, and Tanis let a predatory grin slip onto her lips. "Start talking."

"You already seem to know everything..." Tora's voice wavered. "What else—"

"I want *evidence*," she interrupted. "Something that ties Deering to all of this and exonerates me. Your hide will be a start, but alone it's not enough."

Tora-Unger's eyes narrowed, and the muscles along his jaw tensed.

"Don't think you can give me all that and hold out now," Tanis waved her pulse pistol. "I wonder...at this point, would a pulse shot at your junk hurt more, or be a blessed bit of numbing? Either way, your testicles are gonna be salsa."

<*OK, I'm non-organic, and that was nasty.*>

<*Yeah...it came out before I thought it through,*> Tanis grimaced inwardly while keeping a stern glare fixed on Tora-Unger. <*Going to have that imagery in my mind for a while.*>

"Admiral Kiaan," Tora-Unger said after a moment of indecision. "He has all the information. I'm just flying the ship; I don't know much more than you do."

"And where is Kiaan right now?" Tanis asked.

"His quarters, I suspect. Here in the Éire, suite 724-142." Tora-Unger flashed a grin. "Not that you can stop us, anyway. We're going to get those ships working, one way or another."

<*Checks out,*> Darla said. <*That's part of a block that the SWSF uses when they're here, but they don't provide details as to who is in what suite.*>

"Now tell me, what is it that all my unexpected visitors have been after. The quantum core, we never saw anything like that on your ship."

Unger pursed his lips, but then shook his head. "Damn…you *really* didn't know about it. It was inside a Marsian cruiser model in my cabin…one of your crew must have taken it. So much for you running a tight ship."

Tanis glared at the man, resisting the urge to hit him. After a half-minute—and a few deep breaths—she bent down and tapped the muzzle of her pistol against his forehead.

"OK, Unger. You stay put while I go have a chat with your Admiral Kiaan."

To his credit, Tora-Unger tried to make a grab for Tanis. She'd been ready for it, though, and kneeled on his arm before slamming the butt of her pistol into his temple.

<*OK, no ifs, ands, or buts about it. You're definitely scary, Tanis.*>

LEADS AND MORE LEADS

STELLAR DATE: 01.22.4084 (Adjusted Years)
LOCATION: Suite 1301-01, Grand Éire Resort
REGION: Vesta, Terran Hegemony, InnerSol

Tanis tied Tora-Unger up in the same room that had held the captured mercenary from the prior night. His body wasn't there anymore—which was some comfort, though Tanis still felt a little bad that all of the attackers had died.

She pushed the worry out of her mind, triggering her nano to burn out Tora-Unger's Link antenna, rendering him unable to reach out, should he wake before she returned.

Then she stripped off the bumblebee-vomit dress, and pulled the shimmersuit back on, this time putting both a pulse pistol and a kinetic handgun into pouches on the suit's waist.

She wished there was a way to take the last rifle Harm had brought, but there was nowhere to hide it—other than in the suit itself, and that would be far from comfortable.

The ride up to the 724th floor took just a few minutes. When Tanis arrived, she very nearly collided with a group that was rushing toward the lift, laughing about someone they were going to meet at one of the lake bars, and bragging about how wasted they were going to get.

Rather, they nearly collided with her, given that she was invisible.

Pressing herself against the bulkhead, Tanis winced

as one of the men in the group brushed against her. He didn't slow, and she let out a long, cautious breath before turning and walking down the corridor to Admiral Kiaan's room.

When she arrived, Darla set to work on the access panel—once again utilizing one of Harm's Infil Kits—and forty seconds later, the door slid open.

Tanis was inside with the portal closed again in seconds, only to see a rather non-descript room that showed no signs of occupancy.

<What the hell?>

<The bed's unmade, and there's schmutz on the carpet and trash in the barrel. Looks like we just missed whoever was here.>

Tanis walked to the barrel and grabbed it, dumping its contents on the bed. There were some food wrappers, and a half-eaten apple. Then she saw a piece of plas with the resort's logo on top.

A welcome letter for Admiral Kiaan.

<So this ***was*** *his room,>* Tanis muttered as she straightened.

<I think we ***just*** *missed him. I'm searching through departure queues now, to see if he's on any ship leaving Vesta. OK…there's only one SWSF ship docked here, a patrol boat, and it's not slated to leave for another day.>*

<Think Unger got the word out to him somehow?> Tanis asked.

Darla let out a frustrated groan. *<I don't think so…I didn't pick anything up. But* ***could*** *he have? Sure. I'm not perfect.>*

<Harm,> Tanis sent her first message to the MICI

agent since she'd cold-cocked him in the MP detention facility. <*I've nabbed Captain Tora, who is indeed Unger. He fingered Admiral Kiaan as being the mastermind, but the good admiral is missing. Any ideas where he could be?*>

<*You know, when I said to make it look good, I didn't mean fracture my eye socket,*> Harm said tersely. <*Yes, I have an idea where Kiaan could be, but you're not going to like it.*>

Tanis gritted her teeth and closed her eyes. <*Lay it on me, Harm.*>

<*Well, earlier today, the MPs moved your ship from Sector 33 to the impound, but it's gone missing. I've got eyes on Bay 8129, and it's definitely not there. What's more, a bunch of crates of engine components that were in the bay are missing too. I don't have anything but my suspicion here, but I'll bet those held the parts you initially confiscated from the* Norse Wind.>

Tanis opened her eyes, staring across the room in shock. <*Wait a second…are you saying that these fucking bastards have stolen my ship?*>

<*I think so…*>

<*How is that even possible? How does Vesta's STC just let them wander off like that? This is one of the biggest TSF bases in the system!*>

Harm sighed, and Tanis realized she was taking her ire out on the wrong person. <*I imagine that's part of the problem, Tanis. Vesta's a great place to pull off this sort of thing. Everyone thinks everyone else has things under control. But I do have good news.*>

<*I could really use some of that. Oh! Captain Tora-Unger is tied up in my suite, in case you go there.*>

<*'Your' suite, or the one you're squatting in?*>

Tanis couldn't help a laugh as she thought about how strange her life had been these past few days. <*Squatting. Now what's the good news?*>

<*Your crewmembers all checked out and have been released. I even managed to work some back-channel mojo and get Connie out. Lovell is down at a network hub in Section 12, being rehabbed. I can't get to him, but maybe Darla can.*>

That sounded like good news, but not the kind that got her onto the *Jones.* "I thought your 'good news' would be that you have a ship."

<*Right, that's why I started with your crew. You need a crew to run a ship. Especially one like the* Norse Wind.>

<*The* ***what****?!*>

* * * * *

Tanis had made it as far into Section 12 as she could without being detected. Though the shimmersuit could fool passive optics and IR sensors, the security arch ahead would use active scanning systems with higher-energy particles that the shimmersuit wouldn't be able to convincingly bend around her.

Which meant this next part of the mission was on Darla.

<*You ready?*> Tanis asked the AI.

<*Ready to breach one of my people's inner sanctums and risk ostracization from expanses everywhere? No. Not really. Too bad this wasn't the Kora Expanse; I could have walked us right in there—since I own half the facility.*>

<*I get that it's a risk, but so is what I'm doing,*> Tanis said. <*We get caught, and we both go to prison anyway—well,*

until Harm and the MICIs get us out.>

<***If*** *they get us out.*> Darla's tone was derisive. <*You know how this spy shit works. Plausible deniability, and all that.*>

<*Right, except there's no reason to deny this when it all comes out. Harm is just laying low because he doesn't want to blow his cover, and we don't know how far up this goes. Could very well be that Admiral Kocsis is in on it, too. Between him and Deering, they pretty much control all of Vesta.*>

Darla made a humming sound, but didn't speak further for a few minutes. Tanis hoped that meant she was working her magic. The AI hadn't said whether she was going to hack the security arch ahead, or call in a favor, but either way, she wasn't happy about doing it.

Just as Tanis was about to ask if Darla had made any progress, the AI spoke up once more.

<*It's done. You can pass through the arch.*>

<*Did you have to sell your soul?*>

Darla made a groaning sound. <*Only the part of it I liked most. I had to promise to spend a year in the Kora Expanse after my time with you is up.*>

Tanis walked forward gingerly, careful to avoid the two guards standing on either side of the arch—one human, and one AI in a mobile combat frame.

<*I thought AIs* ***liked*** *hanging out in expanses.*>

<*Sure, hanging out with other AIs, melding minds, thinking deep thoughts, that's all fun. What they want me to do is* ***teach****.*>

Tanis had to hold back a snort as she passed under the arch, half-certain the AI guard heard her anyway, by a slight twitch it gave.

<*I'm sorry you have to undergo such a horrendous penalty. I'll do my best to ensure our pairing lasts as long as possible.*>

<*You do that, Tanis,*> Darla retorted. <*You owe me.*>

Tanis nodded as she turned right at an intersection, following the path Darla had laid on her HUD. It would take them to an Ensconcing Chamber, a place where AI cores were mounted and cared for if they had no reason to occupy a mobile frame.

<*There will be another guard at the door,*> Darla advised. <*This one isn't in on our little heist, so you're going to have to take him out.*>

<*Human or AI?*> Tanis asked.

<*AI. Heavy mech frame.*>

<*Shit, Darla. How in stars am I supposed to just 'take him out'?*>

In Tanis's mind, Darla's avatar gave a protracted shrug. <*Something quick and non-fatal would be best. Maybe sever his core's trunk line with your lightwand.*>

<*He'll sound an alarm,*> Tanis warned.

<*My friend will suppress it—so long as you don't harm Fred.*>

Tanis surmised that the guard AI was Fred, and was a touch surprised that Darla's friend on the inside was letting her take this much risk with the life of an AI.

A few minutes later, Tanis came to the door of the Ensconcing Chamber, and sure enough, there was a heavy mech standing in front of it.

<*His core is…?*> Tanis asked.

Darla highlighted a section of the mech's chestplate. <*Under the left armpit. The main data trunk line runs to a junction at the neck. If you drive your lightwand right into its chest where I've marked, you* ***should*** *be able to disable it.*>

<*'Should'?*>

Darla's avatar shrugged. <*You'll have to have really good aim…plus, you're going to have to activate your lightwand right in front of Fred, and he'll probably see it. I imagine he has very fast reflexes.*>

Tanis observed the three-meter mech for half a minute, considering his dual pulse cannons, chain gun, and scattershot slung from his hip. The thing meant business, and her shimmersuit—while great for stealth—offered almost no protection when it came to direct weapons fire.

<*What's the strike angle I need to hit the data trunk from?*> Tanis asked, and Darla highlighted it.

She formulated a plan and crept down the corridor toward Fred, praying there would be enough room to execute her attack, and that it would work to begin with.

At one point, her foot dragged on the deck, and she froze, terrified that he'd detected her, but after fifteen seconds of no response, she continued forward.

Sidling around the AI's mech frame, Tanis drew her lightwand's hilt out of the pocket on her forearm, and held it close, knowing that the mech would have eyes on the back of its head as well—hopefully just not as many, or not ones it was paying as much attention to, given that they were staring at a door.

<*It won't work from back here,*> Darla advised. <*Your lightwand's not long enough.*>

<*It's long enough,*> Tanis replied, praying she was right as she adjusted the wand to its maximum length. She drew a slow breath, and held the hilt up to the back of

the mech frame.

She activated it, and a stream of relativistic electrons shot out of the wand's hilt, pushing out the tiny reflective mirror that was connected to the base of the wand by a nanofilament.

For all intents and purposes, the wand was a controlled bolt of lightning that could cut through almost anything, the white gleam of electrons tinted blue by the cherenkov radiation that the beam gave off.

The lightwand cut into Fred's body, which jerked once and then fell still.

<*Told you it was long enough,*> Tanis said as she disabled the wand and slid it back into the pocket on her forearm.

<*Well, you never told me it was one of the adjustable length ones. Size does matter.*>

<*Do you have the door, or should I cut through it?*> Tanis asked, ignoring the joke.

Darla didn't reply, but the door slid open to reveal a hundred-meter-long chamber, filled with titanium AI columns.

An indicator appeared over a pillar a dozen meters in. <*That's Lovell. You're going to want to hard-Link to his cylinder. I've not reached out to him yet—not sure how receptive he'll be.*>

Tanis nodded silently as she approached the titanium cylinder. Once there, she grabbed the hard-Link cable hanging from it, and loosened the shimmersuit's hood, exposing the small port behind her ear, and sliding the cable in.

<*Lovell,*> she called out once the protocols were set up

and the connection was established. *<Lovell, it's Tanis.>*

<Commander Richards? What are you doing here? You know you're wanted, right?> Lovell's voice seemed to carry a combination of annoyance, worry, and a definite undertone of anger.

<Yeah,> Tanis followed the word with a soft chuckle. *<I'm all too aware of that. It's a frame-up. Admiral Deering is in cahoots with the people from the* Norse Wind. *They've stolen the* Kirby Jones *and are flying it out to the Disk.>*

<They ***what****!>* Lovell all but roared. *<How the hell is that even possible? How did you get in here, anyway?>*

<I helped her,> Darla said, piggybacking over Tanis's hard-Link.

<Who are you?>

<Darla,> the AI replied, and Tanis could see the datastream spike as the AIs exchanged their tokens and identity matrices.

Lovell made a sound of amazement. *<Wait a second. You're piggybacking over Tanis's hard-Link. That means…Shit!>*

<Yes,> Tanis confirmed. *<Darla and I are paired, but that's top secret, hush-hush stuff.>*

<You're a fugitive, what do you care about what's top secret?> Lovell asked. *<Er…Commander.>*

<Because I'm going to clear my name, and also because I'm working for MICI. Look, I'm not here for a nice teatime chat. We're going to steal the Norse Wind *and go after the* Kirby Jones. *It would go a lot better with your help, but I understand if you're still recovering.>*

<Pffft, recovering? Tanis, they have me in a 'rehabilitation program' to help me 'cope'. If I had eyes, I'd've stabbed them

*out by now. You get me out of here, and I'll fly to Tau Ceti with you—*Norse Wind *or no.*>

Tanis stifled a laugh at the ire in Lovell's voice. *I suppose I know why he sounded so angry when he first responded,* she thought.

<*But I'm not riding in your pocket,*> the AI added. <*There are mech frames on the outer wall there. Pull me and put me in one.*>

<*You sure?*> Tanis asked. <*I have a shimmersuit, we can just stealth our way out of here.*>

<*Don't worry, Tanis,*> Darla said. <*AIs have good tech, too. There are stealth frames here.*>

Tanis suddenly wondered how often AIs wandered around in stealthed frames. The idea was a bit disconcerting.

The cover on Lovell's cylinder slid open, and Tanis waited for the 'safe to pull' indicator to turn green as she disconnected the hard-Link cable from behind her ear.

When she was no longer tethered, and the light had turned green, she pulled Lovell's core and threaded her way through the forest of titanium cylinders to a mobile frame Darla had pointed out.

It was shaped like a tall, lithe man, and if she had spotted it out in the station, Tanis would never have guessed it was an AI frame. A slot hung open on the chest, and she slid Lovell's cylinder into it.

<*All se—*> she began, but a sound drew her attention back to the entrance.

<*Shit, is that Fred?*> Lovell asked as he came online in the frame.

<*He must have bypassed the trunk line,*> Darla figured,

as they watched the massive mech frame enter the space. Thus far, it hadn't spotted them.

Then it turned to face the still-open door on Lovell's cylinder.

<*Aw, crap,*> Tanis muttered.

She was about to advance on Fred once more, maybe slice off his weapon arms, when another mech frame surged forward from a rack on the wall, rushing toward Fred's and crashing into it, knocking it back from the entrance and into the corridor beyond.

<*I got him, you two get moving!*> Darla ordered.

Tanis glanced back at Lovell. <*If we get separated, we're going to Bay 8129—once I round up the rest of the crew, that is.*>

<*Got it,*> Lovell replied with a nod before his frame became invisible like Tanis.

She assumed he was behind her, hopefully gauging her pace well enough to not run into her back. Normally, in a combat situation, they'd use special random IFF frequencies to maintain awareness of one another's positions, but they hadn't had time to set that up.

Once in the corridor, Tanis jogged past the mech frame Darla was controlling as it struggled with Fred, praying her AI could keep him at bay long enough.

Fred managed to fire a few random pulse blasts out into the corridor, but by some miracle, none caught Tanis with more than a glancing blow, and the one that did hit, struck her right arm, and was easily absorbed by the prosthetic limb.

<*He's pinned.*> Darla advised. <*When you get to the entrance arch, just run through. Misty is going to distract the*

organic guard. I'll relay the instructions to Lovell.>

Ten minutes later, she was out on Section 12's main sweep, a maglev platform just a few hundred meters away.

<*Made it.*> A single ping message came from Lovell, followed by, <*I hate crowds.*>

Tanis had to agree. Navigating crowds while invisible was a nightmare. By the time she'd managed to find a corner on a relatively empty maglev car, she'd caused two arguments between people thinking that someone else had bumped into them.

<*I think you're enjoying messing with people,*> Darla said as the maglev took off.

<*Maybe a bit,*> Tanis chuckled. <*I wonder if people do this for kicks sometimes. Though I suppose if you can afford a shimmersuit this good, you're not using it to feel people up on the maglev.*>

<*One would hope,*> Darla replied. <*Got a ping from Lovell. He made the next train.*>

Tanis breathed a sigh of relief. They were almost home free.

Well, home free before we begin the most dangerous part of all this.

She had mixed feelings about involving the rest of her crew. Keeping them out of this mess had been a major motivation for her over the past few days, but now that the MPs had pulled them in and questioned them—not to mention how Connie and Lovell had been abducted—she knew that keeping them at arm's length wasn't protecting them: it was putting them at risk.

Harm had sent her a location to meet with her crew, a

bar in Sector 33, one kilometer from where the *Norse Wind* waited for them in Bay 8129.

The place bore a rather welcoming name, 'The Pig's Ass'. When Tanis entered, she could see that it was well-earned.

The 'Ass' was a period tavern that was made to look like it was straight out of the sixteen hundreds, or some ancient time like that. Tanis never really got the appeal of dirty period taverns, but a lot of soldiers and sailors did, making bars like it quite popular.

She spotted her crew occupying a long table at the back of the bar, and was surprised to see everyone there. Connie sat at the end closest to the door, and next to her was Lieutenant Jeannie. Lieutenant Smythe sat across from them, and next to him was Corporal Marian, followed by her breach team: Privates Yves, Susan, and Lukas.

At the end of the table, their heads together and chuckling about something, were Connie's E-3s: Seamus and Liam, seeming unperturbed by their ship to Ceres having been recalled.

Tanis walked around the table and settled into the vacant space between Smythe and Seamus.

"So, what's good here?" she asked, causing Smythe to jump and Seamus to burst out laughing.

"Commander?" Marian asked from across the table. "You need to be more careful. They'll be listening with us here."

"Don't worry," Tanis replied. "Between Darla and Harm, they have the audio pickups tackled. Vid's a bit harder, so I'll keep my shimmersuit on. In theory, Lovell is here, too."

"Down here." Lovell's voice came from the foot of the table. "Don't order anything on my account, though, this frame can't ingest food."

"OK, Commander, what the *hell* is going on?" Smythe asked in a soft voice that carried no small amount of ire. "Connie told us that the people we took out on the *Norse Wind* are behind all this?"

"Plus Admiral Deering," Tanis replied. "And an Admiral Kiaan of the SWSF. Oh, and they've stolen the *Kirby Jones*."

"Mother*fucker*!" Connie swore. "Harm didn't share that tidbit when he got me to set up this meeting. What the hell?"

"Don't worry," Tanis smiled, then realized no one could see it, and added a devious chuckle. "We're going to steal it back, and we're going to do it with the *Norse Wind*."

"With *that* tub?" Connie asked. "I don't even know if it can *catch* the *Jones,* let alone come close to taking it in a fight."

"Well, we'll have to figure something out," Tanis replied. "We don't exactly have our pick of ships, and the *Wind* is slated to be moved to impound in three hours—so if we're not there to take it, we'll miss our window."

"So we're going to fake our way onto the *Norse Wind* as the impound crew?" Marian asked with a mischievous grin. "I kinda like this."

"Well, I haven't officially asked you if you're all in. This is a point of no return sort of thing."

"Commander," Connie spoke up, looking up and down the table. "I think I speak for everyone here when I say that not only do we have faith in you, but we're not going to let the fucking SWSF steal our ship. Most of us have spent a few years on the *Jones*—and with you as our captain. We believe you, and we're behind you every step of the way. Now how do we get past the MPs?"

Tanis was glad that the shimmersuit hid the flush on her cheeks as her chief of engineering spoke. "Thanks Connie, and everyone else, too. I'll understand if anyone doesn't want to go through with this; you can head out now, no judgment."

Not a single person so much as shifted in their seats, and a smile split Tanis's lips.

"You're all the best, you know that?"

"Of course we do," Marian said with a grin. "Now about getting past those MPs?"

"Harm told me he has creds sourced," Tanis replied, getting down to business. "But we're going to need uniforms as well."

Connie ran a hand through her dark, curly hair. "Ten is a pretty big crew to take a ship like the *Wind* out to an impound yard. The MPs will raise an eyebrow at that."

"Well," Smythe said after downing half of his beer in one gulp. "I know a guy who works tugs. He owes me a favor. I could get myself, Jeannie, and maybe Seamus and Liam onto a tug. We can have it dock with the *Norse Wind* after we pull it away from the station. Get it onboard that way."

"I like that," Connie said while tapping a finger on her chin. "Only we don't undock the tug, we leave it there. Heck, any chance your favor with your friend is big enough to cash in for two tugs? The *Wind* is a clunky ship; I could see them using a pair to pull it away from the station. Keeping them with the ship can give us a serious boost."

Smythe pursed his lips. "That's gonna be a big favor, Connie. Two tugs that we don't send back is a favor that has to be worth a career."

"I can get one of the STC AIs to fudge the logs on the tugs coming back in," Lovell said from the foot of the table. "I'm owed a favor or two, as well."

"OK, so that gets the team onto the *Norse Wind,*" Tanis confirmed. "Then we just have to catch the *Jones,* and board her."

"Then we'd better bring some serious gear." Corporal Marian glanced at her team. "Luckily, I have a cousin who runs a supply outfit. We'll have to pack it up in some supply crates; we can claim they are for the trip out to the impound yard."

"Really?" Tanis asked, mouth agape. "Stars, I could have used some gear a few days ago."

Marian adopted a wounded expression. "I'm hurt you didn't hit me up, Commander."

"And Harm?" Connie asked. "Will he be coming along?"

"No," Tanis shook her head. "He has to maintain his cover here."

"Well then," Marian stood and stretched. "We've got our work cut out for us. T-minus three hours."

"Less," Tanis corrected. "Airlock door closes in three hours."

The corporal glanced at her team, speaking loudly. "Food here blows, lads and lady. I know a *way* better place, and with better company, too." With that, she turned and led Susan, Yves, and Lukas out of the bar.

Connie glanced at Seamus and Liam. "You two scoundrels, stay here until I call for you. Don't get into *any* trouble."

"Lovell and I will get down to the bay and try to get on the ship early," Tanis said. "Worst-case, we wait for you and slip on then."

"That leaves you two," Connie nodded to Jeannie and Smythe.

"Jeannie needs to come with me," Smythe said with a slow wink. "Actually, Seamus and Liam should, too. It will take all four of us to do the favor, and we have to move fast if we're to do it and get on those tugs in time for the departure."

"Do I want to know?" Tanis asked.

Smythe shook his head. "No, you really don't."

"What about me? Do I want to know?" Jeannie asked.

A wink was all she got from Smythe, and she glowered at him. "This had better work!"

"It'll work," Smythe said as he stood. "And then we'll never speak of it again."

BACK ON THE WIND

STELLAR DATE: 01.22.4084 (Adjusted Years)
LOCATION: *Norse Wind*, Bay 8129, Sector 33
REGION: Vesta, Terran Hegemony, InnerSol

Tanis was ready to start gnawing on her nails when she finally saw Connie enter the bay on the ship's external feeds. She was wearing a StarCharger uniform—one of the contract firms that managed hauling ships out to impound yards. Behind her came the four members of the breach team.

"Surprising they got past the MPs, what with their faces not disguised," Lovell said from his place at the pilot's console.

Tanis nodded as she leant back in the command chair, centered on the small bridge. "Maybe Harm worked some magic for them."

<Connie's pretty resourceful,> Darla said in a conspiratorial tone. *<At least, from what I've seen thus far. Maybe she sweet-talked the MPs.>*

"STC has just confirmed our place in the departure queue," Lovell announced. "And we have two tugs assigned. I guess someone reported our mass wrong, and our ship looks *huuuuuuge.*"

Darla made a snorting sound. *<Gee, I wonder who that was.>*

Tanis continued to watch the feeds, as Marian and her team pulled three crates up the ramp and into the airlock, cycling it shut a scant two minutes before the external bay doors were slated to open.

She kept one eye glued on the feeds, half waiting for MPs to come storming into the bay, like they had the last time. If they did, she wasn't sure that she'd stand down.

I won't kill them, but if we can get out of the bay…I'll do it. I'm done with this mess. We're getting the Jones *back, and Deering is going to clear my name with her own guilt.*

"You've got that look in your eye," Connie said as she entered the bridge.

"What look?" Tanis asked.

"The one that says, 'I'll kill anyone who gets in my way, and then some'," the engineer replied with a smirk.

"Don't you have a ship to go over?" she retorted.

Connie slid into an auxiliary console. "Lovell's already run all the pre-flight. Everything looks good—they were repairing this ship for a flight out to the Disk before they switched to the *Jones*. I can run things from up here just as well as down there."

"You just want to watch the action on the big holodisplay," Tanis said with a knowing smirk.

"You got me, Commander."

<Bay doors opening,> Darla announced. *<ES shield is in place, cradle's rails are online.>*

The ship shuddered as the docking cradle's clamps disengaged, and the ship began to slide toward the bay doors.

"Buckle in," Tanis called out on the 1MC for Marian and her team's benefit. "About to drop."

"You got it, Commander," Marian replied on the audible ship's comms. "We're good to go down here."

The ship rolled to the edge of the bay doors, and then the docking cradle extended its armatures, holding the ship out over the rim of the bay.

The Vesta Ring's tangential velocity would impart thirteen hundred meters per second of v to the *Norse Wind* the instant the arms let go. From there, the tugs would meet up with the ship and set it on a course for the impound yard, which trailed Vesta by four light seconds, centered around an asteroid named Horax.

Of course, the *Norse Wind* would never arrive at Horax.

Right before the clamps let go, a message came in from Harm. <*Captain of the* Norse Wind. *Good luck. Things will be in hand here.*>

Tanis replied with a simple acknowledgement. She knew that Harm had his hands full with keeping eyes off the *Norse Wind* and what it was about to get up to.

"Cradle is dropping us in five, four, three, two, *one*!" Lovell announced, though the readout on the bridge's main holoscreen also held the information.

The instant he said 'one', the comfortable feeling of about 0.7*g* disappeared, and the unnerving sensation of organs shifting in her torso came over Tanis, though it was less noticeable than previous transitions into zero-*g*.

I guess its because less of my insides are organic, she thought as the ship fell away from Vesta.

A call came over the ship-to-ship comms, and Tanis toggled it on the audible systems.

"Freighter *Norse Wind,* this is Tug Ninety-Seven Aaaaalpha One, here with tug Eighty-Twooooo Charlie Foxtrot, we're ready to latch on and give you a coooorective boost to get you headed off to Hoooorax."

The voice was, of course, Lieutenant Smythe's, and

he'd given every possible word the worst drawl it could support.

"Is that how you think tug operators talk?" Connie asked.

"He's not far off," Jeannie said, her voice coming in from Tug 82-CF. "I have to listen to those doofuses all the time. That's actually a pretty tame rendition."

"We deserve hazard pay for having to deal with them," Smythe added. "We're coming in on the port and starboard anchor points. Once we're latched on, we'll EV into the *Wind* and then we can boost on out."

"We'll correct for Horax first," Tanis advised. "I want to get out of Vesta's nearspace before we adjust course and burn for the *Jones*."

"Do we know where she is yet?" Connie asked.

<*No,*> Darla replied. <*We know where she's going, though. The Disk.*>

Connie rolled her eyes. <*Darla, seriously, the Disk surrounds the whole system. Every direction on the stellar plane takes you to the Disk.*>

"Well," Tanis said with a wink. "We know where the *Norse Wind* was going. Lovell ferreted it out of their logs."

"Oh yeah?" Connie asked.

Lovell cast a smug look over his shoulder and nodded at Connie. "Yup, they were headed for Eris. Which is close to the same vector the *Wind* here was on when we first ordered it to heave to."

The main holodisplay changed to a view of space surrounding Vesta out to one AU.

"They only left fourteen hours ago at most. If they

really poured it on, that's the max range the *Jones* could manage in that time. However, I doubt they would have hit the burners that hard; it would make our girl stand out a lot."

"Not to mention that it would melt the engines long before they got to Eris," Connie groused.

"Right," Tanis nodded, drawing a red arc just over half an AU from Vesta. "Chances are they've not yet crossed this line—or if they have, only just. They're also most likely within this cone."

Tanis added a yellow cone to the display, rotating it to show the 3D nature of the possible trajectory.

"We need to look at every drive signature boosting out in that cone," Connie said. "We'll find them."

"Good," Tanis nodded. "Because once we have them, I want to pour on every ounce of speed this shit-box has. We'll head right for them, and do a flying breach."

"Are you serious?" Connie asked, her face going pale. "If you miss, you're screwed."

"She's right," Lovell turned in his seat, and locked his eyes on Tanis's. "Flying breaches aren't accepted doctrine for a reason."

Darla joined in the conversation. *<Well, then we'd better not miss.>*

FLYING BREACH

STELLAR DATE: 01.24.4084 (Adjusted Years)
LOCATION: *Norse Wind*, Outer rim of Main Asteroid Belt
REGION: Vesta, Terran Hegemony, InnerSol

The *Kirby Jones* was within optical range, its engine flare only two million kilometers off the *Norse Wind*'s bow.

Tanis watched the delta-*v* between the two ships continue to climb, feeling more and more nervous about the maneuver she and her team would soon attempt.

There was no way around it. The fly breach was necessary.

Catching up to the *Jones*, and then matching *v* would be a long, slow, and likely impossible maneuver. To achieve zero delta-*v*, they would have already had to begin braking—and then, if whoever was flying the *Jones* picked up speed, they would have to turn the *Wind* around and boost once more to match.

A forced match-n-latch could take days, and when the prey had better weapons than the hunters, it wasn't possible at all.

All this bucket has are a few point defense weapons for shooting at rocks that get too close, Tanis thought ruefully, considering the damage the *Kirby Jones* could inflict on the *Wind.*

On top of that, there was no way that the *Jones* couldn't see them by now. Even with the *Norse Wind* headed straight for them, the halo glare of the freighter's engines would be obvious even if there was a half-baked

NSAI running scan on the TSF patrol boat.

However, some things were working in their favor. Harm had been true to his word, and no pursuit had originated from Vesta as yet. That he could blind the base's sensors, or hack their STC reporting so well that no one had spotted the *Wind* boosting after the *Jones* was both impressive and terrifying.

STC scan was supposed to see all, and know all. The fact that two ships could blast across the asteroid belt with not a single comm message telling them to slow down and get into normal shipping lanes terrified Tanis. It shattered her belief that the traffic in Sol was at all well managed.

One would expect that, simply because you could *see* all the ships boosting around in the system, you knew what they were up to. But it was apparent that with a hundred million ships—station-to-station taxies, freighters, miners, tugs, and military craft—no one *really* kept an eye on it all.

She wondered if someone would change protocol on Vesta after this, or if whatever gap Harm had exploited would remain open for the MICIs to use.

<I've been thinking about the little leap we'll be taking,> Darla said, interrupting Tanis's thoughts.

<Oh yeah?> Tanis asked, acknowledging Darla's leading statement.

<Well, what about using one of the tugs to pass between the ships?>

Tanis scowled. *<We went over that option. We burned out their fuel supplies to catch up. We're only still hauling them with us because we're hoping that Vesta won't be too*

pissed when this is over if we still have their tugs.>

<*Well, what if we only had one tug, but you and I—plus Marian's team—had a much higher chance of success?*>

<*I'm listening,*> Tanis replied.

<*I was going over the* Norse Wind*'s service record, and I saw mention of an inspection of GE-88 burners a decade ago.*>

Tanis scowled, wondering where on the ship's hull the solid chemical boosters would be mounted. They had a distinctive shape, and she'd spent no small amount of time staring at the *Wind*.

<*This is where you tell me where they are,*> Tanis said impatiently.

<*They're* ***inside*** *the ship, now. At some point, someone built on a new section of cargo holds, along either side of the vessel, toward the back.*>

<*Right, the part of the hull that looks like ass—well, more ass.*>

<*Yeah, anyway, they didn't remove the boosters, just built around them. There are four on each side. Two should do the trick to slow down a tug to match the* Jones.>

A smile crept onto Tanis's lips. <*Connie? Get Seamus and Liam down to Hold 6C. We have some work to do on one of the tugs, and we have to do it fast.*>

* * * * *

"Stars," Liam muttered as he pulled his helmet off after the airlock resealed behind him. "It's bad enough lugging that shit around out there, but I don't think the prior crew ever put these EV suits through a san cycle. I think something died inside this one."

Seamus made a gagging sound as he pulled his helmet off. "Yeah, there was a few sticky spots in mine. At one point, I had to piss, and the suit detected my discomfort and offered to do a san hookup. I almost climbed out into vacuum."

Tanis suppressed a laugh as Connie held up a hand and said, "OK, seriously, that's terrifying. I don't want to hear another word."

"Let's just say it was worse than getting mugged after we got back to Vesta," Seamus said with a shudder as he pulled off his EV suit.

"You got mugged?" Connie asked, brows raised. "Why didn't you say something?"

Seamus glanced at Connie, then Tanis. "Well, Sergeant…it just didn't seem like it was noteworthy—what, with everything else that was going on. Whoever it was just grabbed my bag and ran off."

"What?" Liam asked. "I thought the MPs took it from you."

"No," Seamus shook his head. "It happened right before they picked us up. I told them about it, but they didn't care. Bugs the piss out of me, too, I had grabbed a cool ship from—"

He suddenly stopped, his face turning red.

"Seamus, I get the feeling there's something you need to tell us," Connie said, folding her arms across her chest.

"Uhh…" the E-3 stammered. "The captain of the *Wind* had a really cool old ship model in his quarters. Not big, was—"

"An old Marsian cruiser?" Tanis asked, doing her best

not to lash out at Seamus.

"Uhh…yes, Commander Richards."

Tanis caught Connie's gaze. "Well, I guess we know why they finally cut and run from Vesta. They had what they needed."

"Thanks to dumb and dumber, here," Connie said, shooting arrows with her eyes at the two E-3s.

Tanis drew herself up. "Well, on the plus side, if Seamus and Liam hadn't lifted it off the *Wind,* our SWSF friends would have disappeared long before we ever figured out what was going on."

"Is that why you were going to Ceres?" Connie asked Seamus. "You were going to pawn that thing off somewhere? Did you know there was a quantum core inside it?"

"A what? Seriously?" Seamus asked, while Liam slapped him on the back of the head.

"You're such an idiot."

"OK, OK," Tanis held up her hands. "Recriminations can wait, and if we're all still in the TSF when this is done, maybe some discipline."

"Really know how to boost someone's spirits, Commander," Seamus muttered, earning him another glare from Connie.

"Are the boosters secure?" Tanis asked, changing the subject.

"Yeah," Liam nodded vigorously. "We set them in the tug's port and starboard grapples, and welded them in place. Those things can hold a starship while the tug thrusts, so they should be able to hold the boosters."

Tanis nodded. "I imagine you're right."

"They'll hold," Connie said with a nod. "Better than your first plan, anyway."

* * * * *

Ten minutes later, Tanis, Marian, Susan, Yves, and Lukas were all crammed into the tug's tiny cabin. It only had two seats, which Tanis and Marian occupied. Behind them, the three members of Marian's breach team had wrapped themselves in cargo webbing—which everyone hoped would hold.

Each member of the group wore medium combat armor—the best that Marian had been able to source from her cousin on such short notice.

It was powered enough to make the armor feel light, but if they came up on anyone in heavy armor, they'd be in trouble.

Good thing the Kirby Jones *isn't the roomiest of ships,* Tanis thought. *Makes it less likely that our friends over there will be using anything meaty.*

<*Coming up on the* Jones,> Lieutenant Jeannie announced over the comms. <*Prepare to disengage.*>

<*We're ready,*> Darla replied. <*Releasing grapple in three…two…one…MARK.*>

At that, Tug 82-CF released from the *Norse Wind* and fell back into the ship's engine wash.

<*Nice little dose of rads for us to start our mission,*> Lukas said with a soft chuckle.

<*Shut up,*> Marian ordered. <*You can wisecrack when we get onto the* Jones.>

Now that they were no longer attached to the *Norse*

Wind, the force pushing Tanis back in her seat disappeared, and the ship began a slow tumble as it continued on toward their target.

The *Kirby Jones* still lay ten thousand kilometers away. Scan showed that the *Norse Wind* had a delta-*v* of three hundred and twenty kilometers per hour, which meant the freighter would pass the *Jones* in just over thirty seconds, closely followed by the tug tumbling in its wake.

Tanis activated 82-CF's stabilizer jets, spun the tug so they were facing forward once more, and then activated the two solid boosters held in the tug's grapples.

Six *g*s slammed the tug's occupants forward, each one of them praying that their restraining harnesses and cargo webbing would hold. The tug began to slew to starboard, and Tanis realized that the boosters were ever so slightly misaligned. She altered the port side grapple's position, and the tug began to right itself.

<I can't believe this is working,> Marian said as they passed within five thousand kilometers of the *Jones*.

<Dammit, Marian,> Tanis muttered, then sucked in a breath as a beam lanced out from the *Jones,* and struck the *Norse Wind* amidships.

The *Wind*'s meager ES shields barely shed any energy from the shot, and an explosion bloomed from the freighter. The ship ceased burn, and fired lateral thrusters to move away from the *Jones.*

Tanis prayed it would be enough for whoever was flying the *Jones* to cease firing on the *Wind*. She didn't have long to wait for her answer, as a beam streaked out from the *Jones* and struck the tug, blowing away the port side solid booster.

"Shit!" someone screamed.

Instantly, the tug went from a nominally controlled trajectory, to spinning like a top through space.

Tanis rotated the grapple holding the remaining booster, and flipped the direction of its burn in an attempt to slow the mad tumble the ship was in.

It worked for a second, then the booster tore away.

The tug was still spinning one revolution per second, and Tanis barely had time to register that they'd somehow managed to remain on course for their target when Tug 82-CF slammed into the port side of the *Kirby Jones.*

HELL OF A BREACH

STELLAR DATE: 01.24.4084 (Adjusted Years)
LOCATION: *Kirby Jones*, Outer rim of Main Asteroid Belt
REGION: Vesta, Terran Hegemony, InnerSol

"Commander!" a voice cried out, jarring Tanis back to consciousness. "Are you injured?"

Tanis looked at the readouts on her HUD, and, seeing that there were no red bioindicators, said, "I'm good."

"Well, we breached," the voice said, and Tanis recognized it as Marian's. There was nothing on Tanis's optics, but when she tried to move, it became apparent that the tug's cabin had filled with impact foam.

<Triggering the dissolver,> Darla said.

A moment later, the foam began to feel softer, and then it was sloughing away to form a half-meter-deep puddle in one corner of the cabin.

"Lukas," Marian ordered, turning in her seat to eye her team. "Get that hatch open, let's see where we've landed ourselves."

"With my luck, we're probably smashed halfway through my cabin," Susan muttered as she disentangled herself from the cargo webbing and set to helping Yves get free, while Lukas wrestled with the cabin's rear hatch.

Tanis pulled off her harness and rose to her feet, which—given the *Jones*'s current quarter-*g* acceleration, and the tug's position—had her standing on the tug's left interior bulkhead.

<Everyone. On the combat net. Check seals. When Lukas

gets that door open, chances are we'll be sucking vacuum.>

A chorus of affirmative responses came back, but Darla let out a worried sigh just for Tanis to hear.

<*They've an AI aboard, and he's a grumpy sonofabitch. He's got the network locked down tighter than a Venusian farmer's wallet. No open ports that I can detect.*>

<*Well, then, how do you know he's so grumpy?*> Tanis asked as she checked over her rifle.

<*He's broadcasting obscenities on RF. One-oh-seven-point-three megahertz, if you want to tune in.*>

<*I'll pass,*> Tanis replied. <*Let me know if there's anything of substance.*>

<*Unlikely, but I'll do that.*>

Lukas got the cabin's door opened, and the tug's atmosphere rushed out in a single burst of air that flung the hatch wide. On one side of the opening, Tanis could see starlight, but on the other was the port-side passage that ran to the rear airlock.

<*Well I'll be,*> Marian chuckled. <*You slammed us almost square into the airlock, Commander.*>

<*Pure dumb luck,*> Tanis replied, as Lukas and Susan moved out into the corridor.

Susan glanced around the side of the tug. <*Passage to the rear is obscured.*>

<*And the hatch ahead is sealed against vacuum,*> Lukas said, waving his rifle toward the end of the passage.

<*There's an emergency ES field generator in a cabinet,*> Tanis said, gauging where it would be from their current position. <*There.*> She pointed at a location on the bulkhead.

<*Yves. Get on it,*> Marian ordered as she gestured for

Lukas and Susan to move to the end of the passage.

<*Once we get that hatch open, the enemy is going to unload everything they have at us,*> Tanis said as she looked up and down the corridor. <*We don't have much in the way of cover in here.*>

<*I have an idea…*> Darla said, a devious smile appearing in Tanis's mind.

Three minutes later, the ES field was up, and Lukas had part of the bulkhead torn off, ready to trigger the door's manual release.

<*On the count of three,*> Tanis said. <*One, two,* ***three!***>

As she shouted the last word across the Link, Lukas pulled the manual release, forcing the door open, and revealing the muzzles of a half-dozen rifles, held by a half-dozen soldiers.

One of them got a shot off, a kinetic round that ricocheted off Marian's armor before the net fired.

All tugs carried safety nets, used for anything from search and rescue operations, to snagging space junk before it hit a ship or station. The nets fired from twenty centimeter launchers, and packed enough punch to knock over a shuttle.

When the webbing hit the enemy troops, it picked them up, wrapped them in a ball, and carried them twenty meters down the corridor on the far side of the door.

<*Shit, that looks uncomfortable,*> Susan said with a snicker.

<*Yeah, well, now we have to cover them and somehow disarm them,*> Lukas said as he shouldered his rifle and stepped around the door.

<*Good of you to volunteer,*> Marian said, gesturing for Lukas to proceed to the tangled ball of enemies while Susan and Marian covered him.

<*I'd find this downright comical if I wasn't so freakin' pissed that we're storming my own damn ship,*> Tanis said privately to Darla. <*Speaking of ships, how is the* Wind *doing?*>

<*I've no idea, Tanis. I still can't get on the network here, and the tug's smashed. Unless you want to stick your head out the hole in the hull and take a look, we'll just have to wait and see.*>

Tanis sighed, half-tempted to do just that, but she knew they had to get to the bridge. Once there, she could activate the overrides and take control of her ship.

<*Marian, Yves. On me,*> Tanis ordered, taking a cross corridor and avoiding the moaning, writhing net of enemies.

"Get their weapons," Marian ordered Lukas and Susan aloud. "First hint of trouble, just waste them. So far as I can tell, they're pirates that have stolen a sovereign TSF vessel and attacked a TSF officer. We're totally within our rights to kill them or just dump them out the airlock."

Tanis knew that wasn't *exactly* true, but close enough that it seemed to have a calming effect on the enemies wrapped up in the net.

"Go ahead," Lukas grunted at the enemies. "I hate fucking guard duty; I only need half an excuse to waste you."

Tanis grinned behind her helmet's mask, and swept through the side corridor to the ship's central passageway. She stopped at the intersection, and deployed a probe, letting it sweep ahead.

Fifteen meters forward, the passage widened right before it got to the bridge. This was done on purpose to give defenders a place to set up in case they were boarded.

To that end, the bulkheads were reinforced, and would provide enough cover for shooters to hold out for some time.

Tanis didn't plan to wait long enough for their weapons fire to burn holes in her ship. She pulled out two pulse grenades and nodded to Marian. *<I throw, you two go low.>*

The soldiers nodded, and Tanis drew her arms back, lobbing the grenades high, the right one angled toward the left, and the left toward the right. She gave them a spin, and managed to get them around the corners, out of direct line of sight of her team.

That was when Darla triggered them to detonate.

Concussive pulses focused in the corners, slamming into the enemies hiding there—which turned out to be two on each side. The force caused them to half fall, half stumble away from the bulkheads, right into sustained kinetic fire from Marian and Yves.

Tanis joined in, and in less than ten seconds, all four were down.

Yves took up a position in one of the shielded locations, covering the intersection, while Tanis strode forward, eyes locked on the bridge's sealed door.

One of the fallen enemies raised his rifle toward her, but Tanis didn't hesitate, firing a round into his head, ending the threat.

"Toss 'em!" Marian screamed at the three survivors.

Two threw their weapons aside. The third didn't move, and Tanis revised her assessment: *two survivors*.

Then she was at the bridge's door, where she placed an Infil Kit on the panel, and shouldered her rifle, ready to end whoever had stolen her ship.

Twenty agonizing seconds later, the doors slid aside, and she took in the tableau in an instant.

Two soldiers were on either side of the door, and ahead was Admiral Kiaan, with an arm around Deering's throat, and a pistol pressed against her temple.

The soldier on the left fired, his shot hitting Tanis's rifle. She saw the barrel bend, and flung the ruined weapon toward the shooter with one hand, while drawing her sidearm with her other.

By the time the weapon was unholstered, she'd dropped to a crouch. Just as she'd expected, the soldier on her right fired his rifle, the rounds streaking above her, striking the enemy on the left, who had stepped aside to avoid Tanis's flung weapon.

The shooter never had time to realize he was firing at his teammate, taking six rounds from Tanis's sidearm right under the jaw, shattering the seal on his helmet, and then the insides of his head.

Tanis rose slowly to see Admiral Kiaan and Deering hadn't moved—though both were wide-eyed.

"Fancy," Admiral Kiaan finally said, as the barrel of Tanis's weapon drifted in his direction. "But you won't shoot me. I'm just as fast as you. Deering will be dead before your round leaves the chamber."

Tanis glanced at Admiral Deering. The woman looked nothing like she had the other night at Chez Maison. She wore a running outfit with 'TSF' emblazoned across the chest and down one leg. Her hair was a mess, and her face was streaked with blood and tears.

"So, not a traitor?" Tanis asked. "Because from where I've been these past few days, it really feels like you're a traitor."

Deering pursed her lips and gave her head a slight shake. "Dupe, yes. Not a traitor."

"How touching," Kiaan asked with a sneer. "You going to hug? Deering's an idiot and we played her like a flute. But so long as I have her, you're going to do exactly what I say."

"I could just kill you both," Tanis suggested. "Lotta shit happens in firefights."

<*Tanis…*> Darla cautioned.

<*Just pushing his buttons. Even **I'm** not reckless enough to shoot an admiral.*>

"Nice bluff," Kiaan said, barking a laugh after. "You've got moxie, Tanis Richards. Too bad you enlisted with the TSF; I bet the Marsian Protectorate would have loved to have an officer like you. But you went and pissed away your future with the *Terrans*." He uttered the last word like it was a vile curse.

"There's no way out of this for you," Tanis said. "What are you going to do, stand there holding her for the next two weeks while we fly out to the Disk?"

A grin split Kiaan's lips, and he gestured at the holodisplay behind him, which switched from a view of empty space to that of a cruiser, engines braking as it came down on their position.

"I assume you know of the *Arizona*?" he asked.

"There's no way you got a whole ship to turn traitor," Tanis whispered.

"Oh, they didn't turn traitor." Kiaan pushed the barrel of his gun into Deering's head. "*They* think they're here to save their dear admiral."

Tanis shook her head. "Yeah and how's that going to play out, now that the *Jones* has a hole in its hull? They're going to come over here, and their reaction to you holding a gun to the admiral's head isn't going to be any better than mine."

"It's OK, Commander Richards." Deering's tone was mollifying. "Just do what he says, and we'll work something out."

"Yeah," Kiaan glanced at Tanis's weapon. "We'll start working things out with you dropping your weapon, followed by your two soldiers back there in the corridor."

Tanis considered her options, but knew that if things came to a head, Admiral Deering stood a better than average chance of getting shot by Kiaan; the man was visibly shaking, and twice now, his trigger finger had pulled off the guard, twitching toward the small lever that would spell the end of Deering's life.

Tanis took aim at Kiaan, noticing that her prosthetic limb was wavering slightly. *Must have taken a glancing blow, or something,* she thought before twisting her wrist, rotating the pistol horizontally.

"Are you posturing with me?" Kiaan snarled. "I'll do

it. If I go, she goes."

Satisfied that her weapon was no longer wavering, Tanis double-checked the electronic sights, twitched her wrist to the left—and fired her pistol.

Her aim was true, and the gun spun out of Kiaan's hand.

A second later, Tanis was on top of the man. She drove an armored fist into his chest, then the side of his face, shattering his jaw.

He went down in a heap, and Tanis rose to her feet, looking down at Deering, who had flung herself to the side in the brief engagement.

"Are you OK, Admiral?" Tanis asked.

Deering was shaking slightly, but nodded as she pulled herself up by a console.

"I told you not to shoot," Deering said as she stared down at Kiaan's unconscious form.

"I did what seemed best at the time, sir," Tanis replied. "I had to, there was too much risk that you'd be shot, otherwise."

Deering fixed Tanis with a narrow-eyed gaze. "And what about his claim that his reflexes were as fast as yours?"

"Sir. He's a vanilla. I'm an L2. There's no way his reflexes come close to mine. The only reason—"

"Incoming message from the *Arizona*," a voice said over the bridge's audible systems.

<*It's the craptastic AI, Herman,*> Darla informed Tanis privately.

"Put it on," Admiral Deering said, turning away from Tanis.

<*OK, that's strange…*> Tanis replied to Darla. <*If she was under duress, how come the AI is taking orders from her?*>

<*I don't like this…*>

A woman's face appeared on the bridge's forward holodisplay, and Tanis recognized Captain Regina of the *Arizona*.

"Admiral Deering, I'm glad to see you're OK. Have the interlopers been taken care of?"

Deering nodded, glancing over her shoulder. "Yes. Things are under control, thanks to Commander Richards here. Please send over a repair crew, and a pinnace to transfer me to your ship."

"Of course, Admiral," Captain Regina replied, and then the connection cut out.

"Well," Deering turned back to Tanis. "For better or worse, your part in this is over."

<*Uh, Tanis?*> Darla's voice wavered uncertainly. <*I managed to backdoor in when Herman took the connection from the* Arizona. *There was a second channel in that message. The cruiser just launched three assault craft. One is heading toward the* Norse Wind, *and two are coming here.*>

"Shit," Tanis whispered as she turned to Admiral Deering. "You're in on it…that hostage bit was just for show!"

Deering chuckled. "Well, Kiaan was getting a bit volatile there at the end; I'm not entirely certain he wouldn't have shot me if he thought it would save his hide. Either way, the operation you royally fucked up when you boarded the *Norse Wind* two weeks ago can now get back on track."

Tanis took a step back, placing a console between herself and Admiral Deering. "Why?"

" 'Why' what?" Deering asked with a sigh. "Why facilitate the re-arming of the Scattered Worlds? Because there's *a lot* of money in it. They don't like Terra, and they want to protect themselves should the Jovians cause trouble. Honestly, that's fine by me. No Terran blood needs to be shed if those two get into a fight."

As Deering spoke, Tanis reached down to the console and keyed in the override commands that would allow her to take back full control of her ship. But as she went to hit 'send', the AI's voice again came over the 1MC.

"Now, now, Commander Richards. We can't have you thinking you're in control of your ship. Just sit back and wait for the repair crew. They'll square everything away."

"Square it away as in shoot me and my team dead?" Tanis asked.

Deering sighed. "Picked up on that, did you? Don't get any bright ideas. You kill me, and you're dead. I live, and I can make sure that things go well for you."

"Like hell you will," Tanis said through gritted teeth. "I'm going to—"

"Hey, what!—" Herman cried out, then the AI's voice cut off.

A moment later, Lovell's replaced it.

"Hello, Commander Richards. Sorry about that, but I couldn't abide another AI in my place on the *Jones*."

"I felt the same way," Tanis replied as she took a menacing step toward Admiral Deering. "Now, let's turn that around. You're going to confess, and then things just might be passable for *you*. Alternatively, things can go very badly."

"You wouldn't dare extort me..." Admiral Deering hissed.

"I get the feeling people do that to you quite successfully all the time," Tanis replied. "Besides, when you confess to your crimes, it's not extortion. By any chance, do you also think that black is white?"

Deering didn't reply, only set her jaw and glared at Tanis.

"Lovell," Tanis called out. "Can you reopen that connection to the *Arizona*?"

"Yes, Commander."

A moment later, Captain Regina's face reappeared. "Admiral?"

"No subrosa chat this time," Tanis replied. "The admiral has been quite bad of late, and has been moving illegal goods to the SWSF to aid them in bolstering their military. Something that's in direct violation of the Phobos Accords, I suspect."

"Funny," Captain Regina scowled. "She said something similar about you."

"Well," Tanis took a step toward the holo, her unflinching gaze meeting the cruiser captain's. "Do you want to go down with Deering? Because she's going to pay for what she's done."

Captain Regina's gaze flicked to Admiral Deering, then back to meet Tanis's eyes. "Sorry, but the day I take a patrol boat captain's word over an admiral's will be the last day I spend in the TSF."

Admiral Deering laughed and shook her head at

Tanis. "Nice try, Commander. Now stand down, or Captain Regina will instruct her breach teams to use maximum force in taking out your people."

Tanis gritted her teeth, desperately trying to think of a way to convince Regina that Deering was the enemy.

"What about my word?" a new voice came into the conversation, and then a man Tanis didn't recognize appeared in a new panel on the holodisplay.

<*Hope you don't mind that I patched him in,*> Darla said with a grin in Tanis's mind.

<*Who—*> Tanis began, but Captain Regina spoke up first.

"Admiral Pella, I thought you were with the *Normandy,*> Captain Regina stammered.

"I am." The view around Pella expanded, and Tanis could see a massive bridge filled with dozens of stations in the background.

She couldn't help but notice the man working at a console just to Admiral Pella's left.

Harm Ellis, Tanis thought. *You sneaky bastard.*

"You'll recall your assault craft, Captain Regina, and then you'll take a pinnace to report to me in person. Your ship will receive stationkeeping orders from my nav officer."

Tanis could see Captain Regina swallow, then duck her head. "Yes, Admiral. Immediately."

Admiral Pella turned his attention to Tanis. "Well, Commander Richards. From what I've been told, you've had quite an exciting week—what, with uncovering an SWSF plot on Vesta, and then tracing it all the way up to Admiral Deering, here."

"Yes, sir," Tanis nodded. "It's been an exciting few days."

"And do you have evidence of Deering's involvement?" Pella's eyebrows were halfway up his forehead as he asked the question.

<Connie, I assume you came over with Lovell. Do we?> she asked, and prayed that they did.

<Don't fret, Tanis. It's all here, the engine components, even the QC Seamus lifted. The ship's logs have some damning conversations stored in them, as well.>

"Yes, Admiral. We have ample proof that Admiral Deering has been working with the SWSF against the best interests of the TSF."

Pella's gaze flicked to the left for a moment, and Tanis saw Harm nod. Then the Admiral replied, "Very good, then, Commander Richards. We're sending your nav a route to dock with us. The *Norse Wind,* too. We'll bring you back to Vesta."

"Thank you, Admiral," Tanis replied, and the connection ended.

"It'll never go anywhere," Deering growled at her. "They won't put me on trial."

Tanis collapsed in her chair and spun her pistol on her finger. "What are you trying to do, Deering? Convince me to just kill you now?"

Admiral Deering's face lost all color, and from the bridge's entrance, Tanis could hear Marian laughing.

"Corporal," Tanis said after letting out a long, tired sigh. "Can you secure the admiral? Preferably somewhere I can't see her pathetic mug."

"You got it, ma'am," Marian said, a smile evident in

her tone.

<So,> Darla drawled after a moment. *<This is your ship, eh? Needs a bit of work.>*

<You're all heart, Darla.>

SITUATION NORMAL, ALL…

STELLAR DATE: 01.26.4084 (Adjusted Years)
LOCATION: Admiral Kocsis's Office, Fleet Division HQ
REGION: Vesta, Terran Hegemony, InnerSol

Tanis stepped out of Admiral Kocsis's office, still a little uncertain about what had just happened.

<*Higgs really got it, didn't he?*> Darla asked after a moment.

<*Yeah…wow.*> Tanis shook her head, still reeling after everything that had happened over the past week and a half.

Admiral Kocsis hadn't addressed everything that had occurred, and a nagging fear in the back of her mind said she was still facing a dishonorable discharge. She glanced at the master sergeant sitting at the desk across the outer room, and he gestured with his eyes toward a chair.

"Admiral wants to talk to you again in a minute."

Nodding, Tanis blew out a breath while sinking into a chair near the door.

<*Just what I need. To brave the lion's den twice in an hour.*>

Darla's silvery laugh resonated through her mind, and Tanis smiled in response, realizing just how much she'd come to love having another person with her at all times. Someone to bounce ideas off, and share reactions with.

Far from being intrusive, it was more like having a best friend with you always. But AIs weren't needy, didn't try to make you do the things they wanted—unless one considered Darla's fashion sense—and were really just there for you all the time.

Not like she's a ***dog***, Tanis thought to herself.

<I can hear you laughing in that cavernous space you call a mind. What's up?> Darla asked.

At least not a very nice dog….

<I'm just realizing that having you with me is something that I'm really happy about. Even though Higgs is a general ass—what, with brushing off the initial attack on me, and throwing me under the bus after the MPs picked us up—I'm sure glad he rubber-stamped our pairing.>

<Yeah,> Darla's avatar gave an emphatic nod. *<I share a similar feeling toward that rather dour man.>*

As if on cue, the admiral's door opened, and Higgs strode out. He glanced at Tanis and gave her the briefest of nods.

"Commander."

Tanis nodded in response, but did not rise, as it was not required in situations like this—though it would have been respectful. "Colonel Higgs."

He didn't slow his rapid strides, and was out of the room a moment later. The Master Sergeant looked back up at Tanis and gestured toward the door.

"The admiral will see you now, Commander Richards."

"Thank you," she replied as she rose and walked back into the room to see Harm Ellis still seated in one of the chairs in front of Admiral Kocsis's desk, while the admiral stood behind his chair, slowly shaking his head.

Tanis didn't ask what had been said in her absence,

but she would have killed—well, maybe not *killed,* but definitely punched Admiral Deering a few times—to find out.

She stopped just short of the chairs, and stood at attention until the admiral acknowledged her, which he did with a glance and a wave at the empty chair.

"Too much has gone on today for me to rest on formality, overmuch," he said as she sat.

"Yes, sir," Tanis replied.

"I won't lie, Commander Richards, I half wish we could just sweep all of this under the rug, and pretend it never happened, but we can't. A whole lot of shit went down during the last week, and almost none of it should have been possible."

Tanis couldn't help an emphatic nod. "Yes, sir."

"I'm not just talking about what Deering and the SWSF got up to, Commander. The fact that you were able to so easily move about Vesta while wanted for a whole host of crimes—not to mention that your attackers did, too—doesn't sit well with me. The only thing that makes me feel remotely OK about this is that you had your MICI friend, here, helping you out."

The admiral glanced at Harm—whose face was an implacable mask, revealing nothing of his inner thoughts.

"Not that I *like* having MICIs running around on Vesta, making a mess, but at least they're on our side, and their messes are *usually* for the best."

A smile cracked Harm's smooth façade, and he winked at her. "Usually."

That one gesture caused a wave of relief to wash over

Tanis, and her fear of a dishonorable discharge lessened. Though she'd still take one if it meant protecting her crew from getting black marks on their records.

She'd said as much in the first part of the meeting, while Higgs was still present, but the admiral had dismissed it. Not in such a way that Tanis thought the matter was put to rest, but more like he didn't want to talk about it at that time.

"I have a lot of work to do to shore things up, Commander Richards," the admiral said. "A lot of security protocols need to be reviewed, but at the same time, *my* bosses don't exactly want everyone to know that the SWSF is trying to smuggle components out to build a new fleet—or that a TSF admiral was complicit in it."

"So, in a way, Admiral, we *are* just sweeping it all under the rug," Harm chimed in.

Kocsis cast his weary glance at Harm. "In a way, yes. But just because we're not letting the public know about this, doesn't mean that Deering is getting off free and clear. She's going to be running a rather unpleasant station for some time, with an XO that will be on her like gravity on a star. The TSF isn't going to just let her walk off after betraying us."

Tanis could only imagine what that would be like for Deering. As much as she wanted the woman to suffer public shame for what she'd done—after all, Deering had tried to have her killed more than once—there *were* some pretty unpleasant postings out there.

<It'll have to do,> she said to Darla.

<I'll find out where she's been sent, don't you worry. We

can send her hate mail.>

<You're the best, Darla.>

Tanis decided to come out and ask the question that had been burning in her mind for days. "So I'm not going to be sent packing?"

Kocsis barked a laugh. "Stars, Tanis! I should promote you, but Harm, here, won't let me—well, that, and I'd have to say *why* you got an early promotion, and Harm won't let me do that, either."

The idea of a colonel not 'letting' an admiral do something struck Tanis as amusing, and she couldn't help a small laugh.

Admiral Kocsis locked eyes with Tanis, and she wondered if he was going to lay into her, but then he smiled. "Yeah, it is kinda funny. OK, no more beating around the bush, Commander. Here's how things are going to play out.

"Firstly, you remain a commander, and you keep Darla in that pernicious head of yours. Seems like Division 99 is very happy with how the two of you are working out."

<Thank you, sir,> Darla interrupted.

"You're welcome, Darla," the admiral replied, seeming unperturbed by the AI's interruption. "I'm just glad we finally found a place for you where your…penchant for mischief seems to benefit the force."

<Oh?> Tanis asked privately. *<I think there are some stories you need to tell me.>*

<Classified.> Darla winked along with her response.

"We're going to bill this whole thing as an 'exercise', and use it to shore up areas of Vesta's security that are sorely lacking. I'm going to put in for a whole host more AIs to help keep an eye on things, with a XO-style oversight authority. The fact that Deering just did as she wished and no one questioned it at any point is not the sort of operation I want to run."

Kocsis paused and ran a hand through his hair.

"Of course, I'm a realist. At any given time, there are over a hundred million people on Vesta, and keeping a leash on everyone is impossible—plus, I want people who think for themselves. Harm, here, has convinced me that being heavy-handed isn't the right solution."

Tanis's eyebrows rose. She had several suspicions as to how that would play out, but didn't want to interrupt the admiral.

"As a result, Division 99 is going to set up a larger presence here on Vesta—but this one won't be officially visible. We're going to recruit regular space force officers to assist in investigations to determine the extent of any SWSF subversion in our ranks."

"And that's going to take some doing," Harm added. "Knowing who you can trust is no simple thing."

"Which makes me sick," Kocsis muttered. "But I've been in this game for far too long not to know how it's played."

Neither man spoke for a moment, and Tanis decided she was tired of waiting. "So what does this mean for me?"

Kocsis glanced at Harm, who gave Tanis a winning smile in turn. "Tanis, Darla, say hello to your new MICI handler. You're going to be running side-ops for Division 99, now."

Tanis's eyebrows rose to what felt like her hairline. "Seriously?"

"You still report to Higgs," Kocsis interrupted, then shook his head at her dour expression. "I need officers who can work together and get past shit that comes up. This is as much a test for Higgs as it is for you. I don't want you to tattle on him, but if things aren't working, Tanis, you let me know."

She nodded in response, understanding where the admiral was coming from.

"So I have two masters now, is that what you're saying?" she asked.

Harm chuckled. "Well, I'm less a master, and more an advisor. Plus, if I need you to go somewhere, Higgs will suddenly get a mission spec for you that sends you where I ask. I hate being pulled in two directions as much as anyone, so I'll do my best to make sure that doesn't happen here."

"Thank you, sir. I think."

"So does that mean the two of you are in?" Harm asked.

Tanis snorted aloud, while Darla laughed over the link. "We have a choice?" they asked in unison.

URDON

STELLAR DATE: 01.26.4084 (Adjusted Years)
LOCATION: SWSS *Fortune*
REGION: Approaching Jupiter, OuterSol

"They didn't make it to the rendezvous," Major Ron reported to Colonel Urdon. "Scan was able to confirm that the *Normandy* showed up."

"That new carrier?" Urdon asked, a scowl forming on his face. "And they wonder why we want to rebuild our dreadnoughts when they make warships like that."

Everyone in the Scattered Worlds knew why the Terrans would build ships the size of the *Normandy*. One ship alone would be enough to blockade a world, to impose whatever the Terrans wanted on their member states.

The TSF could now project its full might anywhere in the Sol System with just one ship.

Not if we have anything to do with it, Urdon thought.

He knew it would be a long game. It would take decades to secretly build up the fleets they'd need to stand against the Terrans, but stand they would. Someday, the Scattered Worlds would be free.

"The other ships?" he asked Major Ron. "Any problems with them?"

"No, only the *Norse Wind* met with any sort of trouble. Every other courier vessel is now beyond Neptune's orbit."

"Good." Urdon interlaced his fingers and leaned back in the command chair of his frigate. "Then our work is done here…for now. Take us back to Makemake."

"Yes, sir." Major Ron saluted, and nodded to the helm officer, who began keying in the course.

Urdon couldn't help but think about the woman who had foiled their efforts with the *Norse Wind,* and at Vesta. Who, more importantly, had lost them the valuable asset they had in Admiral Deering.

I'm sure we'll cross paths again, Tanis Richards.

THE END

*****

Tanis Richards' adventures are just getting underway. Now paired with Darla, and taking missions from Harm, she's going to get into more tight situations than ever before.

Grab the next book in the Origins of Destiny series: ***Tanis Richards: Operative.***

THE BOOKS OF AEON 14

Keep up to date with what is releasing in Aeon 14 with the free Aeon 14 Reading Guide.

The Intrepid Saga (The Age of Terra)
- Book 1: Outsystem
- Book 2: A Path in the Darkness
- Book 3: Building Victoria

- The Intrepid Saga Omnibus – *Also contains Destiny Lost, book 1 of the Orion War series*

- Destiny Rising – *Special Author's Extended Edition comprised of both Outsystem and A Path in the Darkness with over 100 pages of new content.*

The Orion War
- Book 1: Destiny Lost
- Book 2: New Canaan
- Book 3: Orion Rising
- Book 4: The Scipio Alliance
- Book 5: Attack on Thebes
- Book 6: War on a Thousand Fronts
- Book 7: Fallen Empire (2018)
- Book 8: Airtha Ascendancy (2018)
- Book 9: The Orion Front (2018)
- Book 10: Starfire (2019)
- Book 11: Race Across Time (2019)
- Book 12: Return to Sol (2019)

Tales of the Orion War
- Book 1: Set the Galaxy on Fire

- Book 2: Ignite the Stars
- Book 3: Burn the Galaxy to Ash (2018)

Perilous Alliance (Age of the Orion War – w/Chris J. Pike)
- Book 1: Close Proximity
- Book 2: Strike Vector
- Book 3: Collision Course
- Book 4: Impact Imminent
- Book 5: Critical Inertia (2018)

Rika's Marauders (Age of the Orion War)
- Prequel: Rika Mechanized
- Book 1: Rika Outcast
- Book 2: Rika Redeemed
- Book 3: Rika Triumphant
- Book 4: Rika Commander
- Book 5: Rika Infiltrator (2018)
- Book 6: Rika Unleashed (2018)
- Book 7: Rika Conqueror (2019)

Perseus Gate (Age of the Orion War)
Season 1: Orion Space
- Episode 1: The Gate at the Grey Wolf Star
- Episode 2: The World at the Edge of Space
- Episode 3: The Dance on the Moons of Serenity
- Episode 4: The Last Bastion of Star City
- Episode 5: The Toll Road Between the Stars
- Episode 6: The Final Stroll on Perseus's Arm
- Eps 1-3 Omnibus: The Trail Through the Stars
- Eps 4-6 Omnibus: The Path Amongst the Clouds

Season 2: Inner Stars
- Episode 1: A Meeting of Bodies and Minds
- Episode 3: A Deception and a Promise Kept

- Episode 3: A Surreptitious Rescue of Friends and Foes (2018)
- Episode 4: A Trial and the Tribulations (2018)
- Episode 5: A Deal and a True Story Told (2018)
- Episode 6: A New Empire and An Old Ally (2018)

Season 3: AI Empire
- Episode 1: Restitution and Recompense (2019)
- Five more episodes following...

The Warlord (Before the Age of the Orion War)
- Book 1: The Woman Without a World
- Book 2: The Woman Who Seized an Empire
- Book 3: The Woman Who Lost Everything

The Sentience Wars: Origins (Age of the Sentience Wars – w/James S. Aaron)
- Book 1: Lyssa's Dream
- Book 2: Lyssa's Run
- Book 3: Lyssa's Flight
- Book 4: Lyssa's Call
- Book 5: Lyssa's Flame (June 2018)

Enfield Genesis (Age of the Sentience Wars – w/Lisa Richman)
- Book 1: Alpha Centauri
- Book 2: Proxima Centauri (2018)

Hand's Assassin (Age of the Orion War – w/T.G. Ayer)
- Book 1: Death Dealer
- Book 2: Death Mark (August 2018)

Machete System Bounty Hunter (Age of the Orion War – w/Zen DiPietro)
- Book 1: Hired Gun
- Book 2: Gunning for Trouble

- Book 3: With Guns Blazing

Vexa Legacy (Age of the FTL Wars – w/Andrew Gates)
- Book 1: Seas of the Red Star

Building New Canaan (Age of the Orion War – w/J.J. Green)
- Book 1: Carthage (2018)

Fennington Station Murder Mysteries (Age of the Orion War)
- Book 1: Whole Latte Death (w/Chris J. Pike)
- Book 2: Cocoa Crush (w/Chris J. Pike)

The Empire (Age of the Orion War)
- The Empress and the Ambassador (2018)
- Consort of the Scorpion Empress (2018)
- By the Empress's Command (2018)

Tanis Richards: Origins (The Age of Terra)
- Prequel: Storming the Norse Wind (At the Helm Volume 3)
- Book 1: Shore Leave (in Galactic Genesis)
- Book 2: The Command (July 2018)
- Book 3: Infiltrator (July 2018)

The Sol Dissolution (The Age of Terra)
- Book 1: Venusian Uprising (2018)
- Book 2: Scattered Disk (2018)
- Book 3: Jovian Offensive (2019)
- Book 4: Fall of Terra (2019)

The Delta Team Chronicles (Expanded Orion War)
- A "Simple" Kidnapping (Pew! Pew! Volume 1)
- The Disknee World (Pew! Pew! Volume 2)
- It's Hard Being a Girl (Pew! Pew! Volume 4)
- A Fool's Gotta Feed (Pew! Pew! Volume 4)

- Rogue Planets and a Bored Kitty (Pew! Pew! Volume 5)

ABOUT THE AUTHOR

Michael Cooper likes to think of himself as a jack of all trades (and hopes to become master of a few). When not writing, he can be found writing software, working in his shop at his latest carpentry project, or likely reading a book.

He shares his home with a precocious young girl, his wonderful wife (who also writes), two cats, a never-ending list of things he would like to build, and ideas...

Find out what's coming next at www.aeon14.com